A Good Dog's Guide to Murder

Krista Davis

BERKLEY PRIME CRIME
New York

BERKLEY PRIME CRIME
Published by Berkley
An imprint of Penguin Random House LLC
penguinrandomhouse.com

ISBN: 9780593436950

First Edition: September 2022

Printed in the United States of America

To all my readers who wish Wagtail existed.
I wish there were a real Wagtail, too!

Dogs need to sniff the ground; it's how they keep abreast of current events. The ground is a giant dog newspaper, containing all kinds of late-breaking dog news items, which, if they are especially urgent, are often continued in the next yard.

—Dave Barry

WAGTAIL RESIDENTS

Holly Miller
Trixie—Holly's Jack Russell terrier
Twinkletoes—Holly's calico cat
Nell DuPuy Miller Goodwin—Holly's mother
Holmes Richardson—Holly's boyfriend
Liesel Miller (Oma)—Holly's paternal grandmother
Gingersnap—Liesel's golden retriever
Shadow Hobbs—Sugar Maple Inn handyman
Bonnie Greene—proprietor of Pawsome Cookies
Sergeant Dave Quinlan (Officer Dave)
Zelda York—desk clerk
Stu and Sue Williams
Barry Williams—Stu and Sue's son, veterinarian
Althea Alcorn
Kent and Jay—Althea's sons
Tony Alcorn—Althea's husband
Penny and Tommy Terrell

ORLY BIFFLE'S FAMILY

Wyatt and Josie Biffle—Orly's son and daughter
Delia Riddle—Orly's sister-in-law
Carter Riddle—Delia's son

VISITORS TO WAGTAIL

Jean Maybury and Kitty—inn guests
Penn Connor
Boomer Jenkins

Trixie's Guide to Murder

So you want to learn how to sniff out murder. In case you're wondering about my qualifications, I have been doing this for a few years now. My lucky break was finding my mom, Holly. She's pretty cool, but I had to be persistent with her or she might have passed me by. And that kind of stick-to-it doggedness is what you'll need to be a successful finder of murdered peoples.

Just to be clear, in general peoples are not as interested in dead squirllies or dead birds. So don't mention them to your mom or dad. They can get a little queasy about stuff like that. Oddly enough, they get very excited when you lead them to murdered peoples. They call other peoples to come, and before you know it, you're surrounded by peoples and they're all telling you what a smart dog you are. You even get special treats. And sometimes a steak for dinner! But that never happens when you take your peoples to a dead squirlley.

Some lucky dogs get trained to find dead peoples. Or peoples in general, dead or alive. It's a real cushy deal. The instructors hide stuff from you all day and reward you for bringing everything back to them. The rewards are usually sticks and toys, though. Someone ought to tell them we would prefer treats. Fun as it might be, that kind of formal training isn't really necessary. Any dog can do it. It comes to us naturally.

Stick with me, pups, and I'll tell you how it's done.

One

"Mom?"

I was busy helping our desk clerk, Zelda York, handle a steady stream of arrivals at the Sugar Maple Inn when I looked up and saw my mother, Nell. It had been a couple of years since we had been together in person, but we Zoomed regularly. My mom lived in California and was the last person I expected to see this Thanksgiving.

I darted around the check-in desk and plowed through the guests as if nothing could stop me. "Mom!" I opened my arms wide for a hug.

"Holly!" She wrapped her arms around me and planted a kiss on my cheek.

She held me so tight, I thought she might not let me go.

Trixie, my Jack Russell terrier, wanted in on the action. She danced around us on her hind legs, whining. When my mom released me, I picked up Trixie. Her fur was all white except for her black ears and a round black spot on her rump that ran one-third of the way down her tail, which had not been docked and now wagged so fast it was only a blur.

"Is this Trixie?"

I was shocked to realize that my mother had never met my sweet little dog. "Of course. What are you doing here? We weren't expecting you."

"Surprise!" said Mom, tilting her head and reaching out to stroke Trixie.

I looked around for her husband and her other children. "Where is everyone?"

"I'll explain over dinner. Is that all right? Can you get away for dinner? It's a zoo in here."

"I wouldn't miss dinner with you. Where are you staying?"

"Holly!" called Zelda, crooking her finger at me.

"I hoped I could stay here at the inn."

Uh-oh. We were booked solid. "Follow me." I picked up her bags and led her behind the registration desk. Trixie followed along.

Zelda shot me a look of surprise. We didn't usually bring anyone behind the desk. "Zelda, this is my mother," I said.

Zelda did a double take, which didn't surprise me. I took after my dad's side of the family. Not to mention that my mom looked younger than her years. My arrival as a baby hadn't exactly been hailed with joy because my mother became pregnant with me while still in high school. Now in her late forties, she wore her hair in a sleek short bob and looked great.

Zelda reached out her hand. "Hi, Mrs.—"

"Nell, just call me Nell, sweetheart. I've heard so much about you. I feel like I know you already!"

The woman in front of Zelda, on the other side of the registration desk, coughed with irritation.

"Is there a problem?" I asked Zelda.

The woman said huffily, "No swimming!"

I smiled at her and glanced at the computer screen. "You don't find Swim suitable?"

"We don't want to swim. For heaven's sake, it's November."

I smiled at her. "All our rooms are named after dog and cat activities. It doesn't mean you have to swim."

"Oh!" The woman pointed at Zelda. "She should have said so. But I do need two beds." She aimed her finger at a little girl who was with her. "Kitty and I can't share a bed. I won the Carolina Gingerbread Contest"—she rustled around in a big bag that hung on her arm, pulled out a Sugar Maple Inn brochure, and thrust it at me—"and they said I would have a double room. I'm entering the Wagtail Dog and Cat Gingerbread House Contest. It has a ten-thousand-dollar prize."

I glanced at the screen again and read, *Jean Maybury. Requests two beds.* She was already sour on the word *Swim*, and would never be happy with it, even if we told her Queen Elizabeth herself had stayed there. I switched her around with someone else and put Jean and Kitty in a room as sweet as gingerbread. I had stayed there many times and knew firsthand how charming it was.

"All right, then, we now have you in a different room. Enjoy your stay, Ms. Maybury." I signaled our handyman, Shadow Hobbs, and handed him the key to Pounce.

Located in the mountains of southwestern Virginia, Wagtail had once been a hot tourist spot. In the 1800s, wealthy people built mansions there as summer homes to escape the heat. In addition, Wagtail was blessed with pure, clean springs that lured the sick and ailing. But all of that had fallen out of favor. Desperate to revive the tourist industry, the town had looked to dogs and cats. It had become the premier location for people who wanted to travel with their beloved pets. No one had expected the exponential growth as a result.

Dogs and cats were welcome everywhere, including restaurants, which offered special menus for canine and feline diners. Veterinarians, dog and cat massage therapists, and animal acupuncturists had arrived in droves. Stores offered every conceivable thing a pampered dog, cat, or bird could possibly want. They featured the latest in beds, clothes, leashes, and artisanal treats. Not to mention the T-shirts, matching pajamas, lamps, and animal-themed bric-a-brac their owners bought for themselves.

The Sugar Maple Inn had embraced the spirit by naming all the guest rooms after dog and cat activities, and by loaning GPS collars to our guests who brought pets.

Thanksgiving week was always busy in Wagtail. Some people returned to their vacation homes for the holiday. Others came for the beginning of the season to see the lighting of the trees, shop at the Christkindlmarket, and get into the holiday spirit. Visitors also came to enter the annual Wagtail Dog and Cat Gingerbread House Contest or to visit family in Wagtail. Which made me wonder again exactly what my mother was doing here.

I finally turned my attention back to her. But she had disappeared.

Happily, I found her in the office, catching up with my father's mother, whom I called Oma, German for *grandma*. Trixie sat beside Mom, gazing up at her face. Twinkletoes, my long-haired calico cat, purred on her lap, and Oma's golden retriever, Gingersnap, struggled to get close enough to be petted.

"I worry about him," Mom was saying. A coffee cup sat before her on a table.

"About whom?" I asked.

"Sam. Your father." In spite of the divorce, Oma appeared to be quite comfortable with her former daughter-in-law. I supposed that wasn't terribly surprising. I had never heard Oma say anything bad or even ill-spirited about my mom. Oma sat comfortably in a cushy chair, sipping coffee. She wore what she liked to call country chic, a white blouse topped by a blue sweater knitted by a local artisan, with a matching blue plaid skirt. Hardly high fashion, but appropriate and attractive.

"Is something wrong?" I asked, holding my breath.

"No." Oma said it a little bit too fast, making me wonder what was up. "Where are you staying, Nell?"

Mom raised her eyebrows. "I stupidly thought you might have room for me here. Holly told me that Wagtail had changed, but I never expected anything like this. Is it just because of the holiday?"

Oma smiled at her. "It is no longer the sleepy town in which you grew up."

A few years ago, when Oma invited me to become her partner at the Sugar Maple Inn, I thought she wanted to relax and travel. But then she went and got herself elected mayor of Wagtail, which meant both of us were roped into the town's troubles. On the plus side, Oma was a respected force behind the town's success.

"I have a guest room," I said. "You can stay with me." It would accommodate Mom and her husband, and we could bring up some rollaway beds for the kids, but it would be tight.

Mom looked relieved. "You're certain I wouldn't cramp your style?"

"Are you kidding? It's been so long! I'm thrilled to have you here." I checked my watch. "I need to go over to the new convention center. Want to come or would you rather relax awhile?"

"Convention center? No one told me about that! How can tiny Wagtail afford it?"

Oma rose and patted Mom's shoulder. In the German accent that annoyed her but that I found charming, she said, "It was about time that you came home for a visit. We have much to catch up on."

Mom seemed happy about staying in my guest room, but I was wondering about her husband and her other children. I didn't want to upset her, though. I tiptoed around that subject by asking brightly, "When is everyone else arriving?"

"It's just me this time, Holly."

"Is everything all right?"

"I'll tell you all about it later on." She gave me a little squeeze.

I arranged for Shadow to bring Mom's luggage up to my quarters when he had the opportunity, and the two of us set off for the convention center, with Trixie and Twinkletoes romping along.

We left through the front door of the inn, which led directly to the center of town. A park that we called "the green" sprawled from north to south. Stores and restaurants lined both sides. Mom literally gaped. "This is charming!"

I'd been surprised, too, when I came back as an adult. We turned and walked along a peaceful street.

"You told me everyone gets around on golf carts, but I never imagined that there wouldn't be *any* cars. I rented a car at the airport," said Mom, gazing around. "But they wouldn't let me drive into Wagtail."

"Permanent residents used to be permitted to keep their cars in their garages, but after someone was hit by a car, the rule was changed. Everyone has to park outside. Kind of like a theme park! Wagtail is a car-free community. It's safer for pedestrians and animals that way," I explained. "We use golf carts, but mostly we walk."

"I love that! It's so healthy. But a convention center?"

"The town is popular, and a lot of companies would like to bring their employees here for a break. So when Orly Biffle died and left land to the town, it seemed the perfect opportunity. It was a most generous donation, especially considering the location overlooking the lake."

"Orly? I remember him. We used to call him Ornery Orly because he was the grumpiest man on the planet. I'm shocked that he would leave anything to the town. He acted like he hated everyone and everything."

"Did you know him well?"

"Not really. His kids, Wyatt and Josie, were in school with me. They must be very upset with their dad for giving the land to the town instead of to them. Do they still live here?"

"They do. They run the family grocery store, Biffle's."

"No kidding? Seems like I remember them helping their dad at a roadside stand where they sold produce and honey when we were kids."

The convention center came into view. A giant two-story post-and-beam building, it suited the mountain setting of tall pines and the lake beyond. Built of stone and local wood, it had opened this morning to submissions for the annual Wagtail Dog and Cat Gingerbread House Contest. Some contestants brought the pieces and assembled them on-site. Others brought their baking equipment and rented houses to bake their masterpieces. A daring few transported their creations complete, hoping they wouldn't be damaged in transit.

The official opening ceremony and judging of the contest were scheduled to take place on Thanksgiving Day. The following day, the town would kick off its Christmas season.

"It's breathtaking!" murmured Mom.

At that exact moment, a cracking sound reverberated through the air and the ground shook beneath our feet.

"Earthquake!" Mom screamed, seizing my arm.

"You've been living in California too long."

"Then what was that?"

We hurried toward the convention center. Stu and Sue Williams bolted out of the front door, along with some people I didn't know.

Trixie and Twinkletoes ran ahead. Trixie zoomed around the base of a beautiful ancient oak tree, barking. A giant limb lay on the ground. It had to be twenty feet long and as big around as a man's thigh. Twinkletoes had already jumped on top of it.

Sue and Stu ran toward us.

"As I live and breathe! Nell DuPuy? Is that really you?" Sue opened her arms.

In case Mom didn't recognize her, I whispered, "Sue and Stu Williams."

"Sue!" They embraced while I walked over to the tree as calmly as I could to retrieve my rascals.

I looked up at it, afraid another branch might give way. When the property had been cleared for the building, this tree had been left in the middle of a semicircular golf cart driveway. It was supposed to be the magnificent focal point of the entrance.

"Trixie, come." She pinned her ears back and howled.

I wanted to believe that she was on the trail of a squirrel who had taken refuge in the huge old tree. But I knew better. Trixie had a nose for murder. And when she smelled it, her bark was mournful and anxious as though she were trying to tell me about it. I scanned the pristine lawn. No one lay on the grass. As far as the eye could see, there simply wasn't a corpse. Not even a wounded person.

Now that I thought about it, she had raced around that tree and howled every time we visited the construction site. Thankfully, no one had been killed during the construction. I wondered what on earth she was trying to tell me. That the tree was dying?

Stu groaned. "It couldn't have happened at a worse time."

"We're lucky no one was underneath it when that limb fell," I said, wondering how to convince Trixie to stop howling and come to me.

My phone rang. When I answered, Oma asked, "Is it true that the oak tree fell?"

"Just one limb. But it's enormous."

"Shadow is on the way. He should be there any moment. I am coming with Officer Dave."

In the next few minutes, townspeople arrived in droves. Mom and Sue were still chatting, but I noticed Mom hugging a number of people whom she probably hadn't seen in years. Shadow walked over to me, a chainsaw in his hand.

"Would it be wrong of me to take that limb for furniture?"

Shadow made beautiful handcrafted furniture in his spare time. "I don't think so. It would only be chopped up for firewood. Check with Oma to be sure."

Shadow nodded and began to measure the length of the limb by walking next to it and counting his strides.

I tried to catch Trixie, but she circled the tree and evaded me in her agitated state. "Trixie!" I scolded. "Come!"

She looked at me, panting.

Trixie was almost always by my side. She had hopped into my previous boyfriend's pristine car on a rainy night, a wet, dirty, scraggily mess. I hadn't thought I would be able to keep her, but as things turned out, she became my wonderful, devoted dog and truly did listen to me—mostly. Chills ran down my spine. The only times she acted like this were when someone had been murdered.

Elvis, Shadow's young bloodhound, ambled over to Trixie and bellowed halfheartedly twice.

Feeling like an idiot, I gazed up at the remaining branches, which were bare because of the time of year, but naturally, no corpses were wedged among them. Why was Trixie being so obstinate?

Oma finally arrived with Dave Quinlan. Wagtail's primary policeman, he was affectionately called Officer Dave, even though he had earned the rank of sergeant. Technically, he was affiliated with the police on Snowball Mountain, but he lived and worked in Wagtail. On the rare occasions when he had to interview people, he used our office at the Sugar Maple Inn. And while I was not a police officer, we had come to rely on each other, and he sometimes called on me to assist him with small tasks rather than wait for someone to come over from Snowball who didn't know the situation in Wagtail.

More people gathered, and everyone around us had an opinion on what to do with the tree.

Mom made her way through the crowd to Oma and me.

"It has to come down, Liesel," Stan Dawson said to Oma. "If that branch had hit somebody, it could have killed them. We can't afford that kind of liability."

"But Stan," said Oma, "it looks healthy to me."

Shadow pointed upward. "It won't make it to spring, Liesel. A healthy tree would have little buds on it even in the autumn, when the leaves have fallen off."

Normally, cutting down a tree wouldn't be such a big deal. But when Orly left the land to the town, his will had also contained one caveat. The old oak tree on the east side was not to be cut down. Of all the trees in Wagtail, and there were a great many—more than a person could count—it was that exact tree from which the giant limb had fallen.

I edged closer to Oma. "Are you afraid cutting down the tree will invalidate the will?"

I shuddered to imagine that the town would have put so much money into the beautiful new convention center and could lose it all because of one tree. Was it even legal to require that the tree couldn't be cut down? No one could guarantee the life of a tree, could they?

"A little bit," said Oma. "I see his children have arrived. We consulted with the town attorney before building. Still, I would rather avoid a court proceeding, not to mention the issue of having to call off the gingerbread house contest and all the events scheduled for the holidays."

"Should I call the lawyer?" I asked.

"I already did. Before I left the inn."

Orly's son and daughter, Wyatt and Josie, stood not twenty feet away, watching the proceedings and grinning like happy hyenas. Rumor had it that they were furious to learn their dad had not left the valuable property to them. Apparently, they had planned to sell it for a handsome sum. And now, I suspected, they thought their dreams would come true.

Oma's phone jingled. She answered it on speakerphone. "Liesel Miller."

A male voice said, "I hear you're having some problems with Orly's will and the provision about the tree."

"Can we cut it down?" Oma asked. "Shadow says it won't make it to spring."

"From a legal standpoint, we think the provision in the will falls outside the parameters of the law against perpetuities."

Everyone stared at the phone Oma held. I hoped what he had just said made sense to someone.

Oma groaned. "Our previous lawyer told us very clearly that the provision about the tree was invalid because of this perpetuity rule. And that we should not worry about it."

The voice said, "And where is this legal genius now?"

Oma sighed. "In the Snowball Mountain nursing home. He's not well. We wouldn't have built the convention center if he hadn't told us we could."

"The rule against perpetuities can be confusing," the male voice admitted.

Oma asked, "The rule aside, then, the question remains. Can we cut it down? What if it is a danger to the public? Doesn't the town have the right to cut down such trees?"

I noticed that Wyatt and Josie had drawn closer. Their smiles had faded.

We heard paper rustling through the speaker. The voice said, "The exact language is blah, blah, blah, *said land to the town of Wagtail, Virginia, provided that the town shall not cut down the old oak tree on the east side of the property* and then it cites coordinates."

Oma sighed. "We know that. Can we cut down the tree?"

"No," said the voice. "Not if you want to keep the

property. This sort of provision is generally upheld so long as it is not an illegal requirement."

"What does that mean?" asked Mom.

"Like if his will had said you could have the land as long as you made and sold moonshine on it without a license. Brewing moonshine is illegal unless you're licensed by the state, and they collect a fee."

The Biffle siblings looked at each other and high-fived.

"It doesn't say it can't be trimmed," shouted one of the women who had gathered.

"Have you got the whole town there, Liesel? It specifies that *the town* shall not cut the tree down. Those are Orly's exact words."

No less than seven people walked over to the tree, yelling things like "I'm not with the town. Do you work for the town?"

My boyfriend, Holmes, strode over to us. Dressed in standard Wagtail fashion for men—jeans and a blue flannel shirt—he looked comfortable and adorable.

Holmes slung his free arm around me. "Oma, what do you want to do?" he asked.

Oma spoke into the phone. "What do you advise?"

"Well, a court—"

"Court?" Oma squawked. "I do not wish to go to court."

"I'm trying to make a point," said the voice. "A court would look to Orly's intent. If a judge decided that 'cut down' meant removing the tree in a broader way that would include, for example, bulldozing, then you could have a problem."

Orly's kids snickered.

"However, I believe you may have an out. The town has an ordinance that permits the removal of trees that could pose a risk to the health or safety of residents and visitors, and that ordinance extends to public and private property within the town limits. Now that you have built a public structure on the property and are inviting people onto the property, I would say you could make a good case for the removal of a dangerous tree. I would certainly argue that protection of human life would supersede Mr. Biffle's wishes regarding the tree. You want me to send Ben up there?"

The mere mention of my former boyfriend's name caused me to stiffen. I hadn't seen Ben in a couple of years. He'd proposed to me by text! I turned him down. I didn't mind that he was a stuffy lawyer, but he didn't particularly care for dogs or cats, which was a deal breaker for me. Besides, now that things were going well with Holmes, I didn't want Ben around causing problems in my love life. I already had my mom making an unexpected visit. I certainly didn't need Ben showing up for the holiday, too.

Oma grumbled softly, "Not the Ben." Into the phone she said in a professional voice, "That will not be necessary." Oma thanked him and ended the call.

She stared at the tree and took a deep breath.

Orly's son shouted, "Too bad. Now you'll have to schedule a meeting and take a vote on this."

If his advice disturbed Oma, she didn't show it.

Dave, Stu, and Shadow moseyed over to us.

"I hate to agree with him," said Stu. "But the right thing to do is to call a meeting and take a vote."

Shadow shook his head. "There's no time for that!"

Oma glanced at Dave, who said, "Leaving it up is a risk."

With her chin up and her shoulders erect, Oma said clearly, "Better that I am removed from office than one person be injured. This is a public safety issue. Shadow, please take photos all the way around the tree. Then we will take the tree down."

I noticed that he was taking close-up shots of decay.

A chainsaw roared to life. Trixie ran to me, and I quickly picked her up so she wouldn't get underfoot. Mom held Twinkletoes firmly in her arms.

"Carter Riddle! You get away from that tree!" yelled his cousin, Josie Biffle.

Carter, who did not look like a lumberjack, with his soft, chubby physique, paused and turned off his chainsaw. "Josie, the tree is dead."

"Then don't you be coming around to my house for turkey this year," yelled Josie. "You cut that tree and you're no kin of mine!"

At that very moment, a loud crack filled the air and a second branch fell to the ground. Thankfully, we had all backed away from the tree in anticipation of it being felled. The branch wasn't as large as the first one, but if it had hit someone, it could have caused serious harm.

Oma gave Carter a nod. "Go ahead. Before anyone is hurt."

Carter shrugged and hit the side of the tree with his chainsaw. He worked hard, his round face turning ruddy. The buzz from his saw was deafening.

Those of us not involved in sawing moved farther away.

Mom smiled as she gazed around at the ridiculous number of people who had turned out to help cut down the tree. Word got around Wagtail fast! The mountain and the town were loaded with trees. They offered privacy between homes and added natural beauty. Most families in town had chainsaws to maintain the trees on their own properties. A lot of them had arrived with chainsaws in hand ready to pitch in.

It was a giant tree. Cutting it up and removing it would go faster with more people helping. But I knew that wasn't why Mom was smiling. Wagtail was that kind of place.

We didn't have a lot of emergencies, but everyone turned out to help when something happened.

After a few minutes, Carter stopped and examined his chainsaw. "Great day! Will you look at that? It ate the teeth plum off."

A large man whom I knew from the live Christmas tree stand waved him away. "You don't know what you're doin', Carter." He started his chainsaw and went to work.

A few minutes later, he too pulled his chainsaw away and examined it. "That tree is eatin' my chain."

People began to close in on the tree.

"It's magic!"

"It's possessed."

"Orly knew it was hexed. That was why he didn't give the land to his kids!"

Three

A few Wagtailites crept away from the oak tree and whispered among themselves.

But Oma and I drew closer for a better look. I touched the bark on the tree. It seemed perfectly normal to me.

And then a little old man stepped out of the crowd. His face was bronzed from the sun, as wrinkled and creased as linen on a hot day. He examined the tree. "Mrs. Mayor, your honor, I have seen this a couple of times before in my life. It's been filled with concrete."

Oma's expression showed her doubt. "Why would anyone do such a thing?"

"To save the tree. When they're hollow and rottin' on the inside, people used to fill 'em with concrete. You can't tell from the outside. There are probably more in Wagtail, but we haven't noticed them. It stops the rot, and the tree continues to grow, 'specially up at the top. Nobody does that much anymore, though."

"Surely you joke," said Oma.

"No, ma'am. That's the truth. You'll need to knock her down. Ain't no chainsaw ever made that can get through concrete like that."

"You can't knock it over!" taunted Wyatt Biffle, Orly's son. Even though he was closing in on fifty, he laughed like a ten-year-old boy tormenting a classmate.

Josie elbowed her brother. "Shut up, Wyatt. I'm calling our lawyer." To Oma she said, "You touch that tree, and we'll see that the land reverts to us."

Poor Oma. She looked so torn.

Holmes set his chainsaw on the ground, pulled out a Swiss Army knife, and pried the bark at the spot where the two men had tried to cut the tree. A small piece of bark flew off the trunk, revealing a solid core. "Looks like he's right."

"Bulldoze it, Holmes," Oma said. "The tree is dying and must go before anyone gets hurt. Yes?"

"Yes, ma'am. I'll be back with the bulldozer within the hour." Holmes squeezed my hand and took off at a trot.

Holmes was currently clearing land for construction of new houses on property owned by his family. I assumed he had a bulldozer. Even if he didn't, Holmes surely knew who had one available.

Josie stepped forward. "Mayor Miller, ma'am. I need to inform you that you are in violation of my father's will, and I protest the removal of this tree."

"Duly noted, Josie," Oma said calmly.

When Josie walked away, Oma whispered to me, "I hope the photographs and the falling of the second branch will be enough to convince a judge that this was necessary."

The crowd dispersed. Mom and I set Trixie and Twinkletoes on the ground. We began to walk back to the inn, though Trixie seemed miffed and didn't want to leave the tree.

Oma ordered lunch for the three of us from the inn kitchen, and I wheeled it down to her office. We clustered around the selection of savory carrot-pumpkin soup, fried chicken, warm potato salad, fall salad with crunchy apple bits and bacon, and several different beverages. Cook had also provided chicken lunches for Trixie, Gingersnap, and Twinkletoes.

After I ate, I filled in for Zelda at the desk so she could grab a bite, too. Naturally, the oak tree and Orly's will were the primary topics of discussion.

With twenty minutes to go until Holmes returned, I escorted Mom to my apartment on the top floor of the inn and showed her to her room. After the excitement of the morning, Twinkletoes curled up with Mom for a nap.

Trixie followed me down the stairs to Oma's office, where I packed some lunch for Holmes. Then I suited Trixie up in a harness and leash and the two of us walked back to the tree.

As promised, Holmes had returned with the bulldozer. His eyes lit up when he saw the packed lunch I had brought. He took a few minutes to eat while other townspeople returned, including Wyatt Biffle, who kept his distance.

After planting a deliciously fried-chicken-y kiss on me, Holmes boarded the bulldozer and stepped inside the cab. He began a slight distance away from the tree, digging up the roots, which were a rotting mess, proving that the tree had to go. I took photos of them, just in case the Biffles took the town to court.

But Holmes didn't even get a chance to push the tree over. It fell on its own with a resounding crash that shook the earth under our feet.

I looked around and made note of the names of the people who were watching. That way it wouldn't just be Holmes and me testifying that the tree fell on its own.

Four

I called Oma and sent her a photograph. Once again, Officer Dave picked her up on his way to the tree.

"They could just be shoes," suggested Barry Williams. Stu and Sue's son, Barry looked a lot like his father, tall but without his dad's generous belly. I'd met Barry through Holmes. The two of them and Carter Riddle had grown up together in Wagtail and gone through the ritual joys and pains of teen years. But Barry always seemed somewhat sad to me. He'd left Wagtail for college and to study veterinary medicine. Enormously popular with his furry patients and their families, Barry had a lot going for him.

Holmes looked over at his friend. "Sure, I can see that. I think I'll mix up concrete and pour it into this tree, but first I'll line up my shoes at the base of the tree."

"Hey!" Carter protested. "Anyone loony enough to pour concrete into a tree might think shoes are some kind of good-luck charm."

Barry gazed at Holmes and me. "Do you know of anyone who went missing from Wagtail? Could have been years ago!"

There was a horrific thought. "No one jumps to mind, but a lot of people come through Wagtail," I said.

My parents had fled Wagtail for California when I was five, but they made a point of sending me back to the Sugar Maple Inn and Oma every summer that I could remember. After college, I had worked as a fund-raiser in Washington, D.C., but when Oma offered to make me part owner of the family inn, I had jumped at the opportunity. Still, I didn't know everyone like Holmes did.

"Don't look at me," said Holmes. "I spent most of the last fifteen years in Chicago. But my folks might have some ideas."

Officer Dave and Oma crossed the grass to us with the town physician, Dr. Engelknecht.

"I've never seen anything like it," said Officer Dave. Formerly in the U.S. Navy, he still walked with regal bearing. But right now, he squatted next to the tree trunk. "Could be that the shoes are empty. I guess we should crack off some of the cement to find out if there's a person in there?"

Trixie barked again and tugged at her leash.

Officer Dave eyed her. "I've heard that bark before. Trixie's picking up a scent."

Dr. Engelknecht lowered his glasses. "I realize that dogs have superior olfactory abilities, but she'd bark just the same if a raccoon were trapped in there."

Officer Dave's eyes met mine. We knew better. "Not this dog," he said. "But you're the local medical examiner, so I'll defer to you. Do we strap it on a truck with the concrete or chip it off first?"

"We have to know if someone's in there before we do anything," said Doc. "I'm not shipping a concrete-filled tree for autopsy unless there's someone inside. Have you got a screwdriver and a hammer?"

The situation was becoming more surreal by the moment. A crowd had gathered around the tree, yet behind them, people were carrying adorable gingerbread houses into the convention center.

The sound of a hammer tapping the screwdriver on the concrete drew my attention. Even Trixie focused on the doctor.

Chunks of concrete fell away, and a crack appeared.

We fell silent as we watched. Doctor Engelknecht kept at it, chipping away wood and concrete with the care and patience of an archaeologist.

"Engelknecht!" said Carter. "Just give it a good whack with a hammer."

"Can't do that, Carter. We could destroy evidence." Doc continued, methodically removing small bits.

The word *evidence* chilled me to the bone.

Doc carefully followed the line of the crack, gently enlarging it. Bigger pieces fell to the ground.

"This is going to take all day," griped Carter.

He had barely finished speaking when a piece of fabric appeared and then, when weakened concrete fell, a hand became visible.

"Ach! Someone *is* in the tree." Oma sighed. "The concrete is not as thick in some places. That Orly! He must have known. This is why he did not want anyone to cut down the tree." She promptly phoned her lawyer to inform him.

Dr. Engelknecht shook his head in disbelief. "We probably shouldn't chip off more. We don't know the condition inside, but the concrete may have blocked air from getting in. Even just chipping off the section where the hand is will cause it to deteriorate more."

Holmes, ever the practical one, asked, "You don't really want to transport the whole tree, do you? If the hand is right there, then I think we can guesstimate that the person inside wouldn't be any taller than"—he walked it off—"right here. Shouldn't we get a jackhammer and break off the concrete above this point?"

"We might damage evidence," said Dave.

We all looked at him.

"Okay. I guess we'll have to do that," he conceded. "We can't transport the whole thing."

"Will you be able to get DNA?" asked Oma.

Doc smiled at her. "Probably. But it would help if you could put together a list of missing persons. From the looks of those shoe soles, I'd start with men who went missing."

Oma's phone rang. She answered, "Liesel Miller here."

She listened for a moment. "I'm going to put you on speaker. Would you repeat that?"

Her lawyer's voice said, "The Biffles' lawyer contacted me. I have informed him that the provision regarding the tree is null and void since its purpose was to hide a crime. He's speechless right now."

Oma thanked him and ended the call just as her phone rang again. Oma answered, listened briefly, and said, "Thank you, Zelda. Just a moment."

She addressed Dave. "People are calling the inn to tell me about missing family members."

Dave took a deep breath. "I'd better stay with the body. Holly, can you make a list of the missing persons for me? I can pursue the likely candidates later today or tomorrow."

Oma explained to Zelda that I would collect the names and should be back soon.

Oma and I left them to the task of figuring out how to transport the body. We walked across the lawn to the convention center and waited in the lobby while Sue and Stu Williams checked in a contestant.

Sue peered at the woman through glasses with translucent pink frames that matched the light pink of her sweater. She looked through a sheaf of papers and pulled out a sheet that listed the entrants. "There you are." She plucked a number from an automated machine, made note of it on a computer, and then handed it to the woman. "Now don't lose your number. None of the judges will know who made the houses. In fact, the judges aren't even permitted to go in there until judging day. Any questions?"

The contestant shook her head and thanked Sue.

When she left, Stu, considerably larger than his petite wife, boomed, "Am I glad to see you two!"

Oma looked wary. "Oh?"

Sue said softly, "Lower your voice, honey."

He complied and said, "My Suzy and I have a good life. We're financially comfortable and all, but I guess you know that our son, Barry, has only provided us with four-legged grandbabies, and he doesn't even have any of those right now. We'd like to spoil a child this Christmas. We don't care if it's a boy or a girl or even two or three children. We thought you might know of a child in need. Or maybe parents who could use a helping hand making the holidays special for their children."

"Oh!" Oma looked at me. "What a lovely gesture. I can't think of anyone. How about you, Holly?"

"Not off the top of my head. But I'm sure we can come up with someone." I eyed them. With Stu's substantial belly and Sue's sweet face, they would make a terrific Santa and Mrs. Claus team. "How would you feel about roaming the Christkindlmarket as Santa Claus and Mrs. Claus?"

Sue clasped her hands. "What fun! Maybe we can hand out small toys or chocolates to the little ones!"

That settled, they peppered us with questions about the

tree. While Oma filled them in, I gazed around. The convention center smelled new and fresh. Holmes, who was an architect, had designed the beautiful post-and-beam building for Wagtail. Windows soared, letting in light, but the wooden beams and rustic stone fireplaces added just the right touch of country mountain comfort and coziness. In addition to the large hall, it featured several smaller meeting rooms, a business center loaded with the latest in office equipment, and a full catering kitchen.

I strolled through the exhibits in the large hall, listening to familiar Christmas carols playing in the background and laughing at the clever dog and cat houses created out of gingerbread. Dog-bone-shaped cookies had been used liberally. One house had a thatched roof made of shredded wheat crackers. Another one mimicked Snoopy's classic doghouse, complete with Christmas lights and the famous dog lying on his back on top of it. Christmas lights were a big favorite, not terribly surprising given that it was already Thanksgiving week.

Some clever person had created a cat gingerbread house that had been made to look like a cardboard box. I couldn't help laughing aloud. Anyone with a cat knew they preferred boxes to fancy plush cat beds.

Several Wagtail residents were setting up their displays, impressing me with the details and precision of the houses. Except for those in the children's categories, these weren't the cute, shabby kind of gingerbread house I had made as a child. The contestants were pros. Out-of-town contestants had filled up the Sugar Maple Inn, and I had seen many of them carrying their gingerbread creations into their rooms ever so carefully before the convention center was open for registration.

My phone rang and the name *Sugar Maple Inn* showed. "Hello?"

"Holly," said Zelda in a hushed and serious tone. "I think you better get back here ASAP."

"What's going on?" I asked.

"There's a line of people here to report missing persons. I called Officer Dave, but he's tied up and said to call you."

"Tell them I'll be there in ten minutes."

I rushed back to Sue and Oma, explained briefly, and took off for the inn with Trixie running ahead of me.

We arrived to chaos. People packed the registration lobby, most of them anxious, some of them carrying sheaves of papers and photographs. They clustered around me, talking simultaneously. I picked up Trixie so no one would accidentally step on her and made my way to the registration desk. "Zelda, send them into Oma's office one at a time."

She brushed back her long blond hair with both hands and nodded. "Is it true that they found a body in the tree?"

"I'm afraid so." I hustled to Oma's office and set Trixie on the floor.

Twinkletoes raced into the office and flew onto the desk. She sat primly and wrapped her black tail around her white paws, as though she intended to assess the people who would enter. On a mostly white base of fur, she had one butterscotch square and one chocolate square on top of her head that always made me think of raised sunglasses. Her intensely green eyes didn't miss much and often looked like they glowed.

I grabbed a legal pad and a pen and settled at the desk.

The first person to enter the office was Matilda Critchfield. The petite woman with short curly hair that was beginning to gray took a seat in front of me. "I think"—she gulped hard and took a deep breath—"the man in the tree may be my uncle, Seth Dobbs."

She handed me a photograph of a smiling man in a fedora. I gazed at the back of the picture. It was dated 1948. I suddenly understood why Dave had relegated this job to me. We were going to go through loads of unlikely candidates. "When did your uncle go missing?"

"1955. I was a little girl at the time."

I paused for a moment to get my thoughts straight. Orly's insistence on not cutting down that particular tree suggested very strongly that he knew about the body in the tree. He'd probably guessed that his children would sell the land and the tree would be razed, thus revealing the body. Which was likely the reason he left the land to the town with the provision that we not cut down the tree. But the tree had finally given up its secret.

If Orly knew about the body in the tree, then it was most likely to have happened during his lifetime. I had no idea how long a tree could live after being filled with concrete, but one had to think he knew about it, even if someone else, a relative like his father, perhaps, had filled the tree. That left a very long span of time to check for missing persons.

I flicked open my phone and reviewed the photo I had taken of the shoes. The deep tread pattern looked fairly modern to me. But rubber soles had probably been around for a long time.

I decided to leave that up to Dave. I would make a note of details, like the date the person was last seen. The police would probably be able to determine the general age of the shoes, and that would narrow down the possibilities.

I took down basic information about Matilda's uncle. He'd been a farmer who was supposedly quite popular with the ladies and was reportedly last seen driving away in a Ford. I made a copy of the photo and thanked her for coming in.

Trixie and Twinkletoes were not impressed. They had

curled up, and neither even opened one eye when Matilda left.

I handled the next six people the same way, wondering why so very many people had gone missing from Wagtail. None of them seemed likely candidates to me, though. Not until Bonnie Greene walked in.

Trixie's Guide to Murder

The truth is that finding murdered peoples is all about your sniffer. Here's a sad fact—peoples have defective sniffers. You already noticed that, didn't you? They're great in so many ways, but their sniffers are broken.

For us doggums, smellin' stuff is what we do. Have you ever noticed that when you stop to smell something, your person will ask real sweet, "Was a squirlley there?" And you're thinking, Really? A squirlley? There's a new dog in town. He's a big guy, about ninety pounds, brown, mostly Labrador. He's four years old and had beef stew at Hot Hog for dinner last night. *But your person just keeps talking about squirllies.*

Don't believe me? Have you ever noticed that a baby has an odiferous mess in his diaper? The peoples don't notice but every dog within a quarter mile knows that baby made a stinko.

Now, don't go thinking your mom or dad is hopeless. Most of the time, they're pretty good at seeing things. They don't hear as well as we do, either, but nobody is perfect. Besides, they have us to help them!

Five

Bonnie Greene's presence awakened Trixie and Twinkletoes.

Most residents of Wagtail knew Bonnie because she owned Pawsome Cookies, which sold cookies made for people, dogs, and cats. I guessed her to be about my mom's age. She wore her blond hair in a loose bun and didn't bother with makeup. She volunteered at WAG, Wagtail Animal Guardians, and had a houseful of her own rescued cats and dogs. She reached over to pat Trixie and Twinkletoes.

Licking her lips nervously, she slid a photograph across the desk. "I'm somewhat embarrassed to be here."

I stared at a photograph of a drop-dead-handsome man. His chestnut hair was longish. I could imagine him brushing it back with a casual hand and letting it fall into place. He smiled, showing straight white teeth and a dimple in the middle of his chin. The kind of guy who made women swoon. The photograph was worn, as though it had been handled a good deal. "Who is he?"

"Boomer Jenkins, at least that was what he went by. I imagine his parents gave him a proper name, but I don't remember it, if I ever knew it."

"He's very handsome."

"Holly, that isn't the half of it. The man was so charming that everyone adored him. He was the love of my life."

"What happened to him?"

"I don't know." She took a deep breath. "He was engaged to Delia Riddle. Do you know her?"

"Orly's sister-in-law?" The connection to Orly pinged my suspicion antenna.

"His wife's sister." Bonnie's face turned as red as fall oak leaves, picking up on the slight reddish tinge in her hair and highlighting her clear blue eyes. "When I look back now, I realize how wrong it was, but I was mad for him. Just completely smitten."

Delia was still a Riddle, not a Jenkins, so I had to ask, "He broke off his engagement to Delia?"

"He was going to. He promised me that he would end the engagement. I'll never forget that moment. We were in the green, sitting underneath a tree. I had baked fresh chocolate chip cookies. They were still warm. You know, when the chocolate is sort of melty. It was a beautiful day in August. We snuggled together and he told me he was going to break off the engagement that evening."

"And did he?"

"I don't know. I never saw or heard from him again. Not a word. I remember him walking across the green and looking back at me. And that was it. I cooked dinner, thinking he would come to my place after he talked to Delia. The candles burned down, the roast chicken and mashed potatoes grew cold. I called him over and over. We had funny little cell phones back in the day, but the reception in Wagtail was so bad that the only way to reach him was to call on a landline." She reflected quietly for a moment, stroking Twinkletoes. "I was a mess. Of course, I thought Delia had managed to change his mind. That when Boomer was with her, he realized that he didn't love me. Or that he loved her more! For a while I thought I might have to leave Wagtail. How could I continue to live in the same town with the man I loved, when he was married to someone else?"

I could relate. I'd had similar thoughts about Holmes. When I saw him again after a decade or more, he had been engaged. His fiancée's family even stayed at the inn one Christmas. Talk about miserable. But I knew he had to make up his own mind. I couldn't come between them. It wouldn't have been right. For a while, though, I had worried just like Bonnie had. "Did you ask Delia about him?"

She gasped. "Seriously? Walk up to his fiancée and ask where he was? I didn't have it in me to do that. What if she didn't know I was seeing him? Or what if they had a fight about me and that was why he left town? I did go to the police, but the old chief blew it off as an unimportant broken heart."

Bonnie came across as genuine, but what if she murdered him when he tried to break off their engagement? Would she report him missing if she had?

"The old chief? How long ago was this?"

"Twenty years."

I guessed the shoes could be that old. "Can you think of anything else that might be helpful?" I asked.

She shook her head. "I hope it's not him. He may have ditched me, but I'd rather think that he's still alive and well somewhere."

I thanked her for coming in and saw her to the door. When I opened it, two men jumped up.

As interesting as it was to talk to everyone, I was getting a little weary. It had been quite a day. But when I saw the hopeful expressions on their faces, I couldn't turn them away.

Two hours later, I was glad to see the last person enter the office. I recognized her as Althea Alcorn. She walked in with a cane and when she sat down, she handled it deftly, as though she used it all the time. I didn't know her well, even though she was active in the community. She had aged considerably since I last saw her. The Alcorns were said to be a wealthy family. I'd heard that her husband lived in a nursing center in Snowball. "Hello, Mrs. Alcorn."

"Thank you for seeing me, Holly." She sat so straight that I forced my own shoulders back.

She shoved a photograph toward me. "The man in the tree is my son."

Six

✿ ✿ ✿ ✿ ✿

The photograph in front of me showed a young man with light brown hair and a sparse mustache. "He looks like your son, Kent."

"He is Kent's brother, Jay, hence the resemblance. I always thought Kent favored me. Jay took after his father."

"When did he go missing?"

Mrs. Alcorn lowered her eyes. "Must have been twenty years ago now. It was the day after Thanksgiving. Jay and Kent were home from university. I learned, quite by accident, that a local girl had been visiting him there. She was coarse and cheap. I'm sure you know the type. I forbade him from dating her." She shook her head. "She would have dragged him down. Jay was smart but bullheaded like me. He could be sly. Probably got that from me, too. Still, he had the smarts to make something of himself. He had a marvelous future ahead of him. But he was drawn to this tawdry girl who would have led him down the wrong path. I'm afraid we had a tiff." She paused and swallowed hard. "He told me he loved her. I told him not to come back if he was involved with her."

"He never came home after that?" I asked.

"I never saw him again." I could tell it pained her deeply, but she was tough and dry-eyed.

"You said the girl was local. Did you talk with her? Ask her where he went?"

Mrs. Alcorn's mouth pulled taut. She sucked in a deep breath. "I have not been a gentle person. I do not suffer fools gladly, and I loathe idle chitchat. I fear my pride has stood in my way on occasion, this being one of them."

She wasn't a warm person, that was for sure. But I found myself feeling quite sorry for her. She clearly had regrets.

"Are you sure he didn't run off with this girl?" I asked.

"Quite certain. I see her around town. Josie Biffle. I make it a point not to shop in their store, though they do carry excellent produce."

It sounded to me as though Jay had simply taken off, but the least I could do was ask Josie if she knew where he was.

"I worry that Orly shot my boy to keep him away from his daughter and then hid his body. Until the tree fell, I feared Jay was at the bottom of the lake."

I blinked at her. "Okay, you didn't like Josie because she wasn't good enough for your son, but why would Orly dislike Jay?"

"Orly was a snake. A despicable, thieving miscreant. I knew something was up when he bequeathed the lake property to the town. That man never gave anyone anything for free. He was a finagler. He and my husband had a run-in over the land where Biffle's Grocery is located."

"Since the store is there, I gather Orly won."

She shook her head. "He did *not*. The Biffles pay me rent on that building."

"Surely he wouldn't have harmed your son because of a land dispute," I said, horrified at the thought.

"I would hope not. But he would have been extremely upset if he knew his daughter was dating my son." Her blazing eyes met mine. "Consider what you're dealing with. Orly *knew* someone was in that tree. He most likely placed the body there himself. There's no other reason to add a provision to his will prohibiting the razing of the tree. What kind of person does that?"

She had a point. I had trouble imagining that anyone could have such a cold heart. I made note of the squabble between the Biffles and the Alcorns.

I wondered if her husband knew more about their son. "I understand that Mr. Alcorn lives in Snowball?"

She nodded. "He's unlikely to recall anything. He has Alzheimer's. I suppose you could ask him. They say he has good days and bad."

I thanked Mrs. Alcorn for coming in.

"You will phone me as soon as you know anything." It was more of a directive than a question.

"I will."

She walked out the door relying heavily on her cane. Her posture was still remarkably good, but I had seen the exhaustion in her eyes.

Whew! I was glad to be done. But then there was a timid knock on the door.

Twinkletoes yawned. Even Trixie rolled her head back to look at me as though she couldn't believe there were more.

"Come in," I called.

The door didn't open. I rose from my seat and swung the door wide to find a woman hurrying away.

"Did you change your mind, Penny?" asked Zelda.

Penny Terrell swung around. When she saw me, she gasped and held her breath.

I felt terrible for her. This had been achingly emotional for all these people who desperately wanted to know what had happened to someone they loved. I smiled at her. She was probably afraid of finding out that it was her relative in the tree.

Trixie barked, ran to Penny, and wagged her tail.

A smile made its way across Penny's lips. "I'm not dead yet, Trixie."

"Come on in," I said cheerfully.

"That's not necessary. I only wanted to know when the judging will be for the gingerbread houses. I hope I haven't missed the deadline."

"Thursday at noon," I said. "Better have your entry there by Wednesday."

"Wonderful. Thank you. Bye now." She departed so fast that she left a wave of wind behind her.

Zelda looked at me. "That was one of the biggest lies I've ever heard."

"Me, too."

"She'll be back." Zelda drummed a pencil against the registration desk.

"She knows something," I said. "Which is more than I can say for most of the people who came through today."

"No leads?"

"Not many. The size and shape of the shoes lead us to think it's an adult man, which means we can eliminate most women and children. A lot of their missing loved ones moved away and people lost contact with them, so they can be excluded, too."

"But with the Internet and Facebook, you can find all kinds of long-lost friends," Zelda observed.

"Unless they don't want to be found. It's hard to stay off the net, but I suppose it can be done."

"Do you think Penny is really entering the contest?" asked Zelda.

"Does she bake?" I asked.

Zelda shrugged. "She works at the bank. And she's married to Tommy Terrell. Talk about a great husband. Someone told me he makes breakfast for them every day and brings her a cup of coffee before she even gets out of bed! Why can't I find a guy like that?"

Poor Zelda had had a long run of bad luck with men. "You will," I said, hoping that would be the case.

My mom strode into the reception lobby, eyeing all the wonderful things for sale in our little gift shop. "I can't believe what Oma has done with the inn. It's amazing. When you were born, Holly, everything was different. Wagtail was a dying town. I don't know that we would have left if it had been like this."

I checked my watch. "Are you ready for dinner? I can give you a guided tour on the way."

"That would be great."

I dashed upstairs to change clothes while Mom checked to see if Oma wanted to join us.

Half an hour later, Oma, Gingersnap, Trixie, Twinkletoes, and I gave Mom a golf cart tour of Wagtail, pointing out the animal medical center, the restaurants along the lake, and the Shire, which was technically outside the center of Wagtail. The cozy community of cottages resembled a mixture of the Cotswolds in England and darling hobbit houses.

"Are they terribly expensive?" asked Mom. "I would love to live there."

I concentrated on driving while Oma tried to talk her into moving back to Wagtail.

We parked behind one of our favorite restaurants, Hot Hog. Trixie leaped from the golf cart and raced into the restaurant, with Gingersnap right behind her. Twinkletoes took a more feline, measured approach, as if she thought she were royalty. Mostly an outdoor dining place, at this time of year they enclosed the seating in glass panels and kept it toasty with heaters.

Trixie chose a table by beating us inside and jumping up on a bench. It was her favorite place to dine. So much so that Mom was astonished when we ordered and the server asked if Trixie would like her usual of pulled chicken for dogs.

Only when we started to eat our dinner did Mom get around to telling us why she had finally come for a visit.

"I'm sorry to say that Todd and I have separated."

My fork clattered to my plate. A second divorce? It wasn't unheard of, but I felt sad for her. I'd thought this marriage would work out.

"The children are spending Thanksgiving with their dad because they'll be with me at Christmas."

That took me back. I was a teen when my parents had divorced and started new families with new spouses. To be honest, I never felt at home with either of them. They were kind to me, but I was a holiday guest, not really family. I had hated rushing to my mom's house in California, then flying to my dad's home in Florida. Most years I felt as though I had spent more time in airports and on planes than enjoying the company of family.

I barely knew my half siblings, but now I felt for them.

"I am very sorry to hear this," said Oma. "What happened?"

Leave it to Oma to get to the bottom of the matter.

"He had other ideas—"

"Ach," said Oma. "Another woman. Your husband is a fool to leave you." She shook her head. "What do your parents say about this?"

Mom looked at us with a hopeful expression. "We'd like to return to Wagtail. All of us."

"But this is wonderful news!" Oma gushed.

I sat back in my chair, taking it all in. My mom? In the same town as me? After all these years? I smiled at her. "I can't believe it. That's terrific!"

"I love you two. I can't wait to be back. I sat out on Holly's terrace a little bit today and it was so peaceful with the lake and the trees. I've missed the mountains. And it will be nice to have relatives nearby again."

And then all three of us muttered the same name, "Birdie."

Mom's older sister, Birdie, was a pill. I conceded that she looked great. Slender and always impeccably dressed, she made a good first impression, except for that Cruella de Vil white streak that flashed through her black hair. It was like the bright colors in nature that warned us to stay away from poisonous creatures. Not that she was actually poisonous, of course, but Birdie had a tendency to be hostile and disagreeable.

I had been around her enough to see her gentler side. Though I often had to remind myself that it existed, which wasn't always easy when she was haranguing me about some perceived and unimportant infraction of her rules of life.

"I've been thinking about this ever since you phoned me from the hospital, Holly. Remember? The night you thought Birdie might die? Your grandparents and I have talked about this ever since. It's not just that we want to be closer to Birdie, something we may live to regret, but there's not anything keeping us in California anymore. Dad would like to have a boat and fish again, and Mom has been in touch with her Wagtail quilting friends on Facebook. The two of them think they would fit right in. Don't get me wrong, we could move to Lake Tahoe or somewhere else, but *you* wouldn't be there."

The lively chatter in the restaurant hushed and the

bang of high heels against the wood floor grew louder as it approached us. Trixie slinked off the bench and hid between my legs. I could feel Gingersnap under the table, too. Only Twinkletoes remained in classic Egyptian cat pose on the bench, her eyes locked onto something.

Seven

Aunt Birdie towered over us. She raised her right arm and placed her hand over her heart. Gazing upward, she said in a voice that everyone could hear, "My only two living relatives. And this is how you treat me. Like the orphan in a Dickens novel."

My eyes met Mom's and it was all I could do to stifle a roar of laughter. I looked away and bit my lower lip in an effort not to smile. Ever the drama queen, Birdie always lowered the number of her living relatives to the number of them present. Today she ignored her parents and her nieces and nephews, not to mention likely second and third cousins I didn't even know about.

"Can you even imagine my pain, a stab through the heart, to have to learn from a *stranger, a stranger!* that my sister is in town." Birdie's hand crept up to her collarbone. "How *could* you?"

Oma interrupted her with a terse and quite loud, "Sit down, Birdie."

"Oh! An invitation to join the exalted. What an honor."

Mom stood up and circled the table to her sister. "Birdie! It's so good to see you." She reached out her hands for a hug.

Birdie hugged her, though somewhat grudgingly. "How long have you been here?" she asked snidely.

Mom ignored her question and held her at arm's length. "You look great!"

Birdie's nostrils flared. "And why wouldn't I? I wasn't going to let myself go just because my family abandoned me here and fled to the other side of the country."

"I mean because you were in the hospital. Do you remember speaking to me on the phone? You thought you were dying."

"Of course I remember. Thank you so much for bringing up the most dreadful and painful event of my entire life, well, except for when my family abandoned me."

Birdie had eaten a salad laced with wolfsbane when she was one of three women chasing the same widower. Luckily, she had survived the deadly ingestion.

Mom was used to ignoring Birdie's slights. "Come sit down, Birdie. I'm eager to hear all about your life here in Wagtail."

I snatched Trixie's dinner plate away so Birdie could sit down.

A server took Aunt Birdie's order and looked around. "Where's Trixie?"

The little scamp poked her nose out from under the table.

"What are you doing under there?" She promptly brought a little bench for Trixie, who jumped up on it immediately, wagging her tail in gratitude.

I placed her dish on the bench. Gingersnap slinked back to her dish on the floor. Flicking her tail, Twinkletoes watched Birdie carefully.

Aunt Birdie looked aghast.

Since I had also been the recipient of a similar I-wasn't-the-first-person-you-saw-on-arrival-to-Wagtail hissy fit, I soon realized that it was best to keep my distance from Birdie. In spite of my efforts, she managed to wiggle her way into my life on a regular basis, mostly to complain to me about some nonsensical thing that she considered an egregious oversight on my part.

I planned to ignore her horror at eating with two dogs and a cat.

"I have written a book," Birdie declared. "And it looks like the publisher might want a sequel."

"A book?" cried Mom. "That's fantastic. What is it? A mystery?"

"I wanted to write about a woman who lost her entire family and was left alone on a deserted mountain to fend for herself."

She had officially worn out that line. None of us reacted.

"But instead, I wrote about antique American furniture from the seventeenth century. It's selling quite well and being used as a reference book."

Birdie, for all her phony drama, was a nationally recognized authority on antiques. I had to throw her a bone. "I'm so proud of you. That's quite an accomplishment."

Birdie's vegetable plate arrived. She stared at it with loathing. "It's packed with photographic examples and means of distinguishing authentic furniture from fraudulent pieces."

"How would you write a sequel to something like that?" asked Mom.

"We're discussing a series of similar books through the twentieth century. A set that would comprise a comprehensive guide."

"That is very impressive," said Oma. "Congratulations, Birdie."

"Have you told Mom and Dad?" asked Mom.

Birdie sighed. "They're not interested."

Mom looked crushed. "Of course they are! Tomorrow, let's call them together and you can tell them all about it."

Birdie glowed with pleasure and speared a piece of broccoli. All she really wanted was to be included and praised. Just like everyone else. Would she ever learn that putting people on the defensive wasn't the way to earn their affection? Probably not.

Trixie had already snarfed her dinner and was eyeing mine. Not a chance! Besides, my pulled pork gleamed with a vinegar-and-tomato barbecue sauce that she shouldn't eat. But I loved it!

"Nell has news, too," said Oma.

"We're moving back to Wagtail."

"You and your family?" asked Birdie.

"Not my husband. The children are up in the air about it. They're teens, which is a difficult time to transition. But they'll be away at college before long anyway. Mom and Dad are excited to come back."

"They're coming home," Birdie murmured. She stopped eating. "My house. It was their house. Will they expect to move back in?"

"We haven't worked all that out yet," said Mom. "Don't worry, there's enough room in Wagtail for all of us."

Birdie didn't seem so sure. After all these years alone, I could only imagine what a change it would be to have her parents living with her again. But they probably wouldn't want to. No one would want to!

The conversation moved on to the corpse in the tree.

"Zelda told me quite a few residents came to tell you about missing people." Oma looked at me.

"A surprising number, actually. But quite a few were most likely about people who left Wagtail. They're probably not dead. It's just that no one knows how to reach them."

They gazed at me in horror.

"Some people have common names like Smith or Jones. That can be hard to track. And other people change their surnames when they marry or divorce."

Birdie frowned. "Even my sister gave me her address when she moved."

Why did she have to phrase it that way, as it if were something unusual? "Sometimes people leave in anger, I guess. Or maybe they simply feel the need to break all ties."

Our server cleared the dishes and asked if we would like their new gingerbread cake for dessert. They developed it in honor of the gingerbread house contest. We all wanted to try it, even Trixie, who reached one gentle paw toward the server as though she were raising her hand, which lightened our mood.

Beautifully spiced, with a creamy frosting, the cake was delicious. Trixie's and Gingersnap's versions were smaller and topped with yogurt, which probably would have been better for all of us. They snarfed it up.

We took the golf cart home in the frigid night air, dropping Aunt Birdie off at her house first.

The lobby was relatively quiet, as it generally was after dinner. Guests usually drifted back in small groups. The night manager had everything under control.

Oma said good night and headed for her quarters with Gingersnap. Mom and I walked up the grand staircase to my apartment on the third floor. Trixie bounded up ahead of us, and Twinkletoes zoomed up around us so fast that she was little more than a flash of white.

Even though Mom was exhausted, we sat down with spiked hot chocolate in my living room. I turned on my gas logs, which crackled a little.

I honestly could not remember the last time I had been alone with my mom. There had always been babies or toddlers needing attention, or her new husband had been with us. I didn't fault her for that, it was her life. I always loved my mother, but I'd forgotten how much fun she was. We gossiped and talked and laughed for hours.

It was after midnight when Mom headed for my guest room and I dragged myself off to bed with Trixie and Twinkletoes.

I let Mom sleep in the next morning. After all, her body clock was probably still set to California time. She hadn't seemed too upset about her pending divorce. Maybe the excitement of moving back to Wagtail had softened the blow for her a little bit.

One of the perks of living at the Sugar Maple Inn was pre-breakfast in bed. Oma had hired Mr. Huckle, a wizened elderly man, when he lost his position as butler to the wealthiest man in town. Alas, thanks to a very bad second marriage, his boss's resources were drained and Mr. Huckle, who was devoted to the family, had to be let go. Oma wanted to help the elderly gentleman who was down on his luck, but she never suspected that he would become the darling of our guests. He was always ready to lend a hand, deliver tea or packages to a room, or even walk the dogs for guests. He knew how to do everything from mending clothes to setting a proper table. And he insisted on wearing his butler's uniform of waistcoat and tie, which gave the inn an air of gentility.

Apparently, it had been his habit to serve his employer coffee and croissants in bed in the morning. Oma and I knew nothing about that until trays magically appeared in our rooms. He slipped in and out, quiet as a mouse. He had brought me a pot of tea and a chocolate croissant carefully tucked inside a glass-domed server so Trixie wouldn't gobble it up. A Sugar Maple Inn dog biscuit in the shape of a turkey for Trixie and a fishy-smelling cat treat for Twinkletoes also lay on the tray.

I wondered if he had brought one for Mom.

I made a point of dressing in an oatmeal-colored sweater that had been a gift from Mom. I paired it with khakis and sneakers, which weren't stylish shoes, but most days I did a lot of walking, and practicality outweighed stylishness.

In the kitchen, I spooned crabmeat bisque into Twinkletoes's bowl. As she settled in to eat, I picked up the scent of coffee, which must have been coming from a tray in the room where Mom was sleeping.

Trixie and I left quietly so we wouldn't disturb her and walked down the grand staircase. I paused on the second-floor landing. The lobby and the dining area already bustled with guests. But one man stood out.

His hands in his pants pockets, he examined the lobby carefully, taking in the details. He had dark hair and wore tortoiseshell glasses.

I hurried down the stairs to ask if I could help him, but he was gone by the time I got there.

After a brief visit to the dog potty outdoors, we joined Oma, Mr. Huckle, and Gingersnap for breakfast.

"Good morning, liebchen." Oma smiled at me. "You are enjoying the visit from your mother?"

"Very much. Have you heard anything from Dave about the corpse?"

At that moment, Shelley Dixon, our chief server, walked up and poured a mug of tea for me. "Morning, Holly. Cook is in full-out gingerbread mania. Gingerbread muffins, gingerbread pancakes, and gingerbread oatmeal, if you can imagine that."

Mr. Huckle laughed. "It's not as bad as it sounds."

I loved the array of delicious breakfasts at the Sugar Maple Inn and always felt quite spoiled by them. When I resided in Arlington, Virginia, I often grabbed a muffin or ate yogurt for breakfast, usually on the run.

Trixie, who had once wanted to eat all the dogs' breakfasts in the dining area, lifted her nose and sniffed the air in the direction of a sweet beagle.

"What's that dog eating?" I pointed at the beagle.

"Poached eggs, a teeny bit of bacon, and a mini dog-safe gingerbread muffin."

"Trixie will have that. And so will I if there's a people version of it."

Shelley nodded. "Sure thing."

When she left, Oma asked, "Are you certain you want to hear about the cement corpse while you eat?"

"Is it gross?" I asked.

"A little bit. It seems that concrete can inhibit the deterioration of the body. Not in all cases, but it can slow it down."

Mr. Huckle piped up. "It's a matter of whether air can get in."

"Because of this," said Oma, "they wrapped the hand airtight and did not chip off any more concrete. It was loaded onto a truck and transported to the medical examiner in Richmond, where they have sophisticated equipment. They will use some high technology to determine what they can through the concrete before chipping it off."

"I guess we won't know much for quite a while with Thanksgiving right around the corner."

"That is the big problem. I am having to pull strings. We can't leave it until the week after Thanksgiving. Who knows what could happen to it with that kind of delay? It's so large they're not sure where to put it." Oma's phone rang. "Excuse me." She glanced at it. "And so my day begins. I will be in the office if anyone needs me."

She bustled away with Gingersnap. Mr. Huckle shook his head. "I don't know how she does it all."

Our breakfasts arrived at the same time as my mother. I introduced her to Mr. Huckle and to Shelley.

Mom took the seat next to me and glanced down at Trixie, who ate ravenously. "Times sure have changed but I love it! When I lived here people would have laughed at me if I suggested dogs should be served in restaurants."

"What can I get you?" asked Shelley. "Would you like to see a menu?"

Mom glanced at my poached eggs on toast. "I'll have what Holly's having, thank you."

Shelley nodded and bustled off.

My mother turned her attention back to me. "Honey, when I left the apartment, this had been shoved under the door for you."

Eight

Mom handed me a manila envelope. On the front side, someone had handwritten *Holly* in a looping script.

Shelley stopped by with a coffeepot to refill mugs.

I ripped the envelope open and slid out a photograph. A good-looking man in a black leather jacket lounged in front of a motorcycle. There was no question in my mind that it was—

"Boomer Jenkins!" exclaimed Shelley, looking at the photo. She rested the coffeepot on the table.

Mr. Huckle shook his head. "My goodness. It has been a long time since I heard that name."

"A handsomer man never lived." Shelley took a deep breath. "He had puppy-dog brown eyes that could melt a girl's heart with a glance."

Mr. Huckle smiled and sipped his coffee. "He certainly caused chaos around here."

"You both knew him?" I asked.

Mr. Huckle was quick to say, "I knew *of* him. I wasn't, er, of interest to him. The man had quite a reputation."

"Did you know him, Mom?"

She shook her head. "I think I'd remember a fellow who looked like that."

"All the women knew him," said Shelley. "Unfortunately, he knew how good-looking he was, and he worked his charm like a magician. That man flirted with everyone. Even me! I must have been around thirteen, but that didn't stop him from winking at me."

"Bonnie Greene mentioned him yesterday. She implied that they had a relationship?"

"I'd say that was highly likely." Shelley chuckled. "Bonnie and half a dozen other young women. Funny how silly it seems all these years later. Everyone was chasing him."

"She thought he might be the man in the tree."

Mom gasped. "Oh my!"

"I can't say that I remember what happened to him. Did he move away?" Shelley asked Mr. Huckle.

"He probably *ran* away," Mr. Huckle joked. "You can't make eyes at all the girls without one of them expecting a monogamous relationship."

Shelley laughed and picked up the coffeepot. "I sure hope it's not him!"

Mr. Huckle excused himself to get to work, leaving Mom and me to finish our meal.

"Holly, when you told me you were moving to Wagtail, I didn't understand. To be honest, I thought you were retreating to Wagtail to recover from breaking up with Ben. I just couldn't imagine you wanting to move to sleepy little Wagtail. But now I see why you're here. Oma is right. It's not the same place I left. Your grandparents will be shocked by all the changes. This morning, I sat on your balcony overlooking the green and the town of Wagtail, with my hot coffee and a delicious gingerbread muffin. That must be one of the best views in town."

"Shh. Not so loud."

She giggled. "It will be our little secret. I thought I would go house shopping today. I phoned Carter Riddle, Delia's son. He was a darling baby. I can't wait to meet him as an adult. It's sort of strange. I've missed such a big piece of people's lives. Delia and I were very close once. She was always so delicate and sweet. But when we moved away, our relationship fizzled to Christmas cards and Facebook."

"She's still like that. She speaks in a soft voice, so I have to really pay attention to her."

"Is he a good Realtor?"

"I imagine so. He's active on the town council and one of the first to pitch in if there's an emergency. In fact, he tried to cut the tree down. I should have introduced you."

"Want to come along?"

"I would love to." We set up a time and I excused myself to get to work.

The first thing Trixie, Twinkletoes, and I did every morning was our rounds through the inn. They were mostly to make sure the inn was tidy and in tip-top shape. We checked that no lightbulbs had gone out in the corridors. That no broken glass or spills were on the floors. I picked up forgotten suitcases, raincoats, briefcases, clothing, toys, and single shoes that were lying about. I had never quite understood how people lost only one shoe. Seemed like that was something you'd notice.

I collected my clipboard from the office and began at the staircase that led from the registration lobby to the second floor. We walked by rooms named for dog activities and headed past the well of the grand staircase to the cat wing in the addition on the far end of the building. I took the rear stairs down on that side, tested the emergency exit, and walked through the rooms named for cat activities on the first floor. Our small library connected the cat wing to the original building.

A fire crackled in the library. The sun shone through the bay window highlighting a girl's coppery locks as she sat on the window seat. I recognized her as Kitty. Trixie shot at her so fast I was afraid she might frighten the girl when she bounded onto the window seat with her. But Kitty hugged Trixie to her. Trixie licked the freckles on the girl's face, and her tail flashed back and forth with joy.

"Hi. This is Trixie. I think she likes you."

"I love dogs. Hi, Trixie!" She buried her face in Trixie's white fur. I guessed her to be around eight or nine.

"Kitty!" The scolding voice came from Jean Maybury, who entered the library from the main lobby pulling a cart behind her. Her red hair had a distinct purple tinge. It was a young color, but her wrinkled jowls suggested she wasn't all that youthful. "What have you done? Honestly, child, now you'll have to take a bath and change your clothes."

"I'm sorry," I apologized. "It's not her fault. My Trixie made a beeline for her. Trixie," I called.

Trixie licked Kitty's nose one more time before running back to me. I picked her up so she wouldn't bother Kitty anymore. "I hope she won't be ill. Is she allergic to dogs?"

Jean Maybury was clearly annoyed by many things, including my question. "She's allergic to everything. Just everything! But, well, circumstances required that I bring her with me to the gingerbread house contest." She looked at her watch. "You don't have time for a bath, but I want you to run upstairs and change your clothes. Hurry, now! You're putting me behind schedule."

Kitty murmured, "I'm sorry, Memaw." She hurried to Jean's side and held out her hand for the room key.

I was under the impression that Kitty got plenty of scolding and could probably use some encouragement instead. I smiled and winked at her.

She grinned and winked back before running to the grand staircase.

"I don't know if you remember me, but I'm Jean Maybury. I'm staying here at the inn. I won a gingerbread house contest, and the prize was a week here at the inn for two, so I could submit a gingerbread house to your contest."

"I do remember you. How do you like your room?"

"It's darlin'. I couldn't have asked for anything more cozy." She spoke in a North Carolina accent, slow and drawn out. "I didn't bring my husband. I call him my old slippers because he's comfortable, but he's plumb worn out and not suitable for public exposure. So I thought I'd bring my granddaughter Kitty along. The poor child never gets to go anywhere. Her mother is all alone. Daddy ran off. She works two jobs, has two children, and never manages to pay the rent on time. And then this week, bless her, she lost her main position. The restaurant she worked for was sold! The man who bought it is planning to put his whole family to work, so all the employees are unemployed. It's not her fault. She just never can catch a break. So I thought I'd bring Kitty with me and take a little stress off her. But it never occurred to me that Kitty would be bored to tears while I put the finishing touches on my gingerbread house. And I have an obligation to the nice people who sent me here and are paying for our trip."

My head was beginning to spin. I tried to bring her to the point of our conversation. "You need a sitter for Kitty?"

Jean gasped. "It's like you read my mind. But the thing is, I have a responsibility to take care of her. I can't hand her off to just anyone."

I was on the verge of telling her we had a list of responsible sitters when I thought of Stu and Sue Williams. "I know the perfect couple."

"Really? How much do they charge?"

"Not a cent."

She gazed at me doubtfully. "Then why would they babysit? They're not . . . criminals or anything?"

"They're perfectly nice people." I found their number on my phone and selected it. Sue let out a little shriek when I told her why I was calling. "We'll be there in ten minutes."

"I suppose I should stay to meet them," Jean fussed.

That was up to her.

She tapped her foot on the floor. "I pride myself on being a very punctual person. I just detest being late for anything."

Kitty returned in a fresh outfit.

"Now, Kitty"—Jean straightened the collar on the little girl's shirt—"some nice people are coming to babysit you. I want you to be on your very best behavior. Do you understand?"

Kitty nodded as if this were an everyday occurrence for her.

Just then, Sue and Stu burst into the main lobby. I waved at them.

"Oh my goodness!" exclaimed Sue. "Aren't you the prettiest girl? What's your name, sugar?"

"Kitty."

"I hope you won't mind spending some time with us," said Stu.

"Thank you so much. I hope she won't be too much trouble." Jean gave Sue and Stu a critical glance up and down.

"Nonsense. An angel like this couldn't be a problem." Sue smiled at Kitty. "Do you like cats and dogs?"

"She's allergic," said Jean. "Maybe this wasn't such a good idea."

Sue looked horrified and reached for Kitty's hand. "We'll take good care of her. When should we have her back?"

"After . . ." Jean hesitated.

"After dinner?" asked Stu. "Do you like barbecue? We can take you to a fun restaurant!"

"Well, all right." Jean looked at me. "I think she might have more fun than I will!"

That settled, I wished them all a good day and returned to the business at hand.

Trixie and I walked through the main lobby to the covered front porch. It ran along the front of the original building of the inn. We stepped out onto it, and I cast a critical eye over the rocking chairs. No one had left morning papers or sweaters, though I did find a couple of Sugar Maple Inn coffee mugs that had been abandoned. I collected them and took them to the kitchen to be washed.

Trixie waited outside. Dogs and cats were not permitted in kitchens where food was prepared for sale, with the noted exception of bed-and-breakfasts. Not a big loss for the animals, actually, since they were welcomed everywhere else and could join their families eating in dining rooms. Wagtail had been exempted from state laws regarding animals in restaurants in a deal made with the state well before I had moved back.

When I emerged, Officer Dave sat in a chair with Trixie at his feet and Twinkletoes on his lap. Dark circles under his eyes told me he hadn't gotten much sleep.

Shelley brought him a steaming cup of coffee, scrambled eggs with ham, and buttered whole wheat toast.

"I thought you must be nearby with these two lingering at the door. Thanks for helping out yesterday. How'd it go?"

The dining room had mostly emptied out. An elderly couple had taken their coffee out on the terrace overlooking Dogwood Lake.

"I made notes. Should I go get them?"

"Probably a good idea. Shelley can keep me company."

I raised an eyebrow at Shelley, but she was too fixated on Dave to notice. I left the two of them, crossed the lobby, and headed down the hallway to the inn office, with Trixie and Twinkletoes springing merrily along ahead of me. Oma was on the phone, but she crooked a finger at me and handed me a sheet of paper. I collected my notes and left, reading the paper Oma had handed me. It contained only one name, *Jay Alcorn*.

I flipped it over. It said nothing else at all. Well, well. It appeared that old Mrs. Alcorn wasn't the only person in town who wondered what had happened to her son.

Back in the dining area, Officer Dave had snarfed his breakfast. He was nearly finished and bit into his last piece of toast as I sat down with him and Shelley.

I ran through most of the names quickly. "Amelia Buckhead would like to find her brother. She had tried one of those genetic companies but didn't get any useful results."

Dave groaned. "I was afraid of that sort of thing. Did her brother ever live in Wagtail?"

"No."

He heaved a sigh.

"You can't blame them for trying. All those people wish you would help them," said Shelley.

"So no leads at all?" asked Dave.

"Two stood out to me." I handed him my notes. "In case you want to revisit any of them. The only two that seemed to have potential were Boomer Jenkins and Jay Alcorn. But they disappeared about twenty years ago."

"Boomer!" Dave exclaimed.

"I had forgotten all about him." Shelley refilled Dave's coffee.

"Me, too." Dave stirred sugar into his coffee. "Wow, it never occurred to me that he might have been murdered."

"Everyone thought he was on the run from some woman . . . or her father." Shelley giggled. "Oh, Holly! He was the smoothest talker you ever met. Charming and dreamy—"

"And slick as grass after a torrential rain," muttered Dave. "I remember my dad forbidding my sister from going out with him."

"Twenty years is a long time. Do you think the corpse in the tree could be that old?" I asked.

Dave shrugged. "Maybe. No one is an expert on this particular situation. I'm told that some bodies have been found in good shape when buried in concrete. But if air or water gets to them, they deteriorate fast."

"So if, say, a woodpecker made a hole, that might be enough for it to decay?" I asked.

"Yeah. I guess so. And some of those knuckleheads are pretty persistent. I don't hold high hopes for finding anything very useful in terms of who put him in there. Maybe a local dentist can match the teeth. And we can hope that his hand or the fabric might reveal DNA. If we're very lucky, we might find the killer's DNA on the fabric." Dave folded his napkin. "Thanks, Shelley, and you, too, Holly."

We always fed Officer Dave on the house. He often dropped by for breakfast to update Oma on various situations in town, and we were grateful for his help.

Shelley beamed, and again I wondered if something could be going on between those two.

Nine

The sun shone brightly, taking the cold nip out of the air when I drove Mom over to the Shire. Trixie went with us, staking a claim between Mom and me on the front seat of the golf cart. I had never been inside one of the hobbitlike homes and looked forward to seeing one. We drove into the tidy community, where Thanksgiving wreaths decorated doors and some windows. Signs of Christmas were beginning to creep in. Lights sparkled on a Christmas tree in one beautiful bay window.

Carter waited for us outside a stone house with a sloping roof that curled at the end. He hustled toward Mom and shook her hand as she stepped out of the golf cart. "Mrs. Goodwin! What a pleasure. My mother is thrilled that you're moving back to Wagtail. I understand you two were good friends." Dimples formed in his beefy face when he smiled.

"I remember when you were born, Carter. You were an

adorable baby. She was so proud of you! How *is* your mother?"

"Well, very well." He handed her a business card. "Mom's number is on the back side. She said she'll never forgive you if you don't call her and have lunch while you're here."

Mom tucked the business card in her purse.

"You're in luck, Mrs.—"

Mom interrupted him. "I may have changed your diaper, but I believe you're old enough to call me Nell now."

"Thank you. I appreciate that. As I was saying, Nell, you're in luck because these houses don't come up for sale very often. This one doesn't have the dirt and grass over the roof like some of the houses toward the back, but I think the inside is the nicest I've seen. And it's a short and easy walk over to Wagtail proper."

We followed him to the front door.

As he unlocked it, he said, "I have to remind you that these cannot be rented out. When the subdivision was built, people wanted to know who their neighbors were. There's no limit on company, of course, or on pet sitters when owners are traveling. But they cannot be used as rental units."

He swung the door open, Trixie raced inside, and Mom murmured, "Oh my!"

I gazed around in awe. A foyer big enough to hold a small crowd led directly into a living room with a vaulted ceiling and a giant window that flooded the room with natural light. Exposed wood beams and an arched stone fireplace brought the outdoors inside.

Mom turned in a slow circle. "This is beautiful."

We passed through a good-sized dining room with French doors that looked out over a private stone patio. Dormant garden beds hinted at lush flowers in the summer.

"All the homes were built on substantial lots and positioned so that no one can look into their neighbors' windows. As you walk through the Shire, you'll notice all the evergreens that were planted to protect privacy."

And then we entered the room that I knew would sell the house. The combination kitchen and family room was possibly the coziest place I had ever seen. Kitchen counters ran along the exterior wall, with windows above the countertops. The cooktop and ovens were housed in a giant island. The opposite wall was stone. A staircase led up to the next floor.

The bedrooms followed the style of the house, with more beams and stone. Even the showers featured stone walls instead of tile.

Mom poked around, opening cabinets and closets.

Carter watched her with a smile. She was acting like a buyer, not a Sunday shopper.

I, meanwhile, was reading the printout on the property. As I expected, the price was substantial.

Mom's face was flushed when we left the house. I was certain Carter could see her excitement, too. When Mom and I were in our golf cart, following Carter to another home closer to the inn, I had to ask her about the price.

"Honey, I'm getting half of the value of the house in the divorce. Real estate in California is crazy expensive. Not to mention that we've been there for quite a while, so the prices have gone up and our mortgage has been paid off." She reached over and patted my hand on the steering wheel. "Don't worry, sweetie. I'm not out of my price range yet."

Carter pulled up in front of a large white colonial. I thought it seemed too big for my mom, but maybe it would work if her parents lived with her.

Trixie bounded out of the golf cart and sniffed the ground while running in a strange path that led her to the front door, where she barked.

"This house is a Wagtail classic. Can't you just imagine it decorated for the holidays?" Carter waved at it with both hands.

"Didn't the Alcorns live here?" Mom shielded her eyes from the sun and gazed up at the roof.

"They did! How clever of you to remember. Mr. Alcorn has lived at the Snowball Retirement Center for years. They say he has Alzheimer's, but he seemed okay to me. I went over there to have him sign the listing so his wife could put the house up for sale. His lawyer was present with a power of attorney so he could sign for Mr. Alcorn." Carter lowered his voice. "He may be old but he's not missing a beat. He hates his wife. He actually asked me if 'the old biddy' had signed it yet."

Trixie pawed the front door impatiently. I scooped her up so she wouldn't leave scratches on the wood. She wriggled frantically.

Carter kept talking as he slid the key into the door. "Mrs. Alcorn has already moved to a cottage on the other side of Wagtail. She told me the only way they would get her into the Snowball Retirement Center would be to drag her 'lifeless, dead body' inside. That's a quote! I don't know what happened to those two, but I don't believe they had a happy marriage."

He paused and tried the door handle. "Will you look at that? I must have locked it instead of unlocking it." He tried again and was able to open the door.

Trixie squirmed right out of my arms. She leaped to the floor and ran like crazy into another room.

"I think Trixie likes this house," Carter joked. "It was originally built around 1902 as a summer retreat for the family of a lumber baron. You'll note the extra-large room sizes and high ceilings. I don't know of another house in Wagtail built with as much attention to window and door locations to get a draft through the house. Try to imagine it without all this furniture in it. Mrs. Alcorn took what she wanted, and there's a garage sale planned for everything else. I'm afraid their furniture is dated and quite worn. The house will show better when everything is out. The garage sale is planned for the Saturday after Thanksgiving, but I had to show it to you now so you could have first dibs on it."

"It appears to need some work." Mom eyed a foggy window that needed replacing.

"Indeed, it does. But it has such wonderful bones. You'll want to refresh the bathrooms and the kitchen." Carter checked his watch. "That would give you the opportunity to make them your style. Put your own imprint on the house."

Mom tilted her head. "That could be fun. And it's a lot closer to the inn."

"In fact"—Carter pulled out his phone and punched in a number—"I called someone who I thought might help you with that. He was supposed to meet us here."

We heard the soft ring on his phone followed almost immediately by Indiana Jones theme music playing in the house.

I knew that ringtone. "Holmes!"

Trixie ran back into the living room and danced around my feet. "She knows his name. Isn't that sweet?"

Trixie muttered something at me. It wasn't a bark so much as a snuffly growl. I bent to pet her, but she took off again.

"Trixie?" I called. "Excuse me, I'd better go find my little rascal before she gets into trouble."

I could hear Mom and Carter chatting while I went in search of Trixie.

Holmes had to be here somewhere. That was definitely

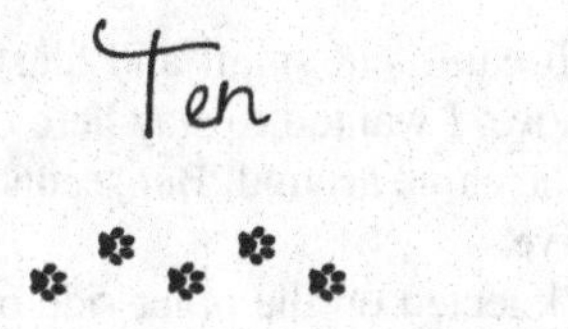

Ten

The clatter of hurried footsteps neared behind me. I kneeled on the floor, my heart fluttering in panic. Why hadn't he made a sound? No! No, no, no. Holmes could not be dead! Not my Holmes!

His beautiful blue eyes were closed.

"Holmes!" I cried louder, in the hope it might wake him.

My scream had brought Mom and Carter into the kitchen. Their voices tumbled over each other asking what had happened.

"Call 911," I said, patting Holmes's cheek.

He still didn't come around. I winced. I had checked for pulses on a few people in my life. But I didn't want to do it now. I didn't want to know that he didn't have a pulse. As long as I didn't know, there was the possibility that he was still alive.

"Holmes," I cried softly. "Please, just move. Make a motion. Open one eye. Just one."

"Better check for a pulse," said Carter.

In that moment, I hated Carter. I knew in my heart that it was ridiculous, but he was pushing me to do the one thing I was afraid of doing. I didn't want to know the truth.

"Holly, sweetheart," said Mom, "do you want me to do it?"

"No." It came out small and fearful. Mostly I didn't want to move. I wanted to stay here on the floor close to him until he came around. But seconds ticked by, and he didn't revive.

Carter kneeled on the other side of Holmes, and all I wanted to do was bat him away. "I'll do it!"

I reached for Holmes's neck as Carter stretched out his hand.

"Stop. Just stop." I sounded harsh, but at that moment, I really didn't care.

Dread filled me to the core as I touched Holmes's throat. It was still warm, and the rhythmic sensation of his blood coursing through his body was strong. "He's alive," I said with relief. "He's alive."

I wasn't much of a crier, but tears flooded my eyes and a few plopped onto Holmes. I wiped them away with my hands. "Holmes." I spoke softly but near his ear. And that was when I noticed the blood. Not much, but enough to make his sandy hair a little bit sticky. "Holmes!" I said it louder and stroked his cheek. "Holmes, can you hear me?"

The front door flung open with a creak, and a noisy rush of footsteps sounded behind me. They would pull me away from him in a matter of seconds. "Holmes!"

Kent Alcorn, the son of the couple selling the house, kneeled beside me. I felt him shoving me aside. "We'll take good care of him, Holly, but you've got to give us some room." He smiled at me, but I quaked from head to toe.

Hands from behind pulled me away, and Mom wrapped her arms around me.

"Whoa. Holmes!" said Buck Sayers. "I did not see that coming. I expected it to be old Mrs. Alcorn."

"He has a wound on the back of his head," I said, trying to be helpful.

Dr. Engelknecht sprinted into the kitchen carrying an old-fashioned doctor's satchel in his hand. Kent moved out of his way. Within minutes, Holmes groaned. I didn't know if that was a good thing or not, but it was about the loveliest music I'd ever heard.

I hadn't noticed Officer Dave until he asked me what happened.

"Trixie found him," I said, watching as a host of Holmes's friends lifted him onto a stretcher and carried him out of the house. "He was just lying there."

I broke away from Mom and Dave and followed them out to the four-wheeler that had been modified as an ambulance of sorts to transport injured people to Dr. Engelknecht's office or to a waiting ambulance just outside town for transport to Snowball Hospital.

Dr. Engelknecht sat in the back with Holmes, and one of Holmes's old friends drove them away. The rest of the volunteer rescue squad piled out of the house, passing me and saying sweet things like, *Holmes will be fine. He only got a knock on the head. That Holmes, he better be okay.*

Suddenly, I stood there alone, holding Trixie, who squirmed. I set her down and she raced back into the house. I followed her.

Mom and Carter were in the foyer talking with Dave.

"There you are," said Officer Dave. "I thought maybe you had gone with Holmes."

"There wasn't room for me. Besides, I didn't want to strand Mom. I thought I'd take her home and then head over to Dr. Engelknecht's. Has anyone called Holmes's parents?"

Officer Dave nodded. "They're on their way to the doc's office. Carter says Holmes was supposed to meet you here. Did you know about that?"

I shook my head. "I hadn't talked with Holmes today."

"I'm sorry to cut short your viewing of this house, Nell," said Dave.

Kent clattered down the elegant staircase. "I don't see a thing out of place, Dave. It looks like it did before. Besides, I'm sure Mom took everything of value when she moved. If someone desperately needed a toaster or an old pillow, then I'd have gladly given it to them."

"Who has a key?" Dave asked.

"Golly. The place belonged to my mom's parents. I imagine all kinds of friends had keys over the decades."

I wasn't so sure about that. If his grandparents were as surly as his mom, they might not have had many friends.

"Is there anyone who would want to harm you or your parents?" Dave inquired.

Kent's eyes opened wide. "Oh. I see what you mean. Someone managed to get into the house and was waiting to attack one of *us*. Gee," he said as he joined our little circle, "nobody comes to mind right away. I would have to think on that. My dad can't be bothering anyone anymore. He's been in a senior residence for years. And my mom, well, she's aggravated a lot of people in her life, but I think those days are done."

It made sense that someone had meant to harm one of the Alcorns. I couldn't know what Officer Dave was thinking, but Holmes was a beloved hometown guy in Wagtail. The town might have expanded considerably since he was a kid, but he was very involved with the community and ready to help anyone in need. It was far more likely that the perpetrator had meant to knock out one of the Alcorn family members. A bash on the back of the head like that to Mrs. Alcorn would have done her in. Kent had described his mom kindly. In all honesty, people walking along the sidewalk parted to make way for the grouch. Everyone except Oma groaned when Mrs. Alcorn showed up at a town meeting. Oma probably groaned inwardly, but she was far too judicious to do so publicly.

Still, now that Mrs. Alcorn was old enough to leave her beloved home and move into something easier to manage, perhaps her curmudgeonly days were over. She'd been civil to me the day before. My own aunt Birdie treated me worse than Mrs. Alcorn had.

"May I peek in the kitchen?" asked Mom. "I won't touch anything."

I tried not to show my irritation. I wanted to get over to Dr. Engelknecht's office as soon as possible to check on Holmes.

Officer Dave nodded.

I followed Mom, hoping she wouldn't take long. I hadn't paid much attention to the kitchen when Holmes lay on the floor. A yellow measuring tape had been left behind. I pointed at it. "Looks like Holmes had some ideas for remodeling."

"I don't mean to be rude," said Mom, "but the whole kitchen would have to be torn out. Kent, your parents took good care of the house, but kitchens get outdated so fast."

Carter looked back at Officer Dave. "When can we come back to see the rest of the house?"

"Maybe tomorrow. I'll have to let you know."

Mom, Carter, Trixie, and I finally made our exit, leaving Kent behind with Officer Dave.

"What do you think, Nell?" asked Carter.

"It's a lot to take in. The two houses and their locations are so different. And I need to consider my parents and whether we'll live together or separately. If they live in town and I buy the place in the Shire, it will take me longer to hop over and check on them if they need something. I'm going to take a long walk around Wagtail today. The two houses you've shown me are definitely contenders. But I feel like I need to get a grip on Wagtail and the neighborhoods. Reacquaint myself with the town a little bit."

"If those two don't grab you, I can show you more houses."

"Thanks, Carter. I'll be in touch." Mom stepped into our golf cart, where Trixie already waited in the middle of the front seat.

As I joined them, a text came in from Holmes's mom. *Taking Holmes to Snowball for a CAT scan. He thinks it's nonsense, and is arguing, which I figure is a good sign. He doesn't want you to know, so don't text back. We should be home in a few hours. Will keep you posted.*

I read it aloud to Mom, and Trixie growled softly as though she understood, which broke some of the tension and made us laugh at her.

"Honey, let's drive back to the inn. You can pick up your car keys and drive to Snowball to be with Holmes. I'll explain to Oma and see if she needs help at the inn. If she doesn't, then Trixie and I will take a nice long walk through Wagtail."

"Thanks, Mom." I was beginning to think it might be better than I had imagined to have Mom around.

It was late afternoon by the time I left Holmes in the care of his parents, even though he wanted to go home. I couldn't blame him. He lived in a cozy A-frame in the woods. But the doctor insisted that he shouldn't be alone that night, even though the CAT scan turned out fine. I offered to stay with him at his place, but there was no convincing his parents. In the end, I agreed that it would be kinder of him to stay at their house so they wouldn't worry about him all night. After all, it was just one night. And it wasn't as though he'd be terribly inconvenienced.

I entered the inn through the registration lobby. Trixie waited for me at the sliding glass doors and danced in circles until I picked her up and held her. "How's my sweetie pie?"

She rewarded me with a kiss on my chin. When I set her down, she scampered into the office. I could hear the murmur of voices and found Oma with Officer Dave and Mom.

"How is our Holmes?" asked Oma.

"He's fine. The CAT scan was clear. They shaved a little bit of hair on the back of his head to stitch it up. Somebody walloped him hard. He's incredibly lucky. The doctor speculated that someone hit him with a shovel."

"He didn't see the person who attacked him?" asked Oma.

I glanced at Trixie. "His parents and I talked about that. We think it might have scared the perpetrator when we arrived. He must have run out the back door. Trixie shot through the house barking when Carter unlocked the front door."

"She did, didn't she? I hadn't thought about that." Mom reached down and patted Trixie. "Thank you for saving Holmes so I can have human grandchildren."

And there it was. Mom had been in Wagtail for less than forty-eight hours. Good grief. I noticed Dave grinning slyly, and I quickly tried to drag us away from *that* topic. "Any word from Richmond about the person in the tree?"

"They have been very responsive. They took X-rays before they started the laborious process of chipping off concrete. They were able to determine that it was a man, and his leg was broken. They have already taken bone samples for DNA. But it will be days, if not weeks, before we get those results."

"That's a lot more than I expected," I said. "And it was fast."

"They're very concerned about decomposition."

"And rightly so," said Oma.

Mom looked at her watch. "Oma and I are meeting with an old friend for dinner. We'd better get going. Holly, would you like to come?"

I supposed I should.

"I need to get going, too. The sun has set and we're full up with visitors to Wagtail. No telling what crazy things they'll do." Dave took off.

"You'll come, won't you, Holly? It's just a casual dinner at Delia Riddle's house." Mom cocked her head.

Oma, always practical, added, "Mr. Huckle will be here watching the inn."

Delia Riddle, the woman who had been engaged to marry Boomer. That might just be very interesting. Trixie and I brought a golf cart around to pick up Oma, Gingersnap, and Mom at the door. I'd have rather walked in the chilly November air, but Oma might not be up to walking home later on.

Delia lived close to our new convention center, in a white farmhouse surrounded by pine trees. I parked in the driveway, and we walked up four stairs to her front porch.

Eleven

I didn't know much about Delia, other than she was Carter's mother and my mom's best friend in high school. I had seen her around town, of course. She'd always been cordial, but our lives hadn't intersected much.

When she opened the door, her border collie, Pepper, ran out to greet Trixie and Gingersnap. They politely sniffed one another, then romped wildly through the yard, playing like old friends.

Blond with a rosy complexion, Delia seemed older than Mom, even though they were about the same age. Deeper wrinkles creased her face, which made her appear tired. I knew she'd been widowed when Carter was nine. She had taken the insurance money from her husband's death and opened a real estate rental management company. Owners of vacation homes in Wagtail signed up with her to make some money off their homes when they weren't using them. She booked reservations and cleaned the houses. A couple of other real estate companies did the same sort of thing, but Delia had been the first, and her business mushroomed when Wagtail became a hot spot for animal lovers.

She hugged my mom and the two of them teared up, making jokes about how old they'd gotten.

Meanwhile, I admired Delia's living room, decorated in true farmhouse style, with modern beige furniture, glitzy accents, and rustic touches everywhere I looked. She had an eye for decorating.

Oma and I listened as the two old friends gabbed non-stop. Delia offered a tray of Apple Cider Cocktails and led us into the dining room, where moss green upholstered chairs flanked a table that appeared to be made of upcycled wood. Matching green runners crossed the table and harvest-themed dishes sat on them.

She fed Pepper, Trixie, and Gingersnap a hamburger-and-rice dish she had cooked for them. It must have been good because they ate like piggies before settling at our feet under the table while Delia served us savory smothered pork chops, corn bread pudding, brussels sprouts, and homemade bread with creamy butter from a local farm.

I hadn't realized until that moment that I had skipped lunch and was ravenous. I listened to them reminisce about people—what had happened to them and where they were now. Many of the names were unfamiliar to me.

Mom unloaded her story about getting divorced for the second time and concluded it with, "I'm surprised you never married again, Delia."

An awkward silence followed. It was long enough to make me pay attention.

"I was engaged," said Delia. "He was wonderful, but"—she smiled sadly—"I guess it didn't work out."

"Who was it?" asked Mom. "That good-looking guy

with the wavy chestnut hair who used to work at the drugstore?"

"I don't think you knew him, Nell. Boomer Jenkins."

I nearly choked. Oma patted me on the back, and I gulped my water. "Sorry," I croaked. "Everything is so good. I've been eating too fast."

"Boomer? Didn't we see a picture of him this morning? He was quite good-looking. I think I would remember a guy with a name like that if I had met him." Mom flashed me a look. She turned her attention to Delia and smiled. "So what happened?"

I tried not to be too obvious as I watched Delia's face.

She shook her head from side to side and murmured, "I don't know."

We all stared at her.

"I still have my engagement ring. We were planning the wedding, something small and simple. We had told the kids and they were excited. You should have seen Mellie. She was nine. You remember how exciting weddings were at that age. She thought it was like something out of a book or a movie. I think she was more thrilled about her dress than mine." She stopped again and sipped her drink. "And then he just left town. He was here for dinner one night. Everything was fine as far as I could tell. I walked him to his motorcycle, he kissed me, and then he left. I didn't know it was goodbye. But I never saw him again."

"What?" Mom gaped at her. "You must have called him."

"We all had cell phones back then, but they were largely useless in Wagtail. For that matter, there are still dead zones in Wagtail. It wasn't unusual for calls not to go through. I had met him because he rented an apartment through my company. There was a landline phone in his apartment, but he didn't answer that either."

"Ach! Boomer!" exclaimed Oma. "Ja, I know now who

you mean. You were engaged to him? I never knew this. He had that noisy motorcycle. They called him something else—Funnsie?"

Delia laughed aloud. "Fonzie. It was a joke because he was that type of guy. In charge and very cool. Leather jackets and motorcycles."

Oma watched her with large round eyes that showed her alarm. "Could he be the man in the tree?"

She chuckled weakly. "Good grief, I hope not. Although, I always did suspect Bonnie Greene of knowing something. When I couldn't reach him, I waited a day, then went over to his apartment. He didn't have much in the way of belongings. I guess there's only so much a person can carry on a motorcycle. His neighbor told me that Bonnie Greene had picked his lock the day before when he didn't answer his phone! I always thought that was odd. What was she after? Did he have pictures of her? You know, the sleazy kind? I never did find out what she was doing there. But the motorcycle was gone. That was the one thing he never would have abandoned. He had left Wagtail." She forced a laugh. "Worst case of cold feet I've ever heard of!"

"Did you go to the police?" I asked.

"Honey, his motorcycle was gone. He rode off into the night and kept going. What could the police have done? Dragged him back here?"

"I'm so sorry that you had to go through that." Mom laid her hand over Delia's.

"Oh heavens, we're talking ancient history!" Delia glanced around the table. "Seconds, anyone?"

"You know," said Oma, "I didn't think about it until just now, but we had a guest at the inn some years ago who never retrieved his belongings. Penn Connor. I think we still have his things in a box upstairs. Holly, we must check on this."

"I don't believe I ever met him," said Delia. "Things have changed. Used to be that I knew everyone in this town."

Delia served delicious homemade apple crisp for dessert, and the conversation shifted to which restaurants were the best and the challenges of shedding dogs.

"I don't know how you manage with all the dogs who come to the inn," said Delia. "I did a quick sweep through before you arrived, and I see yet another clump of Pepper's fur on the floor."

Trixie's short fur didn't shed much, so I really couldn't complain, but Oma nodded.

"I understand completely. I try to brush the loose fur from Gingersnap. I always think I'm done, but just yesterday, I saw more lovely, soft fur ready to fall off again. Fur on the floor is but a small price to pay for the love they give us."

Delia seemed relieved that we didn't think she was a terrible housekeeper.

It was past ten by the time we returned to the inn.

When I opened my eyes early Wednesday morning, my first thoughts were of Holmes. Mr. Huckle should have taken the day off, yet a steaming pot of tea and a chocolate croissant awaited me. I wrapped my plush Sugar Maple Inn robe around me, handed Trixie and Twinkletoes their treats, and opened the French doors in my bedroom, letting in a cold blast of air. I strode outside with a mug of tea in one hand and the croissant in the other and gazed out at the town of Wagtail.

It was still dark outside, but bright lights glowed in bakeries and restaurants where people were already hard at work. A sprinkling of Christmas lights twinkled. Thursday would be crazy with Thanksgiving and the gingerbread house contest. A lot of us would work through Thursday night so that the German-style Christkindlmarket would be up and running on Friday morning and the town of Wagtail would look festive. The job of decorating the inn fell to me so that it would be decked out with Christmas cheer when our guests rose for breakfast on Friday morning.

It was a little too early to go over to Holmes's parents' house. I would shower and dress, and by the time Trixie and I walked over there, the first rays of the sun should be etching the sky.

Wearing jeans, a red turtleneck, a long white sweater, and a red-and-white-plaid blanket scarf that I could pull tight if the wind was crazy cold, I skipped eating more breakfast and headed to see Holmes. To my surprise, Twinkletoes sprang along the sidewalk with Trixie and me. The two of them stopped occasionally to sniff their four-legged friends who were out for a morning stroll. Lights were on at the Richardsons' house. It worried me a little. I hoped nothing was wrong. I knocked gently on the front door in case Holmes was still asleep.

His father, Doyle, answered the door. To my embarrassment, Trixie and Twinkletoes ran past him into the house as though they owned the place. Happily, he laughed about it. "Think they're looking for Holmes?"

"*I* am! I hope I'm not too early."

"Naw, I'd have worried if you didn't show up to see him. We were all so exhausted when we came home last night. Anxiety takes a toll on a person. Grace didn't even cook! She ordered in from Hot Hog, and we all went to bed early."

We heard Holmes ask from another room, "What are you two doing here?"

Trixie and Twinkletoes had found him.

Holmes ambled through a hallway and hugged me fiercely. He bent his head toward mine and whispered in my ear, "I'm being held prisoner. Don't you dare leave without me."

He released me and said cheerily, "Why don't we all go to the Wagtail Diner for breakfast? It's on me."

His dad grumbled, "I've got your favorite, pumpkin French toast, ready to go."

Holmes slung an arm around his dad. "You didn't have to do that. You're acting like I almost died."

His dad paled at the thought. "You could have, son."

Holmes sighed. "Look at me. I'm fine. Apparently, I inherited your hard head."

Doyle laughed. "Come on, you two, I need coffee."

I tried to be helpful in the kitchen, but Doyle had everything under control.

We were eating when Holmes's mother, Grace, came in, looking the worse for wear. She kissed the top of Holmes's head. "How are you, baby? Did you get any sleep?"

"Slept like a rock, Mom. I'm fine."

Their doorbell rang. I jumped to my feet. "I'll get it."

I walked through the house to the front door and opened it. Barry Williams stood on the doorstep. "Holly! I didn't expect to see you."

"I guess we're both checking on Holmes. Come on in." I followed him to the kitchen, where everyone greeted him.

Grace poured mugs of coffee for Barry and herself, and when they sat down, her husband placed a plate of French toast before each of them.

"Holly, darlin'," said Grace, "why would anyone want to hurt Holmes?"

"I suspect Holmes would be the one who might know the answer to that," I said.

Holmes's happy demeanor faded. "I don't know. I've been trying to think of who might have known I would be there."

Barry nodded. "That makes sense. Was the door unlocked when you arrived?"

Holmes gulped some coffee. "Yeah, it was. I knocked first because that's what you do, right? When no one answered, I opened the door without any problem. And I yelled, 'Hello?' When no one answered that, I thought I'd have a look at the kitchen to get some ideas for Nell. The next thing I knew, I was on the floor, and Holly was looking at me."

"You didn't see anyone at all?" asked his dad.

"Didn't see anyone, didn't smell anyone, didn't hear footsteps. Just whammo and I was out."

His mother winced when he said "whammo."

To make her feel better, I said, "Officer Dave thinks someone might have mistaken Holmes for Kent Alcorn."

The tightness and worry in Grace's face relaxed. "Really? Well now, that might make more sense." She gazed at Holmes. "Although Holmes is taller than Kent, isn't he?"

Holmes seemed relieved by the turn the conversation had taken. "Maybe the perpetrator didn't really look. He just assumed it had to be Kent."

"He could have killed old Mrs. Alcorn if he had encountered her," said Barry.

"Carter said she had moved out. She bought a smaller place somewhere in Wagtail. All on one floor." I helped myself to another slice of the heavenly French toast.

"We know all about that, don't we, dear?" Doyle placed a hand over his wife's. Not too long ago, he'd been the one who was seriously ill with a heart problem. They'd sold their old home and bought this one, which didn't require Doyle to walk upstairs.

"Carter. Oh my. Too bad he didn't come for breakfast. He's such a sweetheart." To me Grace said, "Carter used to follow Holmes and Barry around." She smiled at them with affection. "Why haven't any of you provided grandchildren for your parents yet?"

Barry shook his head. "You sound just like my mother. My favorite girl left me, and I haven't met anyone else like her."

"Oh, honey. I'm so sorry." Grace patted his arm. "I'll find you someone."

Holmes roared with laughter. "You're in trouble now, Barry!"

Grace made a face at him. I knew what was coming, and it involved me. To get her off the subject of grandchildren, I asked, "Are the Alcorns divorced?"

Grace took the bait. "Oddly enough they aren't. But they probably should be. They're like oil and water. How they ever got together in the first place is beyond me. I might just pay her a visit." Grace's appetite seemed better, and she finally dug into her breakfast.

"You don't even know where she lives now," Doyle pointed out.

"No problem. I've always liked little Kent. He was such a sweet boy. He'll tell me."

"Not the brightest bulb in the box."

"Doyle!" Grace scolded. "He was darling."

"I understand he has a brother named Jay," I said casually.

"Now Jay was a sharp kid," said Doyle. "Didn't he go to an Ivy League school?"

Barry frowned. "I forgot all about him. He was a few years older than us."

"Hmm. I'll ask about him when I see Althea." Grace poured herself more coffee.

"If you find her," muttered Doyle.

Grace didn't seem perturbed. "No matter. If I can't reach Kent, the girls at the salon I go to will know. Not a thing happens in Wagtail that gets by *them*."

I liked Grace. Well, not when she was asking me about grandchildren. It was still a little bit premature for that topic. But she had been kind to me, and she had a spark in her that I liked. She didn't wait around for things to happen. The Richardsons had probably lived in Wagtail when Boomer came through town. "Do any of you remember Boomer Jenkins or Penn Connor?"

All four of them stopped eating, and an uneasy silence fell over the table.

Doyle cleared his throat and spoke first. "Boomer was a troublemaker." He glanced at Holmes. "I warned you to stay away from him."

"Holmes and Barry were teenagers, at an age when kids are easily influenced," explained Grace. "And not necessarily by people who have good judgment themselves. So many people travel through Wagtail. They stay for a while and then they move on. Most of us never know they were here. But Boomer rode into Wagtail on that big motorcycle of his and took the town by storm."

"He was very cool." Holmes laughed. "All the guys wanted to be Boomer. The girls loved him, and he had that bike. It was like Peter Fonda from *Easy Rider* rode into town—"

"And turned everything on its head." Grace finished his sentence.

Barry laughed. "You either loved or hated Boomer. There was no in between with that guy. Gosh, I haven't thought of him in forever. What brought him up?"

"Residents have been coming forward with the names of people who left town abruptly and might be the man in the tree. Several people have mentioned Boomer."

Doyle snorted. "I can tell you what happened to him.

He got run out of town with his tail between his legs by some irate husband. I don't know which one scared him, but I was glad to see him go."

"He was having affairs with married women?" I asked. "What a crumb. He was engaged to Delia."

Grace gasped. "Of course! That would explain everything. Maybe Orly's wife, Mira, who is Delia's sister, had eyes for Boomer, too. Orly killed him out of jealousy and stuffed him in the tree. All these years, no one was the wiser."

Trixie's Guide to Murder

Dead stuff has a smell that you probably already know. Even dogs who live in a city apartment have smelled a dead mouse. And most likely they knew whether the cat murdered it. And then there's the trash can in the kitchen. The scent is a little different, but when your mom or dad throws away meat and it sits in the trash for a day or two, well, you know how stinky that is!

All dogs have buried something to keep for later. You city dogs might have hidden something behind a pillow or under a bed. You have probably stumbled across a bone or a toy that another dog buried for safekeeping. Remember how that bone smelled? Buried stuff starts to develop a strong aroma. Murdered peoples smell kind of like that.

And then there are birds. Most of the time they're up in the air and only puppies are silly enough to chase them. But sometimes they fall out of the air dead. Or they fly into a window and die. They're small, but they still develop that special odor.

Murdered peoples have a similar scent. But because of their defective sniffers, other peoples can't smell them for a day or two.

It's your job to lead your peoples to them.

Twelve

Holmes and his dad stared at Grace. What she said made perfect sense.

"It had to be Orly," said Doyle. "Otherwise, he wouldn't have put that provision in his will about the tree. He knew he had hidden someone's corpse there and thought that was the best way to protect his secret."

"I think you're right, Mom." Holmes shifted his gaze to me when he said, "But it won't be easy figuring out why he killed the person and hid his body."

"How about Penn Connor?" I asked. "Does that name ring any bells?"

"Never heard of him. But I'm concerned about Holmes." Grace shook her forefinger at him. "I don't want you running around town by yourself, now. You hear? Just in case somebody has it in for you."

Holmes smiled at his mom. "You could come with me. Follow me around all day."

"I can't do that! Thanksgiving is coming! And I'm in

charge of the WAG booth at the Christkindlmarket. Oh, you boys. You're always joking." She took a deep breath.

"I hate to break this up, but I need to get back to the inn. Breakfast was wonderful!" I stood up, rinsed my plate, and stashed it in the dishwasher.

They all spoke at once, but Trixie, Twinkletoes, and I managed to escape with Holmes and Barry, who split off to go to his veterinary office.

"What's the deal with Barry?" I asked Holmes. "He's such a nice guy. You'd think women would be chasing him."

"They do," said Holmes. "I don't know a lot of details, but I gather he met someone when he was in vet school. She was the one. I think she had to move home for some reason, a sick parent or something. He stayed to finish school, and he never heard from her again. He says he has searched for her on the Internet but hasn't been able to find her."

"That's so sad!"

"I hope he finds someone else." He stopped walking. "Don't get any matchmaking ideas! Listen, I need a shower, so I'm heading home. See you later?" He bent to kiss me before we went our separate ways.

He probably had a headache from the blow he'd received. He would never admit it, though. I hoped he could relax at home and get some more sleep.

Trixie darted down a street away from me. "Trixie!" I called. "Trixie!" Normally she wouldn't leave my side unless someone had been murdered. Chills ran through me. But she wasn't barking.

Twinkletoes zoomed in the same direction. Oh no! Not both of them. There had better be a really good reason for this terrible behavior! I marched along the street looking for them. We were in an older section of Wagtail, and houses lined both sides of the street. "Trixie!" I called.

I thought I saw Twinkletoes vanish behind a house and realized she had chosen probably the worst house in Wagtail for a dog or cat to trespass in the yard. Aunt Birdie's house! I sighed. But then it occurred to me that Aunt Birdie might be in trouble. What if she had slipped and fallen?

I darted past the front porch and into the backyard. Neither Twinkletoes nor Trixie was anywhere to be seen. I strode deeper into the yard. Still no sign of them. When I ran back toward the street, I thought I heard whining. Fearful of what I might find, I walked slowly, calling Trixie's and Twinkletoes's names. A board hung loose at the west side of the front porch. "Trixie?" I called.

Twinkletoes poked her nose out from under the board, then jumped onto the railing of the porch and sat there watching me. I dropped to my knees to peer under the porch.

"Holly Miller!" shouted Aunt Birdie. "What the devil are you doing in my yard?"

Aunt Birdie didn't miss much. I looked up to see her gazing down at me.

"And why is your cat sitting up here?"

"I wish I knew. I think Trixie is under the porch. But I'm relieved to see that you're all right."

"You get that dog out of there this instant!"

I moved the board aside. In the darkness under the porch, I saw four eyes looking out at me. I could faintly make out the white of Trixie's fur. I didn't know who the other eyes belonged to, which was a little spooky.

"Have you got a flashlight, Aunt Birdie?"

"Is there a skunk under there? You better not scare it. That odor will linger for weeks." She disappeared into the house and returned with a flashlight.

I turned it on and aimed it under the porch. Trixie sat

next to a solid black dog. No wonder I hadn't been able to see her body. It blended in.

"It's a dog, Aunt Birdie."

"Well, get it out of there."

I called Trixie, who came to me. "Come on, sweetie. Come!"

The dog didn't budge. "Do you have a piece of meat? Or cheese?"

"It may come as a surprise to you, but I have things to do today."

"Do you want the dog to stay there?" It was a snotty question, and I knew it. But it produced the desired result. Aunt Birdie went into her house and returned with slices of cheese and steak. And then she dropped a rope on my head.

"You might need that."

I wrangled the rope to the ground. Trixie immediately nosed the food in my hand. I wedged myself closer to the other dog and handed Trixie a tiny bite of steak to show the black dog that it would be safe to eat from my hand. When I held out a slice of steak to her, she edged closer and gently took it. I backed up a little bit and tried with a little slice of cheese. The dog seemed very hungry. She eagerly took the cheese and didn't back away.

She inched closer and took more food, one piece at a time. I backed up more so she would have to emerge from her hiding place. To my complete surprise, the black dog wedged through the opening and wagged her tail! She must belong to someone, but I didn't recognize her. She wasn't wearing a collar.

As I slid the rope around her neck, she didn't object in the slightest. It was then that I realized the poor girl was heavily pregnant. In spite of that, she looked thin. Too thin. Her black fur didn't gleam and appeared dusty. This girl had been on the run for a while.

"Is that dog pregnant?" asked Aunt Birdie.

"Looks like it."

"She needs to see Barry Williams."

"I thought I'd take her over there."

"She can't walk that far." She disappeared into the house. When she returned, she walked down the few stairs and petted the black dog. Handing me keys, she said, "Take my golf cart."

I looked at my aunt with surprise. Sometimes her heart shone through that surly exterior. "Thank you, Aunt Birdie."

Trixie and Twinkletoes clambered onto the golf cart. The black dog tried to follow them, but when it proved too hard to jump, she gazed up at me pitifully. She looked like a black Lab to me, only a little bit smaller. I scooped her up and gently placed her on the front seat. She probably hadn't ridden in a golf cart before, so I backed it up very slowly.

She didn't seem skittish or afraid, she just looked tired. Maybe she was glad that someone was helping her.

I drove over to Barry Williams's veterinary clinic. A picket fence surrounded the two-story white house. I wondered if Trixie and Twinkletoes would decline to go inside. They liked Barry well enough, but I was fairly certain they associated the clinic with unpleasant things like shots.

Moving slowly so I wouldn't spook her, I lifted the dog and placed her on the ground. She readily walked up the ramp, stopping a couple of times to sniff something. When we reached the top, Trixie and Twinkletoes waited for us. I opened the front door and they bolted inside, which I had not expected. The black dog willingly followed them.

The receptionist made a big fuss over the new patient.

Barry emerged from the back and squatted in front of her, speaking to her gently.

I explained where I had found her. "I think she's been wandering for a while."

"I'd agree with that assessment. We'll take good care of her. Can you put up a found-dog announcement on the Wagtail email list and website?"

"Sure. Let me get a picture of her." I stepped back and snapped a photo of the dog.

I gave her one last scratch under her chin. "Don't worry anymore. I promise you'll have all the food you want and a nice soft bed."

She wagged her tail and walked into another room without so much as a backward glance.

I hustled back to the inn, grabbed my clipboard, and went up to my quarters to leave my blanket scarf. Mom was nowhere to be seen.

After collecting a mug of hot tea from the inn kitchen, I settled at the office computer and sent out notices about the black dog. Then Trixie and I did the daily check of all the hallways and community rooms while Twinkletoes napped.

She reappeared when I returned to the third floor, which housed my apartment and the storage attic.

The lock on the storage room clicked loudly when I turned the key. Last January, I had carefully stored Christmas decorations in one corner so they would be easy to locate. I rummaged through boxes, pulling out and testing strings of lights. There were tons of them. Happily, most appeared to be in good working order. Trixie sniffed around and Twinkletoes jumped from box to box. I made a list of items to pick up at the hardware store. Batteries, lightbulbs, some new ribbons.

Done with that job, I pondered where Oma might have

stashed the box of Penn Connor's belongings. If no one had been interested in them, they would probably be toward the rear of the giant room, undisturbed. Most likely under other boxes. I gazed around in dismay. It looked like a used-furniture store. Partial bed frames, extra chairs, rollaway beds, old rolled-up rugs, dressers, desks, and tons of boxes that contained heaven knew what. Maybe straightening it out and having a giant yard sale should be one of my goals for the coming year.

Trixie scampered ahead of me as I made my way through the furniture to a pile of dusty boxes. Twinkletoes leaped from one box to another.

Fortunately, most were labeled with Oma's neat handwriting. I shoved boxes around to see what they contained. China, bedside lamps, receipt pads, candle holders. And suddenly, there it was. *Penn Connor.*

I wrestled it out from under other boxes, but my hopes for finding anything of interest faded when I picked it up. It didn't weigh much. I carried it out into the hallway and pried open the brittle tape covering the top.

Inside I found one pair of jeans, a pair of tarnished cuff links engraved with the initial *C*, a copy of *Harry Potter and the Sorcerer's Stone*, a toothbrush, toothpaste, a bottle of Givenchy Gentleman cologne, an electric razor, a light duffle bag, socks, underwear, a couple of polo shirts, and one tuxedo complete with cummerbund, shirt, and a highly polished pair of dress shoes. A sheet of paper inside read:

Mr. Penn Connor
Reservation August 24–27
Last seen by Inn staff on August 25.
Contacted by email and letter. No response.
Bill paid by credit card. Charges went through.

Thirteen

Maybe Gus Herbst at the hardware store would remember. I stood up and dusted off my jeans. I needed to stop by to pick up the Christmas decorating items anyway.

I returned to the inn office, where Zelda was showing Mom how our computerized management system worked. "What's this?" I asked.

Mom smiled at me. "I thought I should learn. Oma was telling me that you could use a part-timer now and again. It would be such fun for me."

Oma stepped out of the office. "Is it not wonderful? Nell would also like to help us with our Christkindlmarket stall!"

I didn't know how to react. I was happy to have Mom around, but this was all so sudden. I wondered if she would abruptly pack up and be gone, having decided not to move. I tried to muster up cheeriness in my tone. "That's great! Since everything is under control here, I'm heading over to Shutter Dogs to buy some supplies. Do you need anything?"

"Ach, ja!" Oma dashed into the office and returned with a list. "And take a basket of our big soft pretzels to Gus, please?"

"Sure thing." I hustled to the kitchen, nabbed a basket, and lined it with cellophane and a paper napkin that had an autumn leaf theme. Cook shot me a what-are-you-doing-in-my-kitchen scowl. I waved at him and loaded the basket with pretzels. "They're for Gus," I called.

Cook nodded. "Hey, if you're going that way, could you stop by Biffle's for half a dozen lemons and three celery stalks?"

"No problem." I added them to Oma's list.

I tied the cellophane with a ribbon, and we were off to the hardware store.

Trixie usually ran slightly ahead of me, but the sidewalks teemed with visitors, and she wisely stayed close by. On a usual day, I recognized most people, but it was the holiday season and visiting shoppers were keeping the stores busy.

Even the hardware store, Shutter Dogs, was bustling. In addition to hammers, nails, and such, they sold a nice assortment of lamps with cat, dog, and outdoorsy themes. Not to mention clever hooks for coats and leashes.

Trixie knew where the dog cookies were on display. She zoomed ahead of me and disappeared from my sight, but it didn't take a genius to find her. She stood before a selection of large glass cookie jars, her nose in the air and her tail wagging joyfully.

I filled a bag with her favorites. After all, Santa would be coming soon to fill her stocking. I weighed it and marked the weight on the bag.

Giving me a sad puppy look, she placed her tiny front

paws on my knees, pretending she wasn't inhaling the delicious smells in the bag. But I knew what she wanted.

"Maybe after we talk with Gus."

She appeared to understand and took off through the store. I found her in a room in the back I had never seen before. I'd been told that dogs can understand about five hundred words. Since Trixie had found Gus, I now suspected that he might be on her list of favorite people. How else could she have known to look for him?

The white-haired gentleman sat at a rolltop desk peering through glasses at the inner workings of a clock. Stacks of boxes cluttered the room, far worse than the inn attic. A large old tabby slept on top of the desk. He opened one eye to inspect us and closed it again.

Trixie nudged Gus with her nose, and he looked down at her. "Well, if it's not my friend, little Trixie." He fondly scratched behind her ears.

I held out the basket of pretzels. "With Oma's regards."

He grasped it with a shy smile. "If I'd had any sense, I would have married Liesel the minute she was widowed." He pulled a knife from the desk and jabbed the cellophane with it. He bit into one and savored it. "Mmm, mmm, mmm. You can't beat these pretzels."

"I didn't know that you repair clocks."

"I don't! But Eliot down at the jewelry store wants a king's ransom to repair this one. I figured it couldn't be that hard. What brings you here?"

I waved my list. "Needed a few things. But I also wanted to speak with you."

He flashed a bright smile at me. "I figured you'd be by. You and little Dave Quinlan. I still can't get used to him being a cop. It was in late August about twenty years ago."

It unnerved me that he knew why I was there. "What was?"

"When Orly placed a big order for concrete. I told him if he was gonna use that much, he ought to have it poured by the concrete company over in Snowball. But he was a stubborn old coot."

"What did he say it was for?"

"Concrete stairs and a pad outside the door of his house."

I hadn't been to Orly's house. It sat back in the woods, off the roads. "Did you believe him?"

"Sure, I did. Didn't have any reason not to." With a half grin and a twinkle in his eyes, he added, "He came back and bought more. Enough to build those stairs twice."

"You must have wondered why he needed more."

"I did. He said he'd found a nice old tree that was rotting on the inside."

"So you knew! You knew all along."

"I knew he filled *a tree*. Didn't know there was a man in it, nor did I know which tree it was. Pouring concrete into trees wasn't that uncommon back in the day. Some old-timers still do it now. Not to mention that I was pretty happy to be selling him all those bags of concrete."

"It must have been a lot of work," I mused.

"Sure it was. I figure someone helped him."

My breath caught in my throat. "Who?"

"Well now, I don't know anything about that."

"For someone to have kept his secret all these years, they must have been very good friends."

"Don't go lookin' at me. I just sell the stuff."

"You probably have a feel for who his friends were."

Gus took a deep breath. "You didn't hear it from me." He peered at me from under heavy eyelids. "But Orly and Stu Williams were like that." He held up two fingers pressed together. "If anyone knew what Orly was up to, it would have been Stu."

Fourteen

Trixie dawdled when we left Gus and headed to the cashier. I took a deep breath. The store did smell interesting. Scents of lumber and leather mingled with the pine trees that had been cut and waited to be bought, and the fresh popcorn that they gave away to keep kids happy while parents shopped. If I could make out that many scents, then it must be overwhelming to a dog.

I didn't rush her but made my way to the checkout counter. She caught up to me when I had three giant bags in my hands. I probably should have arranged for a delivery.

When I stepped outside, Barry Williams very nearly ran into me.

"Holly! Sorry about that." He reached out to me. "Can I give you a hand?"

"I'm good, thanks."

He licked his lips and looked annoyed. "I have to pick something up and don't have much time, but I wanted to talk with you." He motioned me over, so we wouldn't block the entrance. "Thank you for setting up my parents with Kitty. I don't know who is having more fun. They brought her by the animal hospital this morning, and now they're planning to let her build a gingerbread house to enter in the contest."

"I'm glad it's working out. She's a sweet kid, and her mom is going through a rough time."

"That's what they told me. Do you know her mom? Is there any way we can help her get back on her feet?"

I took a deep breath and blew it into the cold air. "I'll see what I can find out."

"Good. Let me know."

"Uh, Barry. Someone told me your dad was close with Orly."

He frowned at me. "He knows nothing about the man in the tree."

"But they were close friends?"

"Don't get Dad involved in this, Holly." He waved and disappeared into the hardware store.

Trixie and I walked toward Biffle's Grocery. I paused outside the two-story building, remembering what Althea Alcorn had said. She owned the building, but there had been a fight over it with Orly. Cut pine trees leaned against the wall, and stands held decorated wreaths.

The entrance just inside the store had already been decked out for Christmas. Gleaming ribbon candy and colorful straws, waffles, and pillows would attract everyone. Candied fruit slices, red-and-white peppermints, and caramel pecan turtles vied for attention.

The only sour note in the festive store was Josie Biffle herself. She was in the process of scolding an employee who wore a green Biffle's Grocery apron.

"I am not fighting you on this," she said. "Mark those

trees down lower than anyone else in town. Do you understand me?"

I dumped my hardware bags into a cart, and then Trixie and I hurried to the produce department, where I collected the requested lemons and celery. Since we were there, I added a bag of tiny, sweet mandarin oranges to my cart for mom and me.

Josie swept by in a huff, but I wanted to talk with her. "Josie!" I called out cheerfully.

She swung around and glared at me.

"I love the candy display in the front of the store. I don't know how anyone could resist it."

She appeared confused. As though she wanted to be angry, but now she had to deal with praise. "Thank you," she muttered.

Uh-oh. How was I going to bring up Jay? She probably knew that Mrs. Alcorn disliked her and meant to come between them. I should have thought this out ahead of time. The oak tree and her father had to be sore spots, too. Delia was her aunt and Carter was her cousin. Maybe that would work. "We had dinner over at Delia's last night. She's a great cook."

Josie nodded. "Yes, she is."

"Now how does the family tree go? Delia is your mother's sister?"

"A lot of people get confused because Mom is twelve years older than Delia. So I'm only eight years younger than Delia."

"That explains a lot. She mentioned that you dated Jay Alcorn. I never knew that Kent had a brother."

For one long moment, she stiffened. "Oh gosh. It's been ages since I saw Jay. Is he home for the holidays?"

I played dumb. "I have no idea. She said he was very smart."

"And fun, too." She rearranged a pile of oranges. "My dad could be tough. People say I'm like him. But Dad didn't hold a candle to Jay's mom. No parent could have asked for a better son than Jay. But he was never good enough for her. It wounded him to the core. I doubt that he ever got over it."

"I guess not, if he hasn't been back to town."

A smile touched her lips but disappeared quickly. "Well, enjoy your Thanksgiving." She hurried off at a hasty pace.

I paid for my purchases, and we walked home through the green. Trixie zoomed from tree to tree to interesting spots where I could see absolutely nothing. Mostly I was thinking about Stu.

Back at the inn, I delivered the food to the kitchen. Delicious baking scents wafted toward me.

"Pies?" I asked as I set the lemons and celery on a counter.

"Apple, pecan, and pumpkin. I'm getting started on the stuffings."

I gave Cook a thumbs-up. While putting away the Christmas items in the attic, I saw Penn's name again. I hustled across the hall to my apartment and searched Google for this mystery man. I found absolutely no reference to him.

Maybe the man in the tree *was* Penn. But it seemed like someone would have come looking for him. Most people had families who would miss them and mount a search. I guessed not everyone was that lucky. Like Jay Alcorn. I wondered if his mother knew how to look for him. Probably not. Some people couldn't engage in a search. Or maybe they didn't know where to start.

Penn had brought a tuxedo. That certainly implied some sort of fancy function. Had he attended it? Did all his friends or coworkers assume he had gone home?

Surely someone must have missed him. If nothing else, being in possession of Harry Potter indicated a fun person, didn't it?

And what about Boomer? By all accounts he was the life of the party. I knew a little bit more about him than about Penn. Boomer was quite the flirt. I wouldn't be surprised if Doyle was right about some jealous husband knocking him off.

I checked the time on my way back to the inn office. Why did this have to happen right at the holidays? There were so many things to do.

I set Oma's items on a chair where she would see the bag. Then I checked the schedule for the following day. Breakfast would close at ten, giving us two hours to rearrange the dining area for the Thanksgiving feast. The judges would make their decisions about the gingerbread houses between ten and twelve. At noon we had the official grand opening of the convention center, to be followed by viewing of the gingerbread houses. At two, dinner would be served back at the inn. At six, the convention center would reopen for viewing and the awarding of prizes.

It was tight timing, but the flowers for the tables had already been delivered. Cook had the food well in hand, and everything appeared to be on track. Technically, Shadow and I were off on Thanksgiving Day afternoon and early evening because we would be up all night.

When Oma and I couldn't think of another thing that had to be done, I went to buy cookies. Trixie ran slightly ahead of me through the green again but stayed closed as we reached the teeming sidewalks.

I'd thought late afternoon would be a good time to visit Pawsome Cookies, but the darling store was packed. Trixie, who had eaten plenty of cookies that day, studied the assortment of cookies for dogs and people behind the glass while we waited.

Bonnie Greene, the proprietor, helped her employees until a little lull finally developed. She handed me our cookie order, took off her apron, and stepped out from behind the counter. "Let's go outside. I could use a breath of fresh air."

When we had escaped the bakery, she handed each of us a cookie. "Peanut butter for Trixie, and chocolate chip for Holly!"

The chocolate chips in my cookie were just as she had described them the other day. Melty! "Delicious," I murmured with my mouth full.

"Did you find out anything about Boomer?" she asked.

"Not in the way that you probably hoped." I finished the last deliciously gooey bite of cookie.

"Did you talk to Delia?"

"I did."

Bonnie crossed her arms over her chest defiantly. "It wasn't like Delia and I were best friends or anything, but after Boomer disappeared, I've been wary of her. Never have gotten up the courage to ask what happened. Of course, how could I possibly walk up to the woman who was going to marry him and ask what she did to him?"

Delia had been equally distrustful of Bonnie. I supposed it was lucky they'd never come to blows over Boomer. "As I recall, he was supposed to break off his engagement with Delia and then come to your house for dinner."

"Right."

"Did you do anything at all that night? Try to call him or go over to his apartment?"

Bonnie took a deep breath. "Of course! What would you do if Holmes were going to confront someone and then he never came home?"

"I'm not accusing you of anything," I said softly. "I'm just trying to figure out what happened."

"I know. If anyone hurt him, it was Delia." She swallowed hard. "It was dark out, past midnight." Her breath came faster as she remembered. "I took a flashlight. My biggest fear was finding him with Delia."

"You had a key?"

She shook her head. "I picked the lock. Don't look at me like that! It was a lousy lock anyway, so it didn't exactly pose a challenge." She stared at the grass silently. "What I remember the most was a hollow feeling. Like when you walk into a room that you knew was furnished, but everything is gone. You know that echo when a room is bare? Only it wasn't. His clothes and things were scattered around."

"What sort of things?"

"Boomer wasn't the tidiest guy. He walked into his apartment and dropped everything. Didn't hang up a jacket, threw pants over a chair, left his socks on the floor where he took them off. I foolishly thought I would break him of that when we were married. I know better now. As far as I could tell, his apartment was just like it always was. A potato chip bag on the sofa, cereal and spoiled milk on the kitchen table. The apartment came furnished, and he really didn't have a lot of belongings. I guess you can't carry much on a motorcycle."

Delia had said the exact same thing! It didn't help, but it must have been true.

"And then what?" I prompted her.

"I sat down on the sofa and clutched that bag of potato chips like it was a stuffed animal. I guess I finally fell asleep waiting for him to come home. I woke when the sun rose. In the light of day, I had to accept the truth. He must have stayed over at Delia's. He chose her over me. I think I just went through the motions that day. It came as a shock, a terrible blow. I never saw him again. All I can tell you is that he was going to Delia's house to break off their engagement. I don't want to bad-mouth Delia, but I think that's a pretty incriminating situation."

"And you said that you went to the police at the time?"

She nodded. "I went to the old chief. He told me not to interfere in another woman's engagement. I left with my tail tucked between my legs. I knew I shouldn't have pursued a relationship with Boomer, but that was irrelevant. I only wanted to be sure he was okay." Her lips tightened. "What did Delia have to say?"

"Not much. He ate dinner at her house and left. She never saw him again."

Bonnie hissed, "That's a lie." She sounded bitter when she added, "I bet you anything they got in a fight when he broke off the engagement. She killed him. I don't know how, but I know why."

I hated that Delia was my mother's friend because the scenario Bonnie proposed made a lot of sense.

Bonnie sighed and shot me a glance.

I could tell she knew more. "What?"

"It's just that, well, unless she got a sitter, she wasn't the only one there that night."

"Do you mean Carter?" I asked.

"Carter and his sister. The sister married and moved to Montana, but he's still here."

"I've met him. He seems nice."

She smiled broadly. "Such a funny little boy. Carter was my best customer when he was a kid. Still is, now that I think about it. Carter rode an old bike all over Wagtail. He'd stop by to ask if I had any broken cookies that I needed to get rid of. Isn't that darling? I'd see him sitting in the bars, listening to old fellows. No one seemed to mind. He was like a tubby fly on the wall. Never did see him playing with other children. Anyway, he was likely there that night."

"You never asked him about it?"

"I didn't have it in me. He was just a kid. Ten or eleven, maybe? He lost his dad when he was nine. Talk about heartbreaking. The whole town was sick about it. Sweet little Carter was lost without his daddy. He carried his dad's camera everywhere he went. Delia and his little sister were all the family he had left. I guess Orly would have taken the kids in if Delia had gone to prison, but I couldn't bring myself to involve him. Carter might know what happened to Boomer."

It sounded to me like Bonnie and Carter had a fairly good relationship. "Maybe it's time we asked him."

"We?" Bonnie blanched. She gestured toward her store. "I'm swamped today. Tomorrow's Thanksgiving . . ."

I could tell she didn't want to be the one who talked with Carter. I nodded. "I'll see when I can catch up with him. Thanks for talking with me. If you think of anything else, please let me know."

"Part of me wants very much to know what happened to him. But the other part of me hopes it's not Boomer in the tree. Will they know from DNA?"

"As I understand it, they have collected DNA from the man in the tree. But that doesn't necessarily mean they will know who he was. They need something to compare the DNA to. DNA from Boomer or one of his relatives, for instance."

"It's been so long. I wonder if Delia kept anything of Boomer's. Someone must have cleaned up his belongings. Of course, if she murdered him, she probably burned his clothes."

Bonnie looked so dejected that I blurted, "If it's any consolation, it appears a couple of other men went missing around the same time. It's possible that one of them is the man in the tree."

Her breath caught in her throat, and she coughed. "Really? Who?"

"A man named Penn Connor who was staying at the inn. Does the name ring any bells for you?"

"No. Never heard of him. Must have been passing through."

"How about Jay Alcorn?" I asked.

"I'd forgotten all about him. I guess I assumed he was off somewhere being a doctor or something. Doesn't Althea Alcorn know where he is?"

"Nope. But she said he was seeing Josie."

Bonnie raised her eyebrows. "Orly's daughter? Well, well. Maybe it is Jay in the tree! Orly was mighty protective of his little girl."

I thanked her again and let her get back to work. Trixie and I walked through the green. Lanterns already lit the path. I couldn't believe how dark it was even though it wasn't late. I phoned Mom to see if she had dinner plans.

"I was just about to call you! I haven't been to that new place on the lake yet. It has a funny name. Tequila Mockingbird? Think we could get in there?"

"We should call to see if we can get a table—"

Bright lights shone at me as something crashed through the green, breaking twigs and sideswiping benches. "Trixie!" I screamed.

She ran to me, looking as scared as I felt. I swept her up and ran as fast as I could. I slowed when we were out of harm's way and watched as a runaway golf cart slammed into a tree, ejecting the driver.

Fifteen

"Holly! Holly!" Mom's voice sounded small and far away. I held Trixie in both arms and still grasped the phone in my hand. I tried to hit speaker.

"Mom, I'm in the green. Call 911. I'm okay. Call them now."

I could see the golf cart rammed against a huge tree, but I didn't see the person who had been in it. I was sure I saw someone fly out of it. I set Trixie on the ground. "Find the person, Trixie."

Those words weren't part of her vocabulary, but I thought she would instinctively locate the driver in the dark. I switched on the flashlight in my phone. "Hello? Where are you? Can you speak? Hello?"

Trixie found the person first and barked. A short yelp, like she was saying, *Over here, Mom!*

I left the path and walked cautiously in her direction. The last thing I needed was to fall over something.

When I got to them, Trixie was licking the person's

face. I pulled her toward me and shone my flashlight on him. "Can you hear me?"

Lights bobbed through the trees, and people shouted my name.

"Over here!" I yelled. "I'm over here!"

Trixie woofed.

I aimed my flashlight so I could see the person's face without shining the beam in his eyes. I needn't have been worried about that. Carter Riddle was out cold.

"Carter?" I checked for a pulse. Nice and strong, which made me smile. I tapped his cheek lightly. "Carter?"

His mouth opened before his eyes did.

"Carter," I sang. "Are you all right?"

He opened his eyes slowly. "Holly?" He closed them again. "Tell me this is a bad dream."

Suddenly strong lights shone at us. I shielded my eyes. Voices behind me chattered.

"What in blazes happened here?"

"Is that Carter?"

"Jack, bring the ambulance cart."

"Holly, what happened?"

"Holly, are you okay? Were you in the golf cart?"

I wasn't sure who was asking. "I'm fine. We weren't in the golf cart. It seemed like it veered out of control, and then it hit the tree and threw Carter out. This is how he landed. I haven't moved him."

Dr. Engelknecht arrived on the run. "Carter! How are you feeling, buddy?" He flashed a penlight over Carter's eyes. "Let's get him over to the hospital."

"Woah, no!" Carter sat up.

Several people moved a stretcher next to him.

"I don't need that," Carter objected. But as it turned out, he did need a little help to stand up.

"I'm okay. Really," he insisted.

In spite of his protestations, they whisked him away, leaving me alone with Trixie and Officer Dave.

He flashed his light at me. "Did it hit you?"

"No. Just scared me."

"The cart must have malfunctioned." He dialed his phone. "Hey, it's Dave. I've got a runaway golf cart in the green. It hit a tree. Think you could collect it at first light tomorrow?" After a brief pause, he added, "Great. I'll be here." He stashed his phone in a pocket. "I didn't smell alcohol on Carter, did you?"

I hadn't even considered that. "No. I didn't notice anything."

"How about you, Trixie?" asked Dave.

She looked up at him and wagged her tail, which prompted him to scratch behind her ears.

My phone rang. I glanced at it. "Hi, Mom. Trixie and I are fine. We'll be at the inn shortly and I'll tell you all about it." I disconnected the call. "Have you ever seen anything like this?"

"Oh sure. It doesn't happen often, but every once in a while a golf cart will run amok on a football field live on TV! As long as Carter is okay, it's not a big deal."

"Want to come to dinner with Mom and me?"

"Thanks for the offer, but it's my busy season. I'd better hang around."

His phone rang and I could barely hear a voice saying, "A couple of drunks are fighting at Hair of the Dog."

"Ten-four," he responded.

"But you will come to the inn for Thanksgiving dinner tomorrow, right?"

"Wouldn't miss it. See you, Holly." He took off at a jog.

Trixie and I walked back to the inn at a more leisurely pace. Trixie lifted her nose in the air on entering the lobby. Even I could smell the heavenly scents of Thanksgiving dinner preparations. I poked my head into the commercial kitchen, only to discover Oma and Mom savoring a pecan pie.

I folded my arms over my chest and let the door swing shut behind me. They were so intent on the pie that they didn't notice me. I cleared my throat.

Oma let out a little shriek. "Oh, it's just you. What are you doing sneaking around?"

I laughed at the two of them. "It smells delicious. I think we need to get out of here before you two eat tomorrow's dinner."

Mom had the decency to blush. "We had to make sure it was good."

"Did you call Tequila Mockingbird?" I asked.

Oma nodded. She swallowed a bite of the pie. "They're holding a table for us." She looked at her watch. "We'd better go. They won't hold it for long."

Mom wrapped up the pie. "I guess we can't serve this now." She made a mock sad face.

"Go get your coats, I'll stash it in the magic refrigerator." I carried the pie out of the commercial kitchen. Trixie danced along beside me, sniffing all the way across the empty dining area and into the private family kitchen. We had nicknamed the refrigerator *the magic refrigerator* because Cook stashed leftovers there for us, and it seemed like it was never empty. Most of the extra food went to needy families around Wagtail, but there was always plenty for Oma, me, and the employees, too.

Twinkletoes stretched as though she'd been sleeping and we woke her. She sidled along my legs. "Want to go out to dinner with us?"

She jumped on the hearth but didn't see any bowls of cat food. When we walked into the lobby, she followed along.

We walked over to Tequila Mockingbird, where we were shown to a table with a view of the lake. Lights twinkled in houses across the lake, and a few fishing boats idled by on their quiet trolling motors.

We placed our orders, including catfish dinners for Trixie and Twinkletoes, who sat at the floor-to-ceiling window watching the lights on the fishing boats.

"This is quite the upscale place," said Mom, gazing at the huge beams and the fireplace. "Holly, your grandfather can't wait to get back here. He's already checking out fishing boats."

"We were so busy eating pie that I forgot to ask you about the green," said Oma. "What happened?"

I filled them in on the strange golf cart that went wild. "We should probably check on Carter. He insisted he was okay, but I could tell that Dr. Engelknecht was concerned."

Our meals arrived, and we dug in like we hadn't eaten all day. Oma had ordered sea bass, but Mom and I went with steak and mushrooms. Trixie and Twinkletoes ate politely, though I noticed that Trixie cleaned Twinkletoes's bowl when she had finished. Just to make sure nothing was left.

"I'll text Delia," said Mom. "If that's not too rude to do at the table."

Given the circumstances, Oma and I readily agreed that Mom should text. "But put your phone on vibrate, Nell," said Oma. "That way we won't disturb other people if it rings."

Delia texted back immediately, and Mom read her response aloud. *Dr. E insisted we have him checked out at the ER in Snowball. Waiting now for results. So much for cooking ahead for tomorrow's feast. But Carter is more important. Don't know what I would do without my boy.*

"That's just the worst." Mom reached over and clutched my hand. "When your children aren't well, you can't think of anything else."

"Tell her to join us tomorrow," said Oma. "We will have plenty."

Mom was about to text Delia when I stopped her. "She probably invited Orly's wife, Mira, and his children, Wyatt and Josie. You better include them, too."

"The Biffles," Oma said. "Of course we will invite them all. We are not at war with the Biffles."

"I'll remind you of that when Josie makes a fuss." I speared some mushrooms on my plate.

"It is now very clear that Orly killed someone and hid him inside the tree. He thought his secret would be safe if he gave the land to Wagtail," said Oma. "It was a miscalculation, of course. He didn't foresee the tree dying. The Biffles will not be able to undo the gift of the land. We will live with them and be gracious."

I glanced at Mom, who said, "Not everyone has such a wise and kind grandmother."

I got her point, and I hoped Oma did, too. "What's Mira like?"

"She's older than Delia. I always thought she was sort of timid. And I gather she didn't have an easy life with gruff old Orly," said Mom.

Oma sipped her glass of white wine. "Mira is a sweet woman. And for all Orly's rough ways, he took care of his family. When Delia's husband died, Orly looked out for Delia."

I ordered crème brûlée for dessert, and the two who had pigged out on dessert before dinner had the gall to help me eat it!

We strolled back to the inn, admiring holiday displays in shop windows. A feeling of cheer seemed to have infected everyone.

On Thanksgiving morning, Mom, Trixie, Twinkletoes, and I were thoroughly spoiled by Mr. Huckle. When he brought up our prebreakfast coffee and treats, we invited him to stay, and the five of us sat outside, wrapped in warm, fuzzy blankets to block the chilly air, and watched as the sun kissed the lake, leaving little sparkles that glimmered on the water. When the coffee was gone, Mr. Huckle collected the trays and returned to work while Mom and I showered and dressed.

I pulled on a knee-length plaid skirt in shades of cream and brown with a shot of red running through it, then added a red turtleneck and short, comfortable boots. The outfit would be suitable for the various activities of the day.

At ten o'clock, Mr. Huckle and I stood by, waiting for the final diners to leave after breakfast. As soon as they were gone, we rearranged the tables. Mr. Huckle dressed them with lovely cream-colored tablecloths while I set out the flower arrangements. We had decided it would be best to let everyone serve themselves, so we prepared the buffet to receive the food from the kitchen.

We finished up just before noon. Mr. Huckle and I left our night manager snoozing on a sofa and took a golf cart over to the convention center. We arrived just in time to hear Oma thank Holmes for designing the building. Applause rang out, and a few of his friends hooted and whistled.

Holmes took the microphone. "Thanks, everyone. I have been asked to announce the official name of the convention center. It was unanimous. You are standing in the Liesel Miller Center."

Applause and hoots broke out again. Carter stood close to the podium, snapping photographs.

Oma clearly had no idea that any such thing was under discussion. For the first time in my life, my Oma was speechless.

Sixteen

Oma took the microphone, her cheeks blazing. "I am so honored. Never would I have imagined that this could happen to me. I may have been born in Germany, but life brought me to the place of my heart. The place where I am meant to be—Wagtail. I thank all of you, my dear friends, for this unbelievable gesture. It means more to me than you can imagine. Thank you!"

Holmes took the microphone from her. "And now, please enjoy viewing the gingerbread houses and tour the Liesel Miller Center at your leisure."

I pushed through the crowd to hug Oma. "You deserve this!" I planted a kiss on her soft cheek.

"Did you know?"

"Absolutely not. I had no idea!"

I moved out of the way as other people congratulated her.

Across the room, I spotted Stu with Barry. It probably wasn't the best time to ask Stu what he remembered about the concrete. Barry would discourage Stu from talking about it.

Mr. Huckle whispered in my ear. "I don't wish to rush you, but I think we had better return to the inn."

He was right, of course.

On our return, we found a few guests waiting for the Thanksgiving festivities to begin. Jean Maybury was there with Kitty. Officer Dave arrived, and I could see him gazing around.

"Looking for Shelley?" I asked.

He blushed, confirming the spark between them that I had suspected. I poked my head into the kitchen and said, "Dave is here."

Shelley actually primped her hair. "How do I look?"

Her cheeks were rosy from the heat in the kitchen. "Lovely," I said, holding the door open for her.

Zelda came, as did Marina, our trusty housekeeper. Shadow had extended family in Wagtail, so he had declined.

Carter walked in under his own power, with Delia hovering around him.

"How do you feel?" I asked.

"Still a little woozy, but they say I'll be fine."

"What do you think happened?"

Carter sucked in a deep breath. "It was possessed is all I can say. I had no control over the thing."

Our conversation was cut short by the arrival of Josie; her brother, Wyatt; and their mom, Mira. The Biffle family fussed over Carter.

Mira, a small quiet woman, placed her hand on my arm ever so gently, like a ladybug landing. "Thank you for inviting us. We had planned to go to Delia's. She's such a wonderful cook, but under the circumstances, this is a blessing for us."

"We're very pleased you could come."

Her voice barely a whisper, she added, "I didn't know. Orly told me the tree was rotting and that he was filling it with concrete. My dad used to do the same thing, so I didn't give it much thought. But now I can't hold my head up in this town. Orly has brought shame upon all of us through his evil deed. I only hope that you can identify the man inside the tree so his family will get some closure."

Delia coaxed her away. I could only imagine Mira's pain. Orly hadn't considered how many people would suffer. Even his own family.

Aunt Birdie sidled up to me, holding a drink in one hand and toying with her pearls with the other. "Didn't know, my aunt Fanny. You know the scuttlebutt about town is that Mira was seeing another man and he's in that tree."

"I've only identified three possibilities so far, but they were younger than Mira," I mused.

Aunt Birdie raised her eyebrows. "Holly, darling! Surely you're not that naïve. There's no reason a woman can't have a younger admirer."

Fortunately, there wasn't much time to think about that. I couldn't help wondering if Birdie was speaking from personal experience. Shelley made the rounds with drinks. I had opted to offer hors d'oeuvres on a tray because I thought I would spill drinks for sure. I hurried off to pick up my tray.

When I held the tray out to Josie, she selected a delicious-looking salmon canapé.

"I never gave it much thought before, but we're a lot alike," she said.

I had no idea what she meant. "Oh?"

"My father started the grocery store, and I'm running it now. Your grandparents owned the inn, and when your Oma is gone, I guess it will belong to you. Our families rely on us to keep the family businesses going."

"I guess that's true." I smiled at her.

Cook's assistants began to bring out food. I excused myself, set my tray aside, and helped them with the dog and cat buffet. It contained some of the same foods we would be eating, like skinless turkey breast slices and steamed green beans. Cat tuna was also available for persnickety felines. I knew Twinkletoes would want that. Each dog's or cat's person could handpick the contents and amount of their pet's dinner.

Two o'clock came quickly, and thanks to her German heritage, Oma was painfully punctual. At the stroke of two, she rang a little bell and people found seats.

"I have had quite a day," said Oma to everyone. "I am still shaken about the convention center bearing my name! I am so grateful for this town and all the wonderful people who live here as well as those who come to visit. If you haven't heard, my former daughter-in-law, Nell, and her parents are returning to Wagtail."

People applauded. Aunt Birdie beamed.

"Like many of you, I am most thankful for my family. And now—let's eat!"

Cook and his assistants took a bow when they joined us. The next two hours passed quickly as we devoured roast turkey, cranberries, mashed potatoes, sweet potatoes, brussels sprouts with bits of bacon, green beans, three kinds of dressing, gravy that was so delicious I wanted to drink it, and four kinds of pie.

As was our tradition, the Thanksgiving cooks and inn employees didn't have to clean up. Even though they worked for the inn, on Thanksgiving we washed up afterward. Oma, Mom, Holmes, and Delia pitched in. We tried to talk Oma out of it, but she insisted jokingly that she would not let the naming of the convention center go to her head.

We rinsed the dishes, loaded the dishwashers, and

cleaned pots and pans. Delia started us singing Christmas carols. We sang off-key and got the words wrong sometimes, but it was all in good cheer and made our task much easier.

By the time we finished, we had only half an hour before the winners of the gingerbread house contest would be announced. Delia wanted to take Carter home for a rest, but he insisted that he wanted to go.

I dashed upstairs to retrieve a warm red coat. When I unlocked the door, Trixie sniffed the doorway. She trotted inside and sniffled around but returned to the doorway as though something had been there. A guest's pet, perhaps? They often roamed the inn.

Oma drove Delia, Carter, and Mom over in a golf cart, but Holmes and I took a leisurely romantic walk in the dark. A few people had already put up Christmas lights, which we admired along the way.

We stopped when the Liesel Miller Center came into view.

Holmes and I had been holding hands as we walked. He squeezed my hand. "I've never seen it all lit up at night."

"It's gorgeous!" The tall windows glowed majestically. Dark trees on both sides isolated it from other lights. The old-fashioned lampposts leading to the front door added charm.

"I can't imagine how exciting it is to see something you created on paper come to life like this."

He nodded. "One of the perks of being an architect."

We didn't pause long. The temperature had turned bitter. I was glad I had dressed Trixie and Twinkletoes in coats. Twinkletoes had balked. She did have long fur, but I had feared that wasn't enough.

They didn't wander, though. As soon as Holmes opened the door, the two of them bolted inside. Trixie greeted her canine friends, but Twinkletoes stopped and waited for me to remove her coat. Holmes disappeared among friends who praised the building. I collected Trixie's coat, added my own, and took them all to the coat check.

"Could I buy you a hot apple cider?"

I looked around and found Stu Williams petting Trixie.

"That sounds great!" I knew the refreshments were free and that he was using a figure of speech. But I was thrilled to have a chance to ask him about the concrete and Orly.

We walked over to the busy refreshment center. The apple cider warmed my hands when I held it.

"You must be very proud of Holmes," he said.

"I am. This building is amazing."

He didn't say anything for a moment, almost as though he was considering what to say. He finally looked at me and crooked his finger. I followed him away from the crowd. Trixie tailed us, and I saw Twinkletoes watching us from a windowsill.

When we were out of earshot of the crowd, Stu said, "Orly was my friend. I know he upset a lot of people, including his family, but deep down, he was a decent man. I wouldn't have counted him as a friend if he was as cold and brutal as folks are saying. I want you to know that."

Part of me wanted to blurt, *Yes, indeed. Murdering someone and hiding the corpse in a tree is what any decent person would do.* But I knew unkind sarcasm would only alienate Stu. He might clam up, so I didn't say anything.

Stu winced. "What he did was wrong. I can't condone it. Barry tells me you're trying to figure out who was inside the tree." He inhaled and exhaled, his chest rising and falling.

I could see the pain in him.

"I was there," he whispered. "I helped Orly mix the concrete in an old wheelbarrow. I'd put it in buckets, and he would climb a ladder to pour it into the tree. But I never knew anyone was inside." He wiped his eyes roughly. "Never. Who could even imagine such a thing? I've lain awake at night wondering if I knew the real Orly. Never in my wildest imagination would it have occurred to me to hide a body in a tree. Well, I can't even imagine murdering someone. But hiding a body in a tree? That's the act of a demented mind."

I didn't want to justify what Orly had done, but I added, "Or a very desperate person."

His eyes narrowed. "Yes. I think you're right about that."

"There are rumors that his wife might have been having an affair."

"Mira?" He laughed. "It can't have been easy to be married to Orly, but she doesn't have it in her."

I didn't think so, either, but Stu appeared shocked by the actions of his friend Orly. He might be wrong about Mira, too.

"Do you have any idea who the man in the tree could be? Was Orly angry with anyone?"

Stu laughed. "Orly was always ticked off with somebody. I guess that's why we got along. What do they call it? Yin and yang? I always try to see the good side of folks, and he liked to complain about them. Most people have both good and bad in them, I guess. What shocks me the most is that Orly would have been involved with killing anyone. He used to bring home scraggly little animals and nurse them back to health. Baby foxes and a squirrel that followed him around outside and sat on his shoulder. That was something to see."

How could a man like that be so mean to people? Unless he just didn't like people and had a love for animals? "What about the Alcorns?"

He held up his palms. "Now I knew better than to mention that name around Orly. Ever since the argument about the land the grocery store sits on, the Alcorns and the Biffles have been like the Hatfields and the McCoys."

"What happened there?" I asked.

"An old man owned the land and the building. The sneaky old coot had offered to sell it to both of them, in the expectation they'd try to outbid each other! But he died unexpectedly, and since nothing was in writing, his wife sold it to somebody else altogether. Althea Alcorn was on the ball and went straight to that person with a cash offer and a deed ready for signing. Biffle, who had been renting the building, took both of them to court. The judge ruled that the sale to Althea was legit, and the Biffles have been paying her rent ever since."

"So then, Orly Biffle would have been very upset if his daughter, Josie, was sneaking around with Jay Alcorn."

"Noooo," he breathed. "Did that really happen?"

"Mrs. Alcorn thinks it did." I sipped the last of my cider.

"Well now, wouldn't that just beat all? But Josie never married. I don't recall what happened to the Alcorn boy."

"No one knows."

Stu looked at me in sheer horror. He thought for a moment. "No. I knew Orly better than just about anybody except his wife. Orly would not have hurt the Alcorn boy. Not a chance."

I hoped he was right.

Stu's wife, Sue, moseyed over to us. "Honestly, Stu! I have been looking everywhere for you. You need to come and vote for the people's choice winner. Have you even seen all the gingerbread houses?"

He wrapped an affectionate arm around her. "Holly, if

there's anything I can do to help, you just let me know." He walked away with his wife.

It was a kind offer, but some instinct inside me was wary. He had assisted Orly, for Pete's sake. I couldn't help wondering if he knew more than he was saying.

Seventeen

Trixie left my side and pranced over to Penny Terrell. I noticed Penny watching me from across the room and made my way to her. "Did you get your gingerbread house here on time?"

She gazed at me blankly. "Oh. Yes," she said without any enthusiasm. Whispering, she asked, "Have you made any progress identifying the man in the tree?"

"We won't know anything more until next week. Everyone is closed for Thanksgiving. And there is a possibility that we will have difficulty identifying him. Even if they can obtain DNA, we need to crossmatch it with something. Otherwise, it may be a long hunt, waiting for a relative's DNA to pop up."

Her mouth pulled tight. "I might be able to help you with that."

How could she possibly do that? I frowned at her. "Oh?"

"The picture I left for you. Did you get it?" she whispered.

Picture? "I don't think so."

Her eyes widened. "No! Oh no!"

"Penny," I spoke softly to calm her. "What was the picture of?"

"Boomer," she whispered.

"*That* picture! I didn't realize that you were the person who left it. Yes, I did receive it. Thank you."

"I loved Boomer," she breathed.

Not another one! How many women had Boomer seduced?

She gripped my arm. "No one can ever know. Promise me."

That was a problem. If she had killed him, there was no way I would keep her secret. I skipped over her request. "Penny, do you know something about Boomer? Is he the man in the tree?"

She motioned me away from the crowd. "I have lived with guilt all these years."

Oh no! Was she about to confess? I scanned the room and spotted Dave. A wave of relief swept over me. But how to alert him? "I believe that's my phone."

"I didn't hear anything."

"I have it on vibrate. That way it doesn't disturb everyone."

I hit text and quickly selected Officer Dave. *Come over here!!!*

I apologized for the interruption.

"You see, I have the best husband in the world. But Boomer was so handsome and exciting. All I could do was think of Boomer. My husband deserved so much more from me, but I was fixated on Boomer."

I glanced at her husband, Tommy, across the room. Granted, he was pudgy, balding, and short. Not every woman's dream guy. He wore what appeared to be a handknit sweater with a giant turkey on the front. He was laughing and couldn't have had a sweeter expression. I'd only heard nice things about him.

Dave had been waylaid by two women. His eyes met mine and he gave an almost imperceptible nod, so I knew he had received my text.

"Let me guess," I said. "He asked you to marry him."

"Gosh, no! I was already married to Tommy. And Boomer was engaged to be married. It wasn't in the stars for us to be together."

"So you knew he was engaged to Delia?"

"Delia? No, honey, you've got it all wrong. Boomer was getting married to a girl from North Carolina. A summer visitor."

Eighteen

She had to be kidding. "Are you certain about that?"

"Absolutely."

"Did you meet this girl?"

"I couldn't." She sounded like she might cry. "It would have torn me apart. And how would I feel being in love with her husband-to-be? I felt guilty enough for necking with him! I could hardly face Tommy."

"Necking?"

"Do they call it something else these days?"

"I guess people would say *sleeping*."

She gasped. "Nothing like that, honey. Boomer was a respectable guy."

And a top-notch Lothario, saying what he thought women wanted to hear. "When did you see him last?"

"It was a Friday afternoon. He was supposed to be married the next day. I was heartbroken."

Tommy sidled up to us and handed his wife a cup of

hot apple cider. "Have you tried the gingerbread cookies yet? They're delicious! I understand Bonnie from Pawsome Cookies made them."

Penny smiled at him and gently stroked the side of his face. "You know they're my favorite." Before she walked away, she murmured, "Just between us."

Tommy lagged behind her. "Any word on who that was in the tree?"

"Nothing definite yet."

"I like to think of myself as a kind man, but I hope to heaven that it's Boomer Jenkins."

I tried to play innocent. "Did you know him?"

"Everybody in town knew him. A good-looking guy on a flashy motorcycle? Wagtail wasn't as big then. Everybody knew everybody. Penny had a terrible crush on him. I guess I don't really wish him dead. I just hope he stays away from here. I'm not the kind of guy who can compete with a fellow like Boomer." He grinned. "If he does come back, I hope he's fat and bald. Like me!" He laughed and toddled off to join his wife.

Holmes ambled over to me. "Which one is your favorite?"

"You. You're my favorite. How many women are you engaged to?"

Holmes burst out laughing. "At least a dozen," he teased. "I meant the gingerbread houses. What are *you* talking about?"

"Boomer."

"You can't help sleuthing, can you? Even on Thanksgiving?"

"I have a feeling he may have married a girl from out of town and left women weeping in his wake."

"So back to square one, then."

"I'm afraid so." We entered the huge room where the gingerbread houses were on display.

Barry Williams joined us. "This is an incredible building, Holmes. It's amazing."

"Thanks, Barry. I had a lot of fun designing it. Is this the first time you've been here?" asked Holmes.

"Judges weren't allowed inside until today. No early viewing of the gingerbread houses."

Holmes snorted. "*You* were a judge? What qualified you for that? Do you do a lot of baking on the sly?"

Fortunately, Barry took his ribbing in stride. "I think I may have been chosen because of my familiarity with animals?"

"Ah, the veterinarian angle. Of course. But by those standards, I should have judged them for their architecture."

"Get over it, Holmes. Maybe another year," I joked. Turning to Barry, I asked, "How's our pregnant doggie?"

"She is the best. A real love. I assume you would have notified me if someone claimed her?"

"No one recognizes her, but a few people have offered to adopt her."

Barry nodded. "Gotta love the people of Wagtail. Do I get first dibs?"

"You're kidding!"

"Nope. She's been comforting patients who've had surgery. It comes to her naturally. She's a great dog. I don't have one of my own right now. I'm hoping no one claims her so I can keep her!"

At that moment a scream echoed through the room. The three of us ran toward the exhibition where it seemed to originate.

We arrived just in time to see Twinkletoes knock a gingerbread tree off an exhibit, and even worse, Trixie had taken a bite out of the roof of a gingerbread house! The little stinkers jumped from the table and ran. Trixie still clutched the gingerbread in her mouth!

"I'm so sorry!" I said to everyone, since I didn't know whose it was. And then I raced after my little rascals.

I caught up to them at the door. Trixie crunched on her ill-gotten gingerbread and swallowed it fast.

"What have you done? I thought I could trust you."

Trixie wagged her tail slowly, showing her guilt and hope for forgiveness. Twinkletoes groomed her paw, pretending to be completely indifferent to my scolding.

Barry caught up to me. "It's all right. I spoke to the lady who constructed the gingerbread house. She didn't use any ingredients that would be harmful to Trixie." He tsked at the two of them and grinned. "Life with pets means never a dull moment!"

"Whose was it?" I asked. "I feel just awful!"

"It was made by some lady named Jean Maybury."

"Oh great," I said sarcastically. "She's staying at the inn."

"She's not exactly fond of animals. I'm surprised she came here at all. But you're in fine shape. We judged before the incident. It won't affect her chances of winning."

I took a deep breath. "You don't happen to have a couple of leashes on you?"

Barry laughed. "Really? You think all veterinarians carry leashes with them?"

"A girl could hope. Would you mind watching them for a minute while I apologize to Jean?"

"No problem."

I hurried across the room to Jean, who looked mighty miffed. Not that I could blame her. Kitty stood by her side. "Jean, I am so sorry. I wish there were some way I could make it up to you."

"It's ruined!" she wailed.

"Fortunately, the judges made their selections before it happened," I assured her, realizing that Trixie had followed me and lurked at my feet.

"I should sue you!"

"Memaw," said Kitty, "it's okay. You can bake lots more gingerbread houses. Better ones!"

"Wait until my husband hears about this. If he were here, he'd know what to do and wouldn't let you get away with this." She was on the verge of tears.

Officer Dave walked over to us.

"This woman's dog took a bite out of my gingerbread house!" said Jean, sniffling.

Officer Dave looked at it and tried to hide a grin.

"You people are horrible," Jean said loudly. "I worked hard on that. And you should be ashamed. You're the law. It's your responsibility to protect people and gingerbread houses. That dog should be in jail."

"Memaw!" cried Kitty.

Trixie pinned her ears back and fled, with Kitty running after her.

"I guess I'd better take Trixie and Twinkletoes home," I said to Officer Dave.

I could hear a camera clicking. When I turned around, Carter grinned at me. "I got a great shot of Trixie and Twinkletoes with that gingerbread house they wrecked."

As I picked up Twinkletoes from Barry and walked across the room in search of Trixie, Oma took the microphone and began to announce the winners. "In the age category of eight to ten, the winner is Kitty Johnson!"

Jean Maybury barged between people and made her way to the podium.

Oma smiled at her. "Where is Kitty?"

Jean glanced over the crowd. "She was right by my side. Kitty!"

Our Kitty? Where had she gone? I opened the door and shot outside. "Kitty! Kitty!" There was no sign of her.

I returned to the gingerbread house display.

Jean Maybury was accepting on Kitty's behalf. "She

will be so thrilled! Imagine winning a thousand dollars at her age!"

Sue Williams approached me. "Have you seen Kitty?" she asked. "I'm so excited for her. Neither Stu nor I helped her. Well, we might have made a few suggestions. She's very good at using an icing bag. Barry always ate all the decorating candies, but Kitty said she was saving them all for the house. Isn't that darling? She will be so happy!"

Cheers went up around us as Oma named each winner.

"I don't know where she went," I said. "I'm headed back to the inn."

"We'll come with you. Now where is Stu?"

We were scanning the crowd for him when Oma said, "And the grand winner of this year's gingerbread house contest is Kathleen Connor!"

Another round of cheers went up. In one area, a woman emerged from screaming friends and walked up to the podium.

And then it hit me. Connor. Oma had called the name Kathleen Connor.

Trixie's Guide to Murder

How do you know it's murder? Well, first of all, most peoples don't die out in the grass, or under a bush, or on the floor. If there's a person lying in one of those places, be suspicious. Take your time and see if you can detect a second or third peoples presence. That's the biggest telltale sign of murder. If somebody else was there and left, that's who you need to look for.

Try to pick up smells of blood. Murder very often involves blood. That's a big clue. Sometimes peoples get into fights and one of them ends up dead. There's usually blood when that happens.

Poison is another big problem. Sometimes peoples get sick and fall down. That's not murder. It can be hard to distinguish, but be sure to get your mom's or dad's attention anyway. They'll appreciate it. Use your sniffer to determine if there are any scents of poison. There's a big variety of those, and they all smell different. If your instinct says not to eat something that smells like that, it's probably poison. Leave it alone! No licking to taste it!

Nineteen

There had to be a lot of Connors in the world. It wasn't an unusual name. Kathleen looked about my mother's age. She wore her dark brown hair in a short bob, with just a hint of bangs. She verged on plump, with blue eyes that seemed to sparkle.

At my feet, Trixie growled, something she rarely did. I didn't know she had returned. Jean Maybury bustled up to me, looking angry.

"I should have known a contest with a pot this big would be fixed. What is she? Your aunt or something?"

"I don't know her, and I wasn't involved in the judging," I said as calmly as I could.

"Hah! It's a racket!" Jean grumbled as she barged away through the crowd.

"I am so thrilled," Kathleen said into the microphone. "I haven't been back to Wagtail in a very long time, but it has always been one of my most favorite places to visit. When I heard about the gingerbread house contest, I had to give it a shot. I've entered a few contests like this before, but none of them involved cat or dog houses."

The audience laughed.

"Ohh." She smiled and shook her head. "I feel like this is my Oscar moment! I do want to thank my wonderful husband and all six of my children. This is definitely the icing on the cake of a perfect Thanksgiving weekend. Thank you all!"

I looked over at her family as she walked into their embrace. Four girls, two boys, all high school to college age, and a husband whom I recognized.

He was the man who had been scoping out the inn recently.

I glanced at Trixie, who had made friends with a dachshund. Twinkletoes wrestled to get out of my grip. Could I trust them not to harm any more of the gingerbread houses? I knew I should take them home, but I had no idea where this man was staying. This might be my only opportunity to talk with him. Most likely he was not Penn Connor. But it would only take me a moment to find out.

"I'm going to be a minute longer," I said to Sue. "You go ahead without me."

Keeping an eye on Trixie and Twinkletoes, I walked over to Mr. Connor. He was clean-shaven, with dark hair turning silver along the sides of his face. He wore round tortoiseshell glasses on a long nose and had a remarkably rounded jawline. "Mr. Connor?"

"Yes?"

"I know this sounds silly, but would you happen to be Penn Connor?"

His eyes opened wide. "Do I know you?"

"You're alive!"

He laughed at me. "Happily, yes, I *am* alive."

"You stayed at the Sugar Maple Inn about twenty years

ago. We have your things." I held out my hand to him. "I'm Holly Miller, co-owner of the inn. "I've been trying to locate you."

He shook my hand and tilted his head at me. "Whatever for?"

"You disappeared."

His expression changed. "Did I walk out on my bill? I would be happy to pay now. We'll figure out the interest over twenty years. I'm so sorry!"

"No, no, no. You paid your bill." I tried to phrase my reasons gently. "We've been looking for people who disappeared. That's all."

He studied me for a moment. "This is about the man in the tree."

"You know about that?"

"I think everyone does. It's a most curious situation. It's all anyone is talking about."

"Well, you seem like a nice man." I gestured toward his family, some of whom were listening to us, "And you obviously have a lovely family, so I'm glad it's not you."

"You can strike one name off your list now. How many does that leave?"

"Really only two unless someone comes up with another person."

"Who are they?" he asked curiously.

"Jay Alcorn and a fellow named Boomer Jenkins."

His expression turned serious in a heartbeat. He touched his wife's elbow. "Honey, you and the kids go on over to Tequila Mockingbird. I'll catch up to you."

Kathleen blinked at me a couple of times, worry lines creasing her face. "Are you sure?"

"It's fine. I won't be long."

His family started for the door.

"Is there someplace we could talk?" he asked.

"Of course." I led the way to one of the smaller conference rooms. When we passed the beverages on the way, I asked him, "Hot chocolate or hot apple cider?"

"Always chocolate."

I took two hot chocolates, handed him one, and opened the door to a cold room. I pushed a button and gas logs sprang to life in the fireplace, taking away some of the chill. Large glass windows overlooked the dark lake.

We pulled our chairs next to the fire. "I gather you know Boomer?"

"Probably better than just about anyone. I met Boomer in first grade. Even then he was a scamp. But fun, you know? He had no fear of anything. He ran headlong into danger without hesitation. When we were teens, my parents no longer found that amusing. I was an idealist back then and wanted to believe that Boomer had my back. We did everything together, but I can see now that he wasn't a good influence on me. In retrospect, I've wondered why he stuck with me. I didn't have his looks or his charisma. I have come to the conclusion that I had one thing he liked. Money. My folks weren't what you'd call super wealthy, but Boomer's family didn't have much at all."

"How sad for you that he befriended you for that reason."

"Well, I think there were other justifications as well. My family offered security that he didn't get at home. His dad was what I would call gruff. I don't think he was a terrible person, but Boomer's mom left them when we were about ten, so Boomer didn't get much affection. He tried hard to put up a brave front. But it just made him more daring. It was like he had been born without the maybe-this-is-a-bad-idea gene. My mom used to buy us both clothes. She made sure she differentiated them. I'd get a blue shirt, and Boomer's would be green. It wasn't until I was an adult that I understood she'd been taking care of him all along without making a fuss over it."

"Wow. Your mom sounds like an incredible person."

"She is. She always asks if I've heard anything about Boomer. We all lost touch with him, and I feel guilty about that. It's my fault, in a way. And kind of a long story."

"I'd like to hear it. I've learned a lot about Boomer. He must have been quite a character."

Penn took off his glasses and ran a hand over his forehead before replacing them. "My wife, Kathleen, lived down the street from me. She was my dream girl. She's just as pretty and wonderful today as she was then. But I was the nerdy kid with glasses, and Boomer turned out to be a real ladies' man. My mom told me once it was because Boomer's mom abandoned him. He sought approval from women, and once he became a teen, he was unstoppable."

He paused to sip his hot chocolate. "This is good. It's the real thing, not a watery mix. I went away to college and didn't see much of my old friends for a few years. Kathleen was away at school, too, and Boomer drifted from job to job."

He smiled at me. "I'm finally getting to the Wagtail part of the story. The summer Kathleen and I graduated, her family rented a house in Wagtail. Boomer had moved to Wagtail the year before because he landed a decent job installing and repairing TV satellite dishes. The two of them had a nice reunion. Boomer proposed marriage, Kathleen accepted, and her parents were beside themselves. They knew of Boomer's reputation with women and for being reckless. They tried to talk her out of the marriage, but Kathleen can be stubborn."

He clutched the mug in both hands and looked me in the eyes. "Of course, at the time, I knew nothing about any of that. To my great surprise, I received an email from the two of them. They said they were getting married in Wagtail and they wanted me to be the best man. A truly rotten best man, as it turned out. No one else connected to the wedding party was staying at the inn. Kathleen had come up for vacations over the years and loved Wagtail. She wanted to be married here. Her parents refused to be involved, so Kathleen rented a house where a few of her friends could stay and planned a rustic wedding up on the top of Wagtail Mountain."

Sighing, he added, "I had been crazy in love with the bride for a long time. The inn gave me some distance from everyone else to pull myself together and come to terms with the wedding.

"The day before the big event, everyone gathered at the house and partied. Most of them were pretty soused. Except for Kathleen." He paused a moment and seemed to gather his thoughts.

"She came to me in tears. She had found a necklace belonging to another woman in Boomer's apartment. Kathleen was a wreck. She had been so excited about the wedding, and now she couldn't go through with it. She wanted to run away, but you can't easily run from Wagtail. It's not like you can catch a bus or a train. One of her friends had driven her up to Wagtail, so she didn't have her own car here. She begged me to take her away."

"Oh no! What did you do?"

"To me, Kathleen was about as perfect as a woman could be. I didn't even think twice about it. We got in my car and left town without so much as a goodbye to anyone. We were on the run, so to speak. It didn't occur to me that I had failed to collect my belongings from the inn until six months later when *I* was getting married and realized that I had left my tuxedo behind. I certainly did not expect you to have kept it all this time!"

"When was the last time you saw Boomer?"

"In the afternoon, I think. Neither Kathleen nor I ever heard from Boomer again. I suppose that was to be expected. The best man stealing away with the bride isn't exactly proper behavior. And then I married her, which is even worse. We have now returned to the scene of the crime."

I looked at him with a start. "By 'crime' you mean . . . ?"

"Running off with the bride. We thought we might see Boomer when we came up here. It's been a long time. We were hoping we'd been forgiven by now."

"He didn't go after you and Kathleen?" I asked.

"I expected him to, but he never showed up. Kathleen says that meant he never loved her. After we got married, I landed a job in Switzerland, and we lived there for years. Then we moved to California. On a visit home, I went to Boomer's dad's house, but it had been sold and the new owners didn't know where he had gone. A guy like Boomer is bound to show up on social media, but I haven't seen him anywhere. My fear, of course, is that he finally landed in prison for one of his daring exploits."

"Prison?" That had never occurred to me. "Was he doing anything illegal?"

He snorted. "This is Boomer we're talking about. There's no telling what kind of trouble he might have landed in."

"Drugs?"

"Possibly, if he thought he could make money. Most likely, he got into trouble with an irate husband and high-tailed it out of town."

I gazed silently at the nice man before me. He seemed so calm. So together and self-confident. But he hadn't told me a single thing that indicated he had not murdered Boomer.

"Did you know Orly Biffle?" I asked.

"Orly. There's a name you don't hear every day. No, I don't believe I've had the pleasure."

Either he was telling the truth or he was a smooth

operator. But I couldn't tell which. I was glad I could hear the murmuring and scraping of chairs in the building. I wasn't alone.

Notions ran through my head. Who abandoned all their belongings at an inn and left town? Someone who had committed murder and was on the run. Now he had come back? There was no hard evidence against him except for the fact that he fled and his own admission that he was in love with Kathleen.

And then it dawned on me that Delia may have gotten wind of the fact that Boomer was marrying someone else the next day. Would she have poisoned Boomer at dinner that night?

Suddenly I heard my name. "Holly Miller? Are you here somewhere?"

I popped out of my seat. "Excuse me." I ran to the door and opened it.

Dave spied me from the lobby. He waved a sheet of paper and jogged toward me.

Penn had risen from his chair and stood behind me. I introduced the two men.

"Have you seen Jean Maybury or Kitty?" asked Dave, breathless.

"Not since Jean left here in a snit."

He thrust the paper at me.

AMBER ALERT
MISSING CHILD
KITTY JOHNSON

LAST SEEN IN CHARLOTTE, NORTH CAROLINA. MAY BE IN THE COMPANY OF A WOMAN CALLING HERSELF JEAN MAYBURY. KITTY IS NINE YEARS OLD. FOUR FEET, FOUR INCHES TALL, WITH BLUE EYES AND A SCAR ON HER RIGHT SHOULDER.

Twenty

The image in the photo was unquestionably the same Kitty who was staying at the inn.

Stu Williams dashed up behind Dave. "Is it true?"

Dave handed him the flyer.

Stu moaned. "Not our precious little Kitty."

I pulled out my phone and called Zelda at the inn. "Have you seen Jean Maybury or Kitty?"

"Jean came through the registration lobby a while ago with her luggage and checked out, but Kitty wasn't with her. I called her a Wagtail taxi to take her to her car." Fear rippled through me as I relayed that information.

Dave reached for my phone. "Zelda, be very careful around Jean Maybury if she returns. Don't let on that you know anything is wrong and call me immediately."

He listened to Zelda for a moment. "She kidnapped Kitty." We could all hear Zelda's shriek. "Zelda, you have to play along like you don't know anything is wrong. If you see Kitty by herself, I need you to hide her in the office and call me right away. Can you do that?" He thanked her, disconnected the call, and handed me the phone.

"Should I set up a search party?" asked Stu.

"I'd appreciate that," said Dave.

"We can help. My family and I," offered Penn. "Where should we meet?"

"How about right here?" suggested Stu.

"Is there a copier around here?" asked Dave.

I reached out for the flyer. "No problem. How many do you need?"

"Let's start with three hundred," he said.

Stu stopped me. "Is there a computer and a printer?"

"I think so."

The two of us rushed to the business center. Stu pulled up a map of Wagtail on a computer and printed it out. While I ran off copies of the Amber Alert, he marked the map. We made copies of that, too. By the time we returned to the lobby, it had filled with local people, including Sue and Barry, Holmes, Carter, Penn Connor and family, and more.

"I guess no one has a photo of Jean Maybury?" Officer Dave asked me.

"We don't photograph our guests. I suppose she could be in the background of a photo someone took." I held up my palms hopelessly.

Stu stood on a chair. His voice boomed. "Partner up, please. I don't want anyone on their own. It's already dark out there, and it's getting colder. Twos and threes, everyone. I have copies of a map of Wagtail. I've divided it into sections. Each pair or threesome will take one section. My phone number and Officer Dave's are on the map. If you see Jean Maybury or Kitty, call Officer Dave. For anything else, call me."

He dismounted the chair, and Dave jumped up on it.

"We don't want to scare Jean Maybury. I cannot emphasize that enough. Do not try to catch or apprehend her. Call me. Your job is to be our eyes, not to try to arrest her. Is that clear? In addition, we don't know if she's armed. North Carolina police have told me she's very likely confused and may be panicking. Do not approach her. We don't want to frighten her. Act casual and call me."

"What does she look like?" someone shouted.

"Holly?" Dave gazed at me.

"Her most distinctive feature is crimson red hair with purple highlights. She's a little pudgy and probably in her seventies."

Dave repeated the information. "Line up, please. Stu will assign you to an area, so we'll be sure to have every neighborhood covered."

"What about the woods and trails?" someone asked.

"Let's start with Wagtail and go from there." Dave hopped off the chair. "Did she seem like a hiking type to you?"

"No. Not even a little bit," I said. I honestly couldn't imagine her being outdoorsy. As far as I could tell, she didn't like animals, either.

Minutes later, the lobby had emptied save for Officer Dave and me.

"I'd like to go back to the inn with you, if you don't mind," said Dave.

"Sure. No problem." I collected our coats and helped Trixie and Twinkletoes with theirs before sliding on my own warm coat.

We walked back, keeping our eyes open for Jean or Kitty. Thanksgiving Eve was quiet in Wagtail. Most people were probably indoors, watching football games or eating their feasts.

On the way, Dave said, "If it's all right with you, I'd like you to stay at the inn. I know Jean has checked out, but if she doesn't realize that we're looking for her, or if something goes awry with her plans, there's a possibility that Jean will return to a place she's familiar with. The police in North Carolina said she's under the care of a doctor for mental health reasons and may be confused, so just go along with whatever she says—within reason, of course. Don't approach her. Don't grab Kitty. Act as if you still believe that Jean is Kitty's grandmother and that nothing is wrong. But alert me immediately."

"That's fine."

"I'm serious, Holly. Do not take any heroic measures."

"Stop it already. I get what you're saying. Jean probably doesn't realize that we're on to her. I have to play along."

We entered the main lobby of the inn. Dave held out his hand in a motion to stop. We listened. Very soft strains of holiday music played. Otherwise, there was no sign of life.

Dave whispered, "Which room was she in? Maybe she left a clue to her plans behind."

"Pounce," I murmured. "Do you want the key?"

He nodded, and the two of us walked along the corridor to the inn office. I unlocked the door and opened the locked cabinet where we kept the house keys.

I handed him one. "Do you know where Pounce is?"

He shook his head. "Show me the way, but then stand back."

Wordlessly, I locked the office door behind us and led him up the back stairs to the second floor. I pointed out Pounce, which was located close to the grand staircase.

He placed his ear against the door as a precaution. It seemed like forever, but he finally unlocked the door and went inside. He emerged seconds later. "You can come in."

I walked into the pretty room. The only sign of them

having been there was a small stuffed dog sitting on the dresser next to the TV.

Sighing, I picked up the toy. "Do you suppose someone tipped her off?"

Officer Dave shook his head. "I'm guessing that she hoped to collect ten thousand dollars for her gingerbread house. Her reaction to the damage to her gingerbread house may have exacerbated her psychosis."

"Kitty's mom must be flipping out. Do you think anything Jean told us about her was true?"

"Like what?"

"She's a single mom who is newly unemployed?"

Officer Dave shrugged. "I guess we'll know soon. She's on the way here."

"She'll need someplace to stay, but everyone's booked." I gazed around the room. "Is it okay to clean this room?"

Dave gazed around. "Yeah. It's not like this is the scene of a crime. They were here, all right, but we're not going to get anything useful in here. If you find anything, let me know."

"I'll clean this one for Kitty's mom, then. I think it's safe to say Jean will not be returning."

"Looks okay to me."

I chuckled at him. "You'd like to sleep on the sheets a stranger slept on?"

"Eww." Officer Dave grimaced. "I'm going to check a few places she might have gone. Keep an eye out for Jean, just in case."

Officer Dave left the inn. I took a few minutes to send the missing-child alert to the residents and business owners of Wagtail. Then I retrieved fresh linens and the cleaning cart. While I changed the sheets, Trixie and Twinkletoes inspected the room. The only sources of information were the wastebaskets, which contained a surprisingly large number of chocolate wrappers. I checked the pad of paper on the desk for indentations that might reveal any scribbles she had made. Nothing.

It was so cold outside. I tried to remember what Kitty had been wearing. I thought she had a coat on.

I returned the cart to the cleaning closet and walked through the halls of the inn. No one stirred. It was the dinner hour, I reasoned, and a lot of people were out eating their Thanksgiving dinners or grabbing a sandwich, having eaten a big meal earlier in the day.

I felt a little guilty about it, but I was famished! Trixie and Twinkletoes sprang down the grand staircase ahead of me. As though they knew where I was going, they vanished through the dog door into the family kitchen.

When my dad and his sister were growing up, Oma recognized that living in an inn could be hard on children. She had designed a private room on the main floor with a full kitchen, a fireplace with cushy chairs before it, and a dining table. Cozy and just the right size for eating meals, doing homework, playing games, and gathering as a family.

It was my favorite room in the inn. The one place we could relax and catch a few private moments. Not to mention that it housed the magic refrigerator. I had a turkey sandwich loaded with cranberries in mind when I swung open the door, only to find that Oma and Mom had beaten me to it.

The two of them sat at the farmhouse-style table with all the fixings for sandwiches, as well as other leftovers from our huge meal earlier that day.

"Aha! Caught you!"

Their mouths full, neither one could respond.

I opened the magic refrigerator and found containers that said *Turkey Dinner for Trixie* and *Turkey Dinner for*

Twinkletoes. I spooned their meals into dishes and set them on the floor.

"We have a plate for you," said Oma. "And tea is on the counter if you'd like some."

I poured a mug and settled at the table with them.

"Any news on the little girl?" asked Oma.

"Her mother is on the way. Officer Dave and I checked their room. Jean Maybury took everything except for a stuffed dog. I went ahead and cleaned it so Kitty's mother will have a place to stay."

"Gratis," said Oma.

"Of course! It's the least we can do." I didn't feel one bit guilty when I spread mayonnaise on my bread. Right now I needed comfort food. I was stress-mayoing. Was that even a thing? It was now!

"What I don't understand," said Mom, "is why the little girl didn't say anything. How old is she?"

"Eight or nine, I would think." Oma helped herself to some oyster stuffing.

I removed my copy of the Amber Alert from my pocket and placed it on the table.

"I guess that's still young enough to be gullible and believe what people tell you. Is Kitty her real name?" Mom sipped her tea.

"I assume so. That's what's on the flyer." I pulled out my phone. "Excuse me, but I want to see if Jean really won a gingerbread house contest."

"Jean Maybury might not be her name," said Mom.

"It is the name under which she won the contest that sent her here," said Oma. "I took care of that booking myself."

I nodded and handed them the phone so they could see a photograph of Jean Maybury accepting her prize.

"Granted, I would never steal a child, but I'm having

trouble understanding why she did. Who does that?" asked Mom.

"A woman who needs help." Oma shook her head. "Maybe she doesn't have any family left. No one to hug or understand her. She represented Kitty as her granddaughter. Maybe that's a sign of her desperate desire to have someone who cares about her."

"She seemed a little short with Kitty if you ask me. I felt sorry for her. If you want a child badly enough to steal one, wouldn't you dote on the kid?" I asked.

Mom laughed. "Even the most perfect child is a twenty-four-hour-a-day job. Jean might have glamorized motherhood in her mind. She probably thought it would be easy and was annoyed when she had to put her own plans on a back burner to care for Kitty."

"How are you coming with the body in the tree?" asked Oma.

"You'll never believe this, but the woman who won the gingerbread house contest is Penn Connor's wife!"

Oma stopped eating. "No!"

"It's a long story, but basically the girl he loved was marrying someone else. She changed her mind the day before the wedding and asked Penn to drive her home. He did, and they married six months later."

"Ach! A wonderful love story. We will give them a belated honeymoon week at the inn. Yes?"

It wasn't really a question. "Of course. I think they would enjoy that."

"Then you have narrowed it down to Boomer now," said Mom.

"And Jay Alcorn."

"Althea's older son," said Oma. "I assumed he was living elsewhere."

"If he is, she doesn't know about it. She thinks Orly may have killed Jay because he was interested in Josie."

"What does Josie have to say about that?" asked Mom.

"I didn't push her very hard," I admitted. "She played coy, asking where he was living. Mostly she complained about his mother and told me Althea was a cold woman."

I was finishing my heavenly sandwich when Officer Dave poked his head into the private kitchen. "I thought I might find you here."

A slender woman with copper hair the color of Kitty's followed him into the kitchen holding the hand of a little boy.

Trixie's Guide to Murder

Sniffing out murder is the easy part. The most difficult thing is telling your mom or dad. Remember, peoples can't smell the most obvious scents. And that's complicated by the fact that they're prone to misinterpret what we're trying to tell them.

Maybe you were playing outside when you smelled steak cooking in the kitchen. And yet, the peoples around you continued to talk or throw frisbees. So you ran to the door hoping to snag some steak! And your peoples asked, "You don't want to play anymore? Are you tired?" Even though you really wanted to smack your forehead because they didn't get it, you smiled and wagged your tail. Then peoples opened the door and said, "Smells good in here. What's cooking?"

Smelling murder is kind of like that, but harder to convey to peoples. Because very often, peoples can't smell murder even if the victim is only feet away from them. It's your job to teach them to follow you. Unfortunately, peoples can be very difficult to train.

You know how you can tell what other dogs are thinking by looking at their tails? Wagging tails are happy. Tails tucked under and between the hind legs mean a dog is scared or worried. Sadly, peoples don't come with tails. Watch their faces. Run this test to see what I mean. When your mom or dad asks you to do something like "Sit," do it and watch their expression. They might even tell you what a good dog you are. Now pretend you're going to tear up a toy or a pillow. Check out their faces when they say, "No." That expression is equivalent to a doggum tucking his tail between his legs. Your mom or dad is not happy.

Twenty-One

"This is Marie Johnson, Kitty's mother," said Dave.

If he hadn't introduced us, her hair color would have tipped me off.

"And this fine fellow is Stuey," Dave continued. "Could one of you check them in?"

Marie searched our faces. "I really don't care about that. I just want to find my baby."

"Of course that is your main concern," said Oma. "Holly, would you take her luggage and come back with the key? That way Marie can come and go as she pleases without worrying about anything else."

As I walked out the door, I heard Mom asking, "Are you hungry, Stuey?"

They hadn't brought much with them. I could well imagine that they had packed in a rush. I collected the key from the office, dropped off their luggage in Pounce, locked the door, and returned to the private kitchen.

Twinkletoes purred on Marie's lap, and Stuey ate a turkey sandwich ravenously, as though he hadn't eaten all day. His mother watched him anxiously, probably torn between rushing him and giving him an opportunity to eat at his own speed.

"So you saw Kitty?" Marie asked. "Is she all right?"

Oma smiled kindly. "Kitty looked fine. She even won her division in the gingerbread house contest."

Marie blinked. "She made a gingerbread house? This boggles my mind. I suppose I should be grateful that Jean was kind to Kitty. But where are they? If they took their luggage, doesn't that mean they left town?"

Dave poured himself some tea. "I'm afraid it does suggest that. But there's conflicting information. Jean's car has been located, which would indicate they are still here, or they departed by other means. The good news is that the Amber Alert has now been shared in Virginia."

"I can't believe this has happened to us. I did not leave them alone," Marie blurted. "I left Kitty and Stuey with Jean, a neighbor who had babysat for me before. She was nice to you, wasn't she, Stuey?"

He shrugged and swallowed a bite of his sandwich. "She didn't pay much attention to me, but she liked to do Kitty's hair."

Marie clenched her fist. "This is a woman I saw several times a week. How was I supposed to guess that she would take off with my daughter? Now they tell me she's suffering from depression and delusions following the death of her husband. I didn't even know he died. She talks about him as if he's alive. She's not in her right mind!"

Dave nodded. "Dr. Engelknecht tells me the death of a partner can trigger depression and confusion. Especially if they relied heavily on that person. It's as if the rug was pulled out from under them. They might seem perfectly fine and competent enough to build a gingerbread house or to drive across the country, but other times, they can sink into depression and experience psychosis. She probably grew increasingly lonely and wanted Kitty for company."

Marie groaned. "I feel like such a fool! I should have realized what was going on with Jean."

Officer Dave asked, "What happened when Jean left, Stuey?"

"She said she was taking Kitty shopping for girly clothes. I could go with them or stay home and play Super Mario Brothers."

Mom smiled at him. "I know your mom is glad you didn't go with her."

"I guess. But she's not my mom yet."

"Stuey is my nephew," said Marie. "But we're going to change that as soon as we can afford it. Right, Stuey?"

"Right!" He grinned at her, revealing two missing front teeth. "Aunt Marie will officially be my new mom."

"Thank you so much for Stuey's dinner. Can you put it on my bill?" asked Marie.

"My dear," said Oma, "your stay is entirely on us. Meals included. All we want is to find Kitty."

"I can't let you do that."

"Nonsense. I cannot run around looking for your daughter. The least I can do is put you up for free. One less worry for you." Oma smiled graciously.

"Thank you so much. It is a relief not to worry about that. I guess we should get going." She gazed at Officer Dave.

He took a deep breath. "I can't stop you, and to be honest, if it were my child, I would find it difficult to sit around waiting. But just to be clear, there is a possibility that Jean will run or do something drastic if she sees you. Don't forget that she's confused. There's also the possibility that she has begun to realize that she did something wrong."

Marie's chest heaved with each breath she took. Her hand trembled as she grasped Stuey's. "I'm hoping that Kitty will break away from Jean and run to us."

"As I said, I can't stop you. We have people all over town watching for them. We're setting up the Christkindlmarket stalls tonight, so there will be more people out there than usual. It's going to be below freezing, so there's a strong chance that Jean and Kitty will seek shelter somewhere for the night."

Marie nodded. "Thank you."

When they left, Oma said, "I'll clean up and watch the inn. You two grab a nap. You have a lot to do tonight."

Mom and I retreated to our quarters. She seemed to have no problem heading off for a nap, but I was restless and worried about Kitty. Trixie focused on the doorway again. Something must have left a scent. I opened the door to make sure a four-legged guest hadn't peed on it. But I didn't see any sign of that or of anything unusual.

I closed the door and my thoughts returned to Kitty. What could we have done differently? Children usually had different last names than one set of their grandparents. I didn't have the same surname as my mother. I knew it wasn't the norm to quiz people checking in with children, yet I felt terrible guilt.

Where could they have gone? They could have called for a car to transport them down the mountain. But then they would have needed a car to continue their trip. It was possible to walk down the mountain, but I couldn't imagine doing that with a child. They would have had to make their way through trees and brush without a trail. It seemed highly unlikely to me. They must still be in Wagtail.

I settled on the sofa for a nap. Trixie jumped up on the

sofa to snuggle, then settled at my feet with her head across my ankles. Even though there wasn't much room left, Twinkletoes joined us, wedging between me and the back of the sofa. I heard Twinkletoes purring as I drifted off.

"Holly! Holly! It's almost the magic hour." Mom sounded way too cheerful and bubbly for eleven o'clock at night. I groaned.

"Come on, sleepyhead. I made us some strong coffee."

I sat up and she handed me a mug that had been painted with jolly little mice wearing elf hats. "Thanks, Mom. Any word about Kitty?"

"I haven't been downstairs yet. Besides, no one would notify *me*. Have you checked your phone?"

Bleary-eyed, I peered at it. "Nothing about Kitty at all. That poor child."

"It's twenty-eight degrees outside. That Jean woman must have taken shelter somewhere. I wonder how she knew we were on to her?"

"Good question. We don't really know anything about her. She made a joke about her husband, but that wasn't based in reality. Who knows what she might be thinking?"

"Let's take heart that she seems to love Kitty and will take care of her. Wherever they are."

Fortified by our coffee, I changed into jeans, a sweater, and a warm vest. We crossed the hall and discussed our plans for decorating the inn. We placed a tree on the balcony of my bedroom, where it would be visible from the south end of the green, and loaded it with lights. Pleased with ourselves, we continued with the simple task of placing battery-operated lights in the inn windows. Marina, the housekeeper, had set up lights in the guest rooms that morning when she cleaned. Shadow had already been busy outside hanging fresh evergreen wreaths with bold red bows on the windows.

Next, we tackled the grand staircase in the main lobby. Possibly the most important room of all, since most people entered and exited the inn that way. Mom and I made a great team. I attached an evergreen garland along the right side of the handrail while she worked on the left. We added lights and festive red, gold, and green plaid ribbons and bows that made the staircase scream Christmas. Shadow placed five-foot-tall evergreen trees in heavy buckets on each side by the bottom banisters. Twinkletoes immediately climbed one to test its sturdiness. She peered at us through the branches. When she tired of it, we decorated the trees with ornaments to match the ribbons and the lights on the handrails.

That done, we ventured outside. I was standing on the ladder, attaching a lush wide garland of mixed evergreens and eucalyptus, when Marie returned with Stuey.

"I can't keep him out any longer. The poor baby is exhausted."

Indeed, Stuey slept on her shoulder.

"I just wish I could keep looking for Kitty."

"We could watch him for you," Mom offered.

A spark of hope crossed Marie's face, but she shook her head. "You are very kind to offer. But I've already lost one child by leaving her with a neighbor. I really couldn't leave Stuey with strangers. But thank you for offering anyway."

She headed up the stairs to their room.

We wound a ribbon of red and gold through the garland, then added lights and loads of unbreakable ornaments. Twinkletoes sat on the handrail, watching us, but Trixie roamed around, sniffing the ground.

On each side of the front door, we added adorable gnomes with their Santa hats pulled down over their eyes.

While we worked outside, Shadow was setting up ten-foot-tall trees in the dining area and the Dogwood Room. He attached each to the wall so they wouldn't tip over if a dog became too interested in it or a cat climbed it.

Mom and I unrolled a white pine garland and hung it along the railing of the front porch. As we added lights, Mom asked about the sounds coming from the plaza in front of the inn.

"They're setting up the Christkindlmarket. It was Oma's idea. She loved going to them in Germany. The one in Wagtail is a huge hit. People bring their dogs and cats with them to shop."

Mom didn't say anything. She watched as someone tested the lights on one of the little market stalls.

I hung the wreath on the door, and the two of us headed inside to decorate the trees with dog- and cat-themed ornaments.

Mom placed tall candles, fresh greens, and sparkling baubles on the mantel in the Dogwood Room while I wound ribbons on the tree and hung shimmering old-world blown-glass ornaments, including classic pinecones and cats and dogs of all imaginable breeds.

When the two of us began decorating the tree in the dining area, Trixie darted through the door to the private kitchen.

I was up on the ladder when I heard her barking.

She returned, looked up at me, and complained in a whining tone.

"Shh. Don't you bark again. You'll wake up all the guests."

She shot through the doggie door again and howled. I didn't like the sound of that. It was entirely too much like her sad bark and howl when she found a dead person.

Mom chuckled. "She's such a sweet dog. Do you suppose she smells dog cookies in there?"

I looked down at Mom. "Kitty!" I whispered. "Maybe Kitty is hiding there."

I climbed down the ladder in a hurry. The two of us rushed to the kitchen door. I pushed it open, and we tiptoed inside.

Twenty-Two

The lights were off, and I wasn't sure whether to turn them on. The moon provided some light through the windows but not enough to see clearly. I could make out Trixie and Twinkletoes because of their white fur.

Trixie was fixated on the door that led outside.

Mom flicked the light switch on. "Oh, honey. She just needs to go out."

We had been outside long enough for her to do her business. Not to mention that mournful and too-familiar howl that meant bad news.

I turned on the outdoor light and peered through the window in the door.

I didn't see anything unusual, so I dared to open the door. "Kitty?" I called softly.

Trixie and Twinkletoes flashed by my feet, heading outside.

"Kitty?" I called a little louder.

I grabbed a flashlight and felt Mom's presence behind me as I stepped outdoors.

Trixie and Twinkletoes examined something up against the wall behind the bushes.

I rushed back into the kitchen and grabbed a cast-iron frying pan. Not that I would have hit anyone with it, but I didn't know who was there. And if it turned out to be Jean, there was no telling what she might do.

I tiptoed over to see what the animals were fussing about and angled the flashlight behind the bushes.

Jean lay on her back with her eyes open, staring at the night sky.

"Jean?" I watched her for a moment. The last thing I wanted was for her to grab me.

She wasn't blinking, so I didn't have to look for a pulse, but I handed the frying pan to Mom and felt Jean's neck to be certain. I didn't feel anything. In fact, her skin was frighteningly cold. She was dead.

I dialed Officer Dave.

"We found Jean," I blurted. "She was hiding outside the private kitchen of the inn."

"On my way. Is Kitty okay?" he asked.

Chills ran through me. I looked around the grounds, hoping that Kitty was curled up somewhere. I could barely choke out the words. "I don't think she's here."

"I'll be right over."

I slid the phone into my pocket and walked onto the lawn that sloped down to the lake. "Kitty! Kitty!" I called her name softly, not wanting to wake the guests of the inn. "Kitty!"

I flicked my flashlight over the grass.

Mom walked up behind me. "Where is that child? What could Jean have done with her?"

"She ran out of the room when Jean was upset about

Trixie and Twinkletoes damaging the gingerbread house. Did you see her after that?" I asked.

"I wasn't looking for her then," said Mom. "This is just awful!"

Officer Dave strode over to us at that moment. Dressed in a bulky winter coat and boots, he appeared serious and no-nonsense. "Where is she?"

We showed him to the bushes. He yanked off a glove to check her pulse and shine his flashlight over her. "No blood," he mused.

He pulled out his phone and called the Snowball police station. When he hung up, he said, "This is a fine mess. Do you have spotlights back here?"

I supposed there was no avoiding it. Our guests would be awakened by the lights and activity. I nodded reluctantly.

"Go turn them on."

I returned wearing a warm coat and handed one to Mom, along with a knit hat and gloves. She pulled them on immediately. The spotlights lit up the yard. Sadly, there was no sign of Kitty.

"What if she fell in the lake?" Mom whispered.

Dave grumbled. "There are a lot of places to hide in Wagtail. Let's hope she will be found elsewhere."

"Found?" Mom said with a bit of agitation. "It's past three in the morning. If no one has found her by now . . ."

"We can't think that way, Mom."

I could hear people approaching around the far corner of the cat wing. They conferred briefly with Officer Dave and set to work.

Dave directed several of them to the lake. I was glad Marie's room faced the other way. It was brutal for me to watch the lights moving about at the edge of the lake in search of Kitty. It would be unbearable for her mother.

Behind me, I heard a gasp. "Please tell me they're not

looking for my baby! Did someone see her near the water?"

I turned to find Marie with Mom. "It's only a precaution, Marie. No one has seen her."

"Then why are they doing that?"

"Because we found Jean," I explained.

"Where is she? I have to talk to her."

Mom spoke softly. "I'm afraid she has died."

Marie looked around and zeroed in on the photographer. She ran in his direction. A police officer stopped her in her tracks. "I'm sorry, ma'am. This is a crime scene."

Mom and I took Marie inside the kitchen.

She plopped into a chair and just sat there, looking numb.

"I'll make you a cup of chamomile tea," said Mom. "That will make you feel better."

I knew exactly what she was going to say.

"I'll feel better when my little girl is in my arms again!"

I tried to distract her. "Where is Stuey?"

She let out a little scream and ran from the room.

Dave opened the door and strode into the kitchen. "Someone found Jean's suitcases in weeds near the parking lot at the edge of town. I'm going over there to have a look around."

When he left, Mom and I peeled off our coats and hats.

"We might as well finish that tree," said Mom.

There wasn't anything else we could do.

I was on the ladder again when Marie crept down the grand staircase.

"Are there any . . . developments?" she asked.

"Not really," said Mom. "We'll wake you if we hear anything."

"I can't sleep. I'm so tired I can hardly stand straight. I haven't slept in days. Where could she be?"

Mom asked her to hand us some ornaments, and I followed suit.

"Did you see her?" Marie asked.

"Kitty? She was fine this afternoon," said Mom very kindly.

"I mean Jean. How did she die?"

Mom shrugged. "We don't know."

"I don't understand. Do you think Kitty ran from her? Why wouldn't she have been with her? What did she do with my baby? She left Stuey behind all by himself. What kind of person does that? I'm lucky he didn't wander into traffic or burn the apartment down! I'd better go check on him."

She returned carrying a sleeping Stuey.

Mom took Stuey from Marie's arms and led her to the Dogwood Room, where they sat on the sofa and talked softly.

It was getting close to five in the morning. The assistant cook arrived to start setting up breakfast.

Shadow and I made quick work of hanging wreaths along the hallway leading to the reception lobby. He climbed the ladder to hang a giant wreath behind the reception desk while I created a lush décor of pine, berries, and deer on a console. In the office, we placed a small live tree on top of a table and tied it to a hook in the wall as a precaution. The tree filled up the tabletop, effectively catproofing it because there was no room left for a cat to land if one decided to jump up to inspect the tree. We decorated it with Oma's beloved blown-glass ornaments.

An exhausted Shadow finally went home.

I returned to the Dogwood Room, where I tossed Christmas pillows onto the furniture. "I would make some hot chocolate," I said, "but at this point, I can barely move."

"It's a good thing this only happens once a year," Mom muttered. "I'm drained!"

I smiled at her. "Thinking of staying in California now?"

Mom blinked at me. "Oddly enough, quite the contrary. Living in a place is very different from visiting it. But I'm in love with the new Wagtail. This might sound odd to you, but it's filling a void for me. Everyone has been so welcoming. I've seen old friends, and of course, you and Oma. This is where I want to be."

"Holly is your daughter?" Marie asked. "You don't look old enough to have a daughter her age."

Mom beamed even though it wasn't the first time she had heard that. "I started young," she said.

"Shall we hit the sack?" I asked. "People will be getting up soon."

I carried Stuey up the stairs. He had slept through the entire drama. Marie unlocked Pounce, and I was laying him on his bed when my phone rang.

Twenty-Three

“It’s awfully early for a call,” Mom observed. “I hope that means it’s about Kitty.”

I stepped out of the room so I wouldn’t wake Stuey and looked down at my phone. It was Officer Dave calling. I answered it, hoping for good news. “Hi, Dave.”

“I just got a call from Barry Williams. He found Kitty.”

It was all I could do not to scream with joy. “Is . . . is she okay?”

“Sounds like it. Can you bring Marie to the animal clinic?”

“You bet!”

I knocked softly on the door to Pounce.

Marie opened it.

“They found her.”

She gasped and tented her hands over her nose and mouth.

“I’m told she seems to be okay.”

"Thank heaven." She closed her eyes and took a deep breath.

"Meet me downstairs in the reception lobby."

"Would you rather go to bed?" I asked Mom.

"And miss this? Absolutely not!"

Mom and I retrieved our bulky coats and hats to wrap up.

Twinkletoes settled in a chair, having had enough of the night life, but Trixie showed absolutely no sign of exhaustion. Mom, Marie, Stuey, Trixie, and I piled into a golf cart and drove over to the veterinary clinic.

The front lights shone in the night, but most of the windows were still dark, save for the holiday candles that flickered in them. We walked up the stairs to the porch.

I was about to knock when the door opened. A very dim light was on in the foyer. Barry and Dave wore big grins. "You won't believe this."

I was about to introduce Marie when his smile faded. "Marie?"

Her mouth fell open. "Barry?"

"You two know each other?" I asked, filling in the awkward moment between them.

Barry held out his arms and hugged Marie. "And who is this?"

"I'm Stuey."

"It's very nice to meet you, Stuey," said Barry. "Come on in. I didn't wake her."

We quietly followed him to a back room. A black dog lay on a comfy cushion in a large oval bed. Kitty lay with the dog, her little arm draped over the dog's shoulder.

"That's the pregnant dog I brought in!" I whispered.

"Ohh, my baby. Isn't she darling?" Marie kneeled on the floor. "Kitty? Kitty, honey, Mommy is here."

Kitty yawned and stretched. "Mommy!" She climbed out of the bed and into her mother's arms.

Stuey snuggled up with them.

"How do you know each other?" I asked.

Barry shot me a sideways look. "Um, we go way back. Old friends."

"Kitty, honey, how did you get in here?" asked Marie.

"Dr. Barry's mom and dad brought me over here to see the dogs and cats. Their parents went away so they're staying here, and they like to be visited and petted."

Marie looked up at Barry. "Your parents brought her to you?"

"A couple of days ago. They were babysitting her."

"I don't understand," said Marie.

"Jean needed a sitter so she could finish her gingerbread house," I explained. "Kitty won in her age division."

Her eyes widened. "I did? Mommy! I won!"

Marie leaned over and gently stroked the black dog. "Thanks for looking out for my baby." Marie turned to her daughter and asked, "How did you get here, Kitty? Did Jean bring you?"

"I couldn't find her. I left the gingerbread house contest and went outside," said Kitty. "I was just looking around, but it was dark, and I didn't know how to find the inn, so I kept walking. I recognized Dr. Barry's house, so I crawled through the doggy door in the back, and here I am!"

The pregnant dog slapped her tail against the bedding. Trixie approached her cautiously and sniffed.

"Have you given her a name?" I asked.

Before Barry could speak, Kitty said, "It's Poppy."

Barry laughed. "Poppy it is! Who could use a cup of cocoa, or coffee?" asked Barry.

"Cocoa, please!" said Mom. "We've been up all night."

Mom, Dave, and I followed him into the kitchen.

Mom gazed around at the homey room. "Do you live here?"

"I do," said Barry as he stirred cocoa into milk. "The bedrooms are upstairs. That's where I usually sleep, although sometimes I bunk on a sofa down here if I'm worried about a patient. I checked on Poppy last night before I went up to bed. Kitty must have sneaked inside after that. You can imagine my shock at finding her with Poppy this morning when I got up."

"Will she be having her puppies soon?" asked Dave.

"Any day now!"

Trying to be helpful, I handed mugs to Barry.

"Really? All of you want hot chocolate? No coffee?"

"When we leave here, we're going home to crash," said Mom.

Marie wandered into the kitchen. "Can I help?"

Barry smiled at her. "Have a seat. The crisis is over. So where are you living these days?"

"Charlotte. I moved to Florida to take care of my grandmother. After she died, my mom, my brother, and his wife were killed in a boat accident. That was when Stuey came to live with me. He's such a sweet kid. A friend offered me a job in Charlotte, so we moved there."

"Jean told us the restaurant where you work has been sold. Is that true?" I asked.

Marie bobbed her head. "My friend and her husband divorced and sold their restaurant. The new owner plans to put his relatives to work, so all the employees are out of jobs."

I quietly got up to check on Trixie. She had snuggled up to Kitty and Stuey and was enjoying a tummy rub. "Kitty, Stuey, would you like some hot chocolate?"

They followed me into the kitchen.

Kitty clearly had *not* been up all night. The bubbly

child told us all about being lost in the dark. "Did you know there are people who come out at night and build houses? I saw them! A lot of them were wearing red Santa hats, so I suspect they might have been big elves."

We all tried to stifle laughter.

"After a nap," said Marie, "maybe we can visit some of those buildings they made for Santa."

"I hope you can make time for dinner with me tonight," said Barry.

Marie's smile faded. "I think we might have to head back."

"Oh." Barry nodded. "I see."

Dave kicked me under the table. "Didn't Oma say Marie's room is on the house?"

"Oh yes. Absolutely! Wagtail wants to apologize for all the trouble you went through," I babbled. "You are welcome to stay a few more days."

"Can we stay, Mommy? Please? I want to see Poppy's puppies." Kitty had a winsome way about her. I wouldn't have been able to turn her down.

"I don't know if we can stay that long, but maybe one more night."

A short while later, Officer Dave headed home. Everyone except Barry and Poppy squeezed into the golf cart, and I drove us back to the inn.

Staying up all night to create the wonder of Christmas was well worth it when Kitty and Stuey entered the inn. Their eyes wide, they walked through the lobby like it was magical.

I had no idea how Marie would get them to nap. Grateful that wasn't my problem, I trotted up the stairs with Mom and Trixie.

For once my energetic little rascal was as pooped as I was. Twinkletoes jumped onto my bed, and we dozed off.

* * *

I woke at noon, still feeling sleepy, and stumbled into my living room.

Mom handed me a cup of coffee. "I thought you'd be up soon. Our internal clocks are hard to reset. The dining area is packed. Can you get away from the inn? I thought it would be fun to walk through the Christkindlmarket."

"That would be great! The inn has a booth. I think Mr. Huckle is running it this morning. I'll check in with Oma, feed Twinkletoes, and grab a shower, then we can go."

An hour later, we avoided the crowd in the lobby by taking the back stairs to the registration lobby. A few people browsed the small inn store. Twinkletoes jumped up on the registration desk for some attention from Zelda.

"I heard about Kitty!" she gushed. "Who'd have ever expected that? And by the way, the inn looks great."

We thanked her but kept going before someone stopped us. Twinkletoes chose to stick around the inn, but Trixie went with us. Our first stop was the Sugar Maple Inn booth, where we chatted with Mr. Huckle. I admired the items for sale that Oma and I had chosen last summer. Sparkling blown-glass ornaments, adorable dog and cat gifts, and the traditional superlarge German Christmas cookies called *lebkuchen*. We had placed a special order for them through Pawsome Cookies. Bonnie had seen to it that they were wrapped in traditional red cellophane with a red ribbon tying the top.

We ambled on, stopping to buy a few trinkets. We paused at one of the food concessions, where we bought giant pretzels and hot cider for breakfast. I bought a dog-friendly hamburger for Trixie.

Although it was crowded, the spirit of the holiday filled the air. Christmas music tinkled through loudspeakers, and it seemed like everyone was smiling.

Except for Officer Dave, who caught up to us, looking grim. "I need to speak with you. Liesel said I'd find you out here."

"You're like the Grinch, coming to spoil our fun."

"Oh, I'm definitely going to spoil it for you."

"It can't be that bad," said Mom. "We found Kitty and she's all right."

Dave's mouth twitched. "Jean died of gelsemium poisoning."

Mom gasped. "Are you saying someone murdered her?"

Dave didn't sugarcoat it. "Yes."

"Gelsemium?" asked Mom. "What's that? I've never heard of it."

"I'm sure you're familiar with trumpet vines," said Dave.

"With the pretty red and yellow trumpet-shaped flowers. Of course. They grow everywhere. But it's not the season for them," I protested.

"Apparently the roots and vines are highly poisonous as well. They don't need to be in bloom."

"Why would someone kill Jean? That makes no sense at all," I said. "Are you thinking Marie found her, they argued over Kitty, and she . . . what? Injected her with gelsemium?"

"More likely cooked it or ground it, and then hid it in chocolates. We're not sure yet."

"Nooo!" Mom shivered. "What an awful thing to do."

"It gets worse. She had this in her pocket." He pulled out his phone and showed us a photograph of a box in holiday colors from a popular national chocolates company. It could have been bought anywhere. On the top, someone had written *TO HOLLY* in block letters.

A chill ran through me.

Mom shrieked, attracting attention. "They were meant for Holly?"

"Looks like it. We don't know how she got them, but somebody meant to kill *you*, Holly."

Twenty-Four

I had come to the same conclusion when I saw my name on the box. Another ripple of fear ran through me. "There *are* other people named Holly," I pointed out.

His eyes met mine. "Do you really think it means any of the thousands of other Hollys?"

"No," I said sheepishly. I examined the photo again. "It looks like a child's handwriting."

"I'd agree with that," said Dave. "But I seriously doubt that a child has been gathering trumpet vines to poison people."

"Was it a painful death?" asked Mom.

"I don't know about pain. Doc says the dose is high and it probably inhibited her respiration."

"She was a sad, confused woman to steal a child, but I still feel awful that she died." Mom's lips pulled tight. "I suppose I should be grateful that she ate the candy so Holly didn't."

"How did she get hold of your chocolates?" asked Dave.

"I have no idea. This is the first time I have seen them."

Dave nodded. "I'll check with Mr. Huckle and Zelda. Someone may have left them at the front desk or at your door."

"At my door? Trixie was sniffing the door earlier. I thought maybe someone's pet had marked it."

"She just helped herself? What kind of person takes a gift that is clearly for someone else?" Mom huffed.

I didn't think we should be faulting Jean for that. Not this time. If she hadn't taken them, I would be the dead one in the morgue. I made a mental note not to accept food or drink from strangers.

"Do you think this is related to the man in the tree?" asked Mom. "Could this mean you have stumbled onto something?"

"If I have, then I don't know what."

"It's cold out here and I'm hungry. How about we grab a table at Hair of the Dog and talk where it's warm?" asked Dave.

It wasn't exactly what we had planned, but now that someone was trying to kill me, Mom and I readily walked over to the pub with Dave. Exactly as he described, we settled at a table near the fire. Mom and I ordered beef stew, and Dave went for a burger with fries. Trixie whined at me. "And a doggie beef stew for Trixie, please."

As soon as the waitress left, Dave pulled out a pen and notepad and settled back against his chair. "Who have you been talking to about the man in the tree?"

"Stu Williams, who was a close friend of Orly's and helped him with the concrete. He claims he thought they were just saving the tree."

Officer Dave winced. "Yeah, I talked to Stu and got

the same story. He's a good guy. I really can't see him killing anyone."

In spite of that, I noticed that he wrote down Stu's name.

Our food arrived, and Mom pawed through her purse until she found a pen. She nabbed the paper napkin at the fourth place on the table and wrote down Stu's name.

I started eating. The rich, warm stew was exactly what I longed for on this frigid day.

"Who else?" Dave bit into his juicy burger.

"Althea Alcorn. Did you know that her oldest son, Jay, disappeared? She claims that he was dating Josie Biffle at the time and that both she and Orly disapproved."

Dave stopped chewing. He looked like a chipmunk with one side of his mouth full. After a moment, he swallowed and made a note. "I knew she had another son. Wow. That's a definite possibility."

"But why would Althea poison you?" asked Mom.

"I don't know. There's also Penn Connor, who told me a fascinating story about Boomer Jenkins. We thought Penn was missing, but he turned up right here in Wagtail. To sum it up, Boomer Jenkins was engaged to Delia *and* a girl named Kathleen at the same time. Because that wasn't enough, he promised Bonnie Greene that he would break off his engagement so he could be with her, *and* Penny Terrell was completely enamored with Boomer."

Dave wrote rapidly, then dipped a French fry in ketchup.

Mom made her own notes. "Four women. That's a heap of jealousy among them and their beaus."

"And sadly, there may have been more women involved with him," I pointed out. "Starting with the least likely, in my opinion at least, we have Tommy Terrell, Penny's husband. He said something to me about Penny having a crush on Boomer. He's hoping the man in the tree is Boomer. All these years later, he's still jealous."

"Yeah." Dave sipped his water. "Tommy is devoted to Penny. But he can be a little obsessive about her. And I can see him making poison chocolates. He's one of those jolly types. I always wonder what's going on beneath the too-happy cover."

"That leads us to Bonnie, who says she last saw Boomer in the afternoon. He was supposed to break off his engagement to Delia and come back to Bonnie's place for dinner. But he never showed."

"Bonnie definitely knows how to bake. I guess that extends to poisoning chocolate. Do you think she might have murdered Boomer?" Dave picked up another French fry.

"I like Bonnie a lot. I want to think she couldn't have. But it's possible that Boomer returned to Bonnie's place, and she poisoned him for not breaking off his relationship with Delia."

"What a nightmare! Oh, that would have been awful! I can see that happening. But then how would she have gotten Boomer into the tree? Where did Orly come in?" Mom wrote busily.

"That's a good point, Nell," said Dave.

"Delia claims he came to dinner at her house, but Boomer did *not* break off their engagement. She still has her ring. He left after dinner. She must have been one of the last people to see him in Wagtail."

"It's possible that he did break off the engagement, or he tried to, and Delia knocked him off," mused Dave. "And Delia is a good cook. She could have figured out how to poison the chocolates."

Mom's eyes widened. "Now I *know* she did not try to poison my daughter. Delia would never do that!"

Dave looked me in the eyes. "Go on."

"I don't want to think Delia murdered Boomer, either. But it would explain how Orly became involved, since he is married to Delia's sister. One phone call would have brought Orly running."

Mom groaned. "No. That simply can't be."

"We can assume Orly would have helped Tommy Terrell, too. I don't know about Bonnie, though," said Dave. "That's quite a group of suspects."

"I'm not finished. Kathleen was supposed to marry Boomer the next day. She allegedly changed her mind that Friday, because she found evidence that he was cheating on her. That was the same day he had dinner at Delia's house. That was also the night Bonnie was waiting for him. Kathleen asked her friend Penn Connor to take her home. Penn was in love with her, drove her home, and married her six months later."

Mom gasped. "That makes more sense. Kathleen must have found out about Boomer's engagement to Delia. She confronted him, and either she or Penn murdered him. Then they had to flee Wagtail."

"That's a definite possibility, Mom. After they married, they moved to Switzerland. They were intent on getting away."

"But why come back to Wagtail now?" asked Dave. "And how was Orly involved?"

"My money is on them," Mom declared. "Maybe they paid Orly to hide Boomer's body in the tree. I just know one thing. There's no way Delia was involved in this."

Dave smiled at Mom kindly. "You're a loyal friend, Nell. But Delia is up to her ears in this mess."

As I paid the check for our late lunch, Dave said, "It's going to be hard right now because of all the Christmas goodies. I know firsthand how the women in Wagtail love to bake cookies at the holidays. I receive them by the platterful. But for the time being, I don't want either of you eating anything that could have been tampered with. Especially not chocolates, cookies, or holiday treats."

"That's not fair. What about things from the kitchen at the inn?"

Dave stood up. "Your choice, Holly. That's where I'd go to poison something."

On that happy note, we left the pub, and Officer Dave got back to work. Mom and I strolled back to the inn in a glum mood.

"He's right, you know," said Mom softly.

"All the more reason to catch the perpetrator. I don't want to miss out on all the wonderful holiday sweets."

Mom stopped walking and turned to face me. "Holly, someone tried to kill you. I think you can give up most sweets until he's caught."

Mom and I hit the sack early that night, still exhausted from our night of decorating and murder.

I woke early on Saturday. Alas, no elves had brought me hot tea or croissants. Mr. Huckle must have the day off, I thought. He certainly deserved it. We would all be doing double duty over the holidays.

No matter. I showered and dressed in a green V-neck sweater and navy trousers. Zelda had pulled Christkindlmarket stall duty, so I was taking over the registration desk for her. I added a navy-and-green scarf and gold hoop earrings that had been a gift from Oma.

Mom still slept. Not that I could blame her. I fed Twinkletoes a shrimp dish that must have been tasty because she ate ravenously. Trixie was ready to go out, so I threw on a puffy vest and we walked down the grand staircase.

Wonderful aromas of coffee, cinnamon, and bacon danced in the air. Thoughts of Jean and poison tamped my appetite a bit. I opened the front door and Trixie scampered out. She raced ahead to the area reserved as a doggy toilet, while I strolled behind her.

It was another frigidly cold day, but the air felt fresh and clean. Nevertheless, I was pleased that Trixie didn't dally because I was ready to hurry back into the warm inn.

Inside, I poured myself a large mug of steaming coffee from a pot that was serving a lot of people. Then I left Trixie in the dining room for a couple of minutes while I went into the commercial kitchen. I nabbed a bowl for Trixie and a plate for myself.

I was reaching for scrambled eggs when Cook frowned at me. He crooked his finger at me. Taking three fresh eggs, he cracked them on the griddle. "I heard about the poisoned chocolates. You stick with what I cook for you. You hear?"

"Thanks. You don't have to do anything special for me."

"We're not going to let anything happen to you."

He added some oatmeal to Trixie's bowl along with a pinch of crumbled bacon, slid one of the eggs over it, and sliced it deftly into bite-sized pieces. He pulled out a serving tray and placed her bowl on it. He took another small bowl and filled it with Southern-style fried apples, which he knew were one of my favorites, and added it to the tray. He slid the other two eggs onto my plate and scooped up hash browns to go with them. To that he added a pretty heap of warm spinach salad that he sprinkled with a couple of pinches of crumbled bacon.

He shoved the tray toward me on the counter. Holding up his forefinger like he was lecturing a child, he said, "Do not take your eyes off this food. Don't leave it alone for one minute. Do you understand?"

I smiled at him. "Thank you. I wasn't sure what I would eat today."

I gathered silverware and napkins and was at the door

about to leave when he shouted, "Come back at lunch-time. I'll fix you up. Don't eat anything anybody else gives you. You hear me, Holly?"

"Yes, sir!" It was good advice and very comforting to know I could eat without fear of being poisoned.

Trixie pranced at my feet all the way to the reception lobby. Her nose was trained on the tray I carried. She didn't even look where she was going.

I slid behind the reception desk, deposited the tray on top, and lowered Trixie's breakfast to the floor. After unlocking the sliding glass doors, I sat on the high barstool-type chair and guzzled coffee before eating breakfast.

The next hours passed quickly. Oma and Holmes descended upon me, acting like I might keel over any minute. I was actually glad when guests needed my help. At least they were sane and not lecturing me on avoiding poison.

Even when Oma retreated to the office and Holmes departed for work, the problem hung over me. What had I discovered that posed a threat to someone?

I eliminated Bonnie, because I hadn't learned anything that she hadn't told me herself. There was the possibility, I supposed, that Bonnie's story about waiting for Boomer to come to her place was a total fabrication. She could easily have followed him to Delia's and waited for him to leave. If she saw them kissing, she might have launched an attack on him. But that seemed so unlikely. And the issue of Orly's involvement didn't fit, though she could have phoned him for help. No, I didn't think Bonnie had tried to poison me.

Mom thought Delia wouldn't harm me because they were old friends. I wasn't as certain about that. Delia might hold a higher allegiance to protecting herself. But that was okay, I thought. It wouldn't be difficult to avoid food Delia offered me.

Penny and Tommy Terrell could be the culprits, together or separately. They would go to great lengths to protect each other.

And finally, there was Althea or Josie. Althea had come to me about her son Jay. I didn't see what she would gain by killing me. But if it was Jay in the tree, then Josie might be afraid I would uncover her involvement. Or what about her brother, Wyatt? Would he poison me to protect his sister? Had he been there that night? Did he know what happened?

Maybe I should speak with him.

During a slow period, I Googled Jay Alcorn. There were more Jay Alcorns than I expected. Complicating matters, Jay appeared to be taken on frequently as a nickname. Or they went by Jay because they had a *J* as a middle initial. Oy!

I scrolled through them, not finding anyone who fit the bill. Most of them were the wrong age. After reviewing endless pages of Alcorns, I decided there had to be a better way.

It wasn't quite ten in the morning when Zelda called. We had run out of several items at our stall. I found extra boxes in the downstairs storage and cleaning supply room, where I had stashed them when they came in.

Oma took over the desk. "I have paperwork to do, and I can see from the office if anyone needs help. There's no point in you sitting there all day.

Mom helped me lug the boxes out to our stall, where Twinkletoes sat primly on the counter. We spent a few minutes helping unload them and handing them to Zelda to hang decoratively on the walls.

"I'm so glad you had these," she said. "The stall was looking embarrassingly empty."

I crushed the boxes. Trixie accompanied me when I stashed them in the recycling bin. When I returned, Zelda was already swamped with buyers. Twinkletoes had retreated to the back of the stall, where she had curled up in a cat bed that was for sale. I guessed I knew who would be buying that bed!

"Oh look! There's Delia," said Mom. "I didn't know she would have a booth."

We strolled over to say hi. A sign at the top of the booth said *WAG*, identifying it as belonging to Wagtail Animal Guardians, the animal rescue group in Wagtail. I *had* to buy something to support them! I eyed the items they had for sale. Calming jackets for dogs and cats, special licking pads to comfort dogs, a rainbow of assorted collars and leashes, and a row of big jars filled with dog and cat cookies. An open box on the table behind the counter sported the cheerful colors and paw print logo of Pawsome Cookies.

We greeted Delia, who tried to muster enthusiasm at seeing us. "Good morning. Are you two shopping?"

"We had to bring some refills out. Are you okay, Delia?" asked Mom.

I picked up Trixie so she could see the dog treats inside.

"I'm fine. Just tired. Thank you so much for the cookies," said Delia.

She looked pale to me. Granted, it was puffer-coat cold outside, but her complexion had a sickly pallor.

"They're delicious," she said. "Carter met me at the house this morning to help me bring over more goods. The cookies were just what we needed with hot coffee for breakfast."

She felt behind her for a tall chair.

"Cookies?" asked Mom. "What cookies?"

"The ones that you had sent to my house."

Mom's expression reflected confusion. "Now that you mention it, I wish I had sent cookies. We thoroughly enjoyed dinner at your house the other night. But, Delia, I didn't send any cookies."

Now Delia seemed confused. She slid off the chair and reached for the Pawsome Cookies box. "It's right here."

She plucked a note off the box and, still holding it in her hand, crumpled to the floor.

"Delia!" Mom and I scurried around the little building.

Mom opened the door and kneeled beside Delia. "Delia! Can you hear me?"

Delia looked at Mom with heavily lidded eyes. "So tired. So tired . . ."

I was busy calling 911. Stu Williams and Tommy Terrell rushed to the stall.

Stu asked, "What happened? Did she faint?"

The next few minutes flew by in a confusing whirl. I continued to hold Trixie in my arms so she wouldn't be underfoot as people crowded around the stall. Dr. Engelknecht managed to make his way through the crowd, and there were shouts as the golf cart ambulance slowly rolled up.

Officer Dave did his best to disperse the crowd, but people didn't seem able to walk away. Stu and Tommy lifted Delia onto a stretcher and placed her on the makeshift ambulance. Officer Dave cleared the way for it to exit the area.

And then, suddenly, Mom, Trixie, and I stood at the stall all by ourselves.

"What happened?" I placed a squirming Trixie on the ground. "Did Delia say anything?"

"Just that she was very, very sleepy and weak. Dr. Engelknecht said something about respiratory issues. I'm not sure what that means, but it doesn't sound good."

"I wonder if anyone notified Carter," I mused.

"Hi! What on earth happened to Delia?" A woman I

recognized from WAG hurried up to the stall and stepped inside. "I was called to substitute for her. Is she okay?"

Mom explained what had happened.

I phoned Carter, just in case he hadn't heard about his mom, but my call rolled over to his voice mail.

Mom and I continued browsing through the holiday stalls. They were adorable and festive, but a cloud hung over us.

I had just bought Trixie a Santa hat cookie made for dogs when Mom said in a loud voice, "The cookies!"

"The ones you didn't send Delia?"

"We have to go back and get them. What if they've been poisoned?"

Trixie's Guide to Murder

One of the difficulties is that the murderer is likely to go after your mom or dad, especially if they get too close to solving the murder or even begin to consider that person a suspect.

This is another time when your sniffer is really important. You know how you can smell the scent of a fox or a bear on the breeze? You need to pay attention to the smell of the peoples nearby, too, and get your mom or dad to safety if there's someone you don't trust.

Sniff your house carefully to make sure no one has been there. The porch is usually a great place to begin. Sometimes peoples come through windows, so do a patrol around the outside of the house, too.

We can't always perceive evil. However, most wicked murderers will be extremely rude to dogs. They aren't the people who simply ignore you. They actually watch you, as if they know you're onto them. Sometimes they'll grab you by the scruff of your neck and you'll know that's not a kind hand. Or they'll pretend to like you, but you can tell from the way they stroke you that this is a person with a black heart.

Twenty-Five

I had forgotten all about the cookies. The three of us hurried back to the WAG stall. Relief washed over me when I saw Delia's replacement handing a man his purchase.

Mom got right to the point. "Delia left a box of cookies . . ."

The woman turned around. "The ones from Pawsome Cookies? They're so good. There's a flavor in them that I can't quite identify. I'll have to ask Bonnie about her secret ingredient."

"You ate some?" I asked.

"I didn't think Delia would mind. She's always the first to offer goodies."

"How do you feel?" asked Mom.

"Me? I feel fine. I'm getting a headache and I'm tired, but I'll be all right."

"Go straight to Dr. Engelknecht's office," I said. "In fact, we'll take you."

"Nonsense. I'm fine."

"Look, here's the situation," said Mom. "Delia thought I sent her those cookies. But I didn't. She ate some for breakfast. I don't know who sent them to her or what is in them, but you have to go straight to the doctor."

The woman gasped. "But what about the stall?"

"Let's close it until we know more. Okay?" I stepped inside and helped her shut the front. I picked up a paper bag and used it to shove the cookie box into a second paper bag.

When I stepped out, Mom, Trixie, and the woman from WAG were already walking away. I closed the door and snapped on the padlock before dashing to catch up to them.

Officer Dave was walking out of Dr. Engelknecht's office just as we arrived. Mom escorted the WAG lady inside, but I paused on the front porch to talk to Dave.

"How's Delia?"

"Showing all the signs of gelsemium poisoning. Engelknecht is sending her over to the hospital in Snowball."

I opened the bag I carried so he could peer inside and explained about the cookies.

With a huge sigh, Dave took the bag. "You're one hundred percent certain that your mom didn't send these cookies? Or Oma? Maybe she forgot about having done it? It's been crazy around here."

I blinked at him. "You want to take that chance?"

"I'll have these delivered to Snowball for testing."

Mom emerged and closed the front door behind her. "Doc says they haven't been able to locate Carter. It's bad enough that he doesn't know his mom is in the hospital, but she told us he ate some of the cookies, too."

Dave groaned. "If I know Carter, he ate more than some. I'll hand these over to Doc, then go to Carter's house for a wellness check. I'll swing by Pawsome Cookies for a chat with Bonnie, too." Dave waved and stepped back inside the medical office.

"I'd like to have a talk with Bonnie myself," said Mom. "The tag on the box clearly says *Happy Holidays, from Nell!*"

I had no idea my mom was such a sleuth. We headed straight to Pawsome Cookies. Once again, the line of customers extended out the door. In the front window, darling holiday boxes were on display featuring winter wonderlands with deer, Santa Paws themes for dog and cat cookies, and funny gnomes.

I waved at Bonnie, who motioned us to come around to the back door.

Mom and I made our way there.

Bonnie propped the door open, letting cold air in. "Nell DuPuy! I heard you were back in town."

Mom squinted at her. "Bonnie Greene!" She held out her arms to hug her.

Bonnie grinned, and I got the feeling they really liked each other. "Your mother used to help me with my math homework."

Mom nodded. "Seems like a lifetime ago."

"It was," said Bonnie.

"Bonnie, have I ordered any cookies from you in the last few days?" asked Mom.

Bonnie flashed a look at me like she was worried about my mom's sanity. "No, Nell. You haven't. Did you want some?"

"How about Oma or me?" I asked.

Furrows formed on Bonnie's forehead. "Did I mess up a delivery or something?"

Mom told her about the cookie box.

Bonnie paled. "And they're making people sick? Oh

my gosh. I have sold tons of cookies this week. I mean tens of thousands of cookies. I don't know the names of all the customers."

"They were in your logo box," I said.

Bonnie's face contorted with confusion. "That doesn't make any sense. For the last few weeks, we've been using harvest and Happy Thanksgiving boxes. And before that we had a cute Halloween-themed box. Those cookies would have been bought before Halloween, and if there was something wrong with them, I think I would have heard about it before now."

She looked from me to Mom. "Nell, they may have been in one of my empty logo boxes that someone didn't throw away. But I can assure you that the cookies weren't bought here. And I don't recall an order from either of you or Oma."

The news was both heartening and confusing. "You're saying someone probably bought cookies from you and ate them but saved the box. Then that person baked cookies, put them in the box, and added Mom's name so Delia would think they were a gift from Mom?"

Bonnie's eyes widened. "I can't imagine any other logical scenario. Someone wanted to harm Delia and blame it on you, Nell."

"Why me?" asked Mom. "I've only been here a few days." She gazed at me. "Have I ruffled someone's feathers without realizing it?"

"I don't think so!" I hadn't been with her every minute, but I wasn't aware of any unpleasantry involving Mom.

While we were talking, my phone rang. Officer Dave didn't bother introducing himself. He blurted, "It's definitely gelsemium, which is deadly. The WAG lady didn't eat much, and Doc evacuated her stomach, so she should be okay. They say if Delia makes it through the night, she'll probably be all right. But no one can find Carter.

He's not at home. We have to locate him and bring him to the hospital."

"We're not far from his office. I'll stop in and see if anyone knows where he might be." I ended the call. "They still can't find Carter."

Bonnie covered her mouth in horror. "Poor Carter!"

"Where's the office?" asked Mom.

"Just across the green." We thanked Bonnie and hurried away.

Mom picked up the pace.

It wasn't long before we could see the sign that said *Riddle Realty*.

I pushed the door open and held it for my mom.

The woman at the front desk greeted us.

"Hi, Irma. We're looking for Carter. Do you have any idea where he might be?"

"Not at all. I haven't seen him today."

"Would you mind if I took a look at his desk? Maybe he noted something on his calendar?"

"No, I don't think that's a good idea. I'll let him know you came in. Shall I tell him what it's about? Did you decide on a house, Nell?"

"He might be very sick and has to get to the hospital immediately," said Mom.

"Which one is his desk?" I barged past her, looking at the photos and treasures on desks, hoping to see one that could belong to Carter.

"Well . . ." Irma dragged her feet, clearly reluctant to give us any information.

"Mom, call Officer Dave and tell him Irma won't help us."

Irma held up her hand. "Let's not be hasty. If it's that important to you, his desk is the one with the big chocolate kiss on it."

Just as I had hoped, he used a desk calendar, probably

as backup for appointments on his phone. I could hear Mom explaining what happened to Delia. I flipped the calendar to Saturday and read *Mann house, Pine Street.* "Do you have the house number for the Mann house on Pine Street?"

"Oh my." She opened a cabinet that contained keys. "One eleven." She turned toward us, her face grim. "The key is gone."

We thanked her and left.

"It's very close," I assured Mom.

Trixie trotted ahead of us. Even from a distance, we could see the Riddle Realty *For Sale* sign.

"Let's just hope we can get inside, and that he's actually there," I said.

The house had clearly been renovated in recent years. A crisp white porch ran across the front. I knocked on the door and tried the doorknob. It opened.

"Hello?" I called.

Trixie dodged around my legs and ran inside. I heard Mom gasp when she entered.

I looked at her. "Are you all right?"

"I *love* this house!"

"Focus, Mom. We're looking for Carter."

A moan came from the living room. Carter lay on the floor on his back. Trixie was licking his face.

"Carter!" I walked over to him, punching 911 on my phone. I rattled off our location, hung up, and called Officer Dave to let him know we had located Carter.

Mom crouched beside him. "How do you feel, Carter?"

"I've been better."

Mom stroked his hand. "Honey, your mom has the same thing. You'll be okay. Holly is calling the ambulance."

"Same thing? Wha . . . what is it?"

"The cookies you ate had poison in them."

"Poison?" Carter's eyes opened wide.

"Can I bring you a cup of water? How about a cold compress?" She didn't wait for an answer.

"Could I help you up?" I asked.

Carter held his hand out to me.

I thought he meant to sit up or stand, but when I took his hand, he pulled me toward him and gasped. "It's Boomer."

Twenty-Six

“Boomer? What do you mean?”

“He’s back.”

I regarded him with doubt. Was he delirious?

Mom returned and laid a wet cloth across his broad forehead.

“I knew this would happen someday,” Carter murmured.

“You should rest,” I said.

“No! I have to tell you. What if I die? I have to be sure someone knows.”

My phone rang. Officer Dave wanted to know how Carter was doing.

“There’s a delay with the ambulance. Doc says to keep him talking and alert.”

“Okay. We can do that. Keep us posted.” I disconnected the call.

“Are you sure you don’t want to sit up?” I asked.

“Listen to me,” he insisted. “Someone has to know. If I die, it all dies with me. That’s what Boomer wants.”

"Are you saying that Boomer tried to poison your mother and you?" I picked up Trixie and held her in my lap.

"It had to be him. I have lived in terror of his return. But I knew it would happen one day."

"We're listening," Mom said soothingly. "You're safe with us, sugar. You just relax."

"After my dad died, I felt responsible for my mom and my sister. It's hard to explain. I knew I was just a kid, but we were very tight. None of us could imagine losing another family member. It was unthinkable. In *my* mind, my dad was a superhero. Clearly, he wasn't, but to me, he ruled the world. My world, anyway. When he died, I should have been out having a great time with other kids, but it was a tough time for me, and I worried about everything. My dad had the foresight to get a good insurance policy. Money was the one thing we didn't have to be concerned about. Even at that age I understood how vital that was, and I appreciated my father all the more for having provided for us.

"And then Boomer Jenkins showed up in town. Everybody thought he was wonderful. Everybody except for me. It was like I could see things about him that nobody else did. And he knew it. He feared the one chunky little boy who could see straight through his phony demeanor.

"When he started showing up at our house, chasing my mother, I became suspicious. Or maybe I was jealous that he had her attention. I didn't want him there. I wanted my dad back. When I think about it now, I realize how young she was and how lonely she must have been after my dad died. Having a guy like Boomer take an interest in her was flattering. It filled a void in her life. She just didn't realize how he was deceiving her."

He didn't sound delirious as he spoke. I didn't want to stop him, since Dave told me to keep him talking.

"It was almost instinctive. I mean, at eleven, I couldn't really understand just how evil he might be. I'd never been outside of Wagtail, so for the most part, I had only been around people who were kind to me. The funny thing about being a tubby local kid was that nobody noticed me. I hear women at the real estate office talking about being invisible after they turn forty. It was like that for me when I was a kid. I could hang around and listen to people without them noticing me. As long as I kept my mouth shut, they talked freely and usually gave me a soda or something to snack on. I was part of the scenery in Wagtail. I picked up on the fact that Boomer rarely paid for anything. A couple of the restaurant owners thought it was interesting that women always paid for his meals. According to them, he had a habit of conveniently forgetting his wallet. So when he started seeing my mom, and she had just gotten that big insurance payout from my dad's death, I was mighty suspicious."

"Oh, you poor child," Mom cooed. "I'm sure you weren't invisible. I bet you were adorable."

"I . . . I followed Boomer and spied on him. It didn't take me long to understand that he went after every pretty girl in town. My dad had a great camera when he died. I carried it with me all the time. And I used it to take pictures of Boomer with other women."

Uh-oh. This did not sound good.

"He came to our house for dinner regularly. He'd flirt with Mom and make my sister laugh. When they weren't around, he bullied me. He would call me names like Porker and Bacon Butt, and he had this ugly habit of holding up his hand like it was a gun. He'd point it at me and make a weird sound with his mouth like he was shooting me. It scared me to death. I was afraid he would pull out a real gun and shoot me one day. Even now, I can't imagine doing that to a kid. Maybe he did plan to shoot me or eliminate me."

"What a horrid man!" Mom exclaimed. "How could anyone treat a child like that? I'm glad I didn't know him. I can't imagine what Delia was thinking."

"When I look back on it, I'm surprised that Mom didn't notice how reticent I was in Boomer's presence. She just told me not to be such a grouch and gave me an occasional lecture on how it didn't mean I loved my dad less if I liked Boomer. I hated him. Hated with a passion. I knew he was going to drag somebody down with him, and I couldn't let it be us. Mostly, I clammed up when he was around. My mom made excuses for me, but I could see in Boomer's eyes that he knew I was onto him.

"One night, they sat my sister and me down on the fireplace hearth to tell us they were getting married. The diamond on my mom's hand flashed in the light of the fire like a neon alarm. My grandmother used to tell me stories about spirits, and I thought it must be my dad sending me a warning. The wedding date came at me like a locomotive, and I didn't know how to stop it. I had all those pictures. The thing was, I didn't know how to show them to my mom."

Mom looked at me. I didn't know what to think.

"One night, Boomer noticed my dad's camera. He picked it up and admired it. I swear I held my breath until I thought I might explode. It had a little memory card in it, and if he accidentally pressed the right button, he would see all those photographs I took of him smooching with other women. And then he stopped breathing. He stared at it and licked his lips. His eyes met mine, cold and dark and evil, and I knew he had seen the pictures."

"Did you finally tell your mother?" asked Mom.

"I was scared out of my mind. All I had were those

pictures. Mom would never believe me if I told her about the other women without the pictures as proof. So that night, I slipped out the back door and waited for him to leave. Just as I feared, that thief had my camera in his hand. I darted out at him, snatched it, and ran. Now mind you, I have never been much of a runner. But fear is a mighty strong motivator, and I ran until my lungs hurt. I could hear him crashing through the woods behind me. Night was on my side because even though there was a moon, it was pitch black under the evergreens. I was tiring pretty bad by the time I got to the bluff near the lake. You know the one? There's a steep path down to the shore. You can walk down, but you can't run. One slip and you'd crash to the bottom. I was trapped. I could hear him thrashing through the woods, coming closer and closer. I fell. Right there at the edge. All he had to do was push me or give me a kick and I'd have gone over. I could feel the edge of the cliff. I knew I was a goner. At the last minute, just before he was upon me, I grabbed hold of the root of a tree. And then I heard him fire a gun at me."

Mom gasped. "No!"

Carter stopped talking, which scared me more than his story. I could see his chest rising and falling. He was still breathing. "Carter? Are you okay?"

He winced. "Yeah. I guess he saw me in the light of the moon. He came pounding along toward me. He laughed real mean. I still hear him in my head. Then he squatted next to me and said, 'Good try, but you are not going to ruin things for me with your mom.' I tried to talk him out of it. I promised I wouldn't say anything. I had the camera strap over my head and shoulder. And all the while, he was grabbing for it. I kept thinking I would fall over the bluff any second. It was torture! And I don't mean that in a flippant way. He truly was torturing me. And then, I guess my weight broke some dirt along the top edge, and it fell. I thought for sure I would tumble to my death. But I still had hold of those tree roots. He figured that out and started beating my hands with a stick and yelling at me to give him the camera. If he had managed to get hold of it, I knew I would be dead. Once he had it, he would have pushed me. I guess he took a misstep or leaned out too far. He let out a scream that echoed across the lake as he tumbled by me headfirst."

Mom's eyes met mine.

"They say you get a burst of adrenaline in a crisis. You know, women lift cars off their babies, that sort of thing. I know it happens because I managed to pull myself up. I hugged that tree for a long time. Then I got worried that he might be alive. I scrambled to the edge and looked over. In the light of the moon, I could see him lying at the bottom. He wasn't moving and I thought he was dead. I remember being terrified that he would wake up and somehow manage to grab my legs and pull me down with him. Like in movies, ya know? I ran home and went to bed with the camera strap around my neck so no one could take it without waking me. Stupid, I know. But it wasn't necessary. I was up all night anyway, with my blanket over my head. Around three in the morning, I heard his motorcycle start, and I knew he was alive. I got up and shoved my dresser behind my door so he couldn't get in my room to kill me. I sat there quivering until I heard the engine fade away into the night. I never saw him again. To be honest, when he never showed up again, I was kind of proud of myself. He knew the jig was up when he saw my photographs, and there was no getting around them."

"Did you ever tell your mother?" asked Mom.

Carter coughed and struggled to get air. "No. She doesn't know to this day. But I kept the photographs in case he ever returned and my mom fell for him again."

His voice faltered as he said, "And now he has come back to Wagtail."

Mom took his hands into hers. "We'll take care of you and Delia. Besides, you're not that scared little kid anymore. You're a strong, handsome young man now, able to stand up to anyone."

He looked at her as if he thought she were an angel. In spite of the poison in his system, he sounded lucid and convincing. Unfortunately, I didn't think there was anyone who could confirm it. By his account, Delia didn't know what had transpired that night.

We were all startled by a loud knock on the door. Trixie ran to it, barking like she owned the place. I opened the door cautiously, relieved to see Stu and Tommy. Just beyond them on the street, the modified golf cart ambulance waited.

I picked up Trixie and held her while they took care of Carter.

"Mom," I murmured, "we need the key to the house so we can lock up."

"Of course! Good thing you thought of it." She walked out to the ambulance and said something to Carter. He handed it to her, and she returned to the house.

I closed the door as they drove away.

"Poor Carter! What a sad little boy he must have been." Mom eyed the living room and plumped up pillows to straighten it a bit.

I took the water and wet cloth into the kitchen. I had thought the kitchen in the hobbit house had been unique, but this one had clearly been designed by a cook. Mullioned glass cabinets lined the walls. The far wall was solid glass and overlooked woods. Mostly white with touches of pine that brought the outdoors in, the kitchen was big enough for family gatherings around the fireplace, and intimate enough for a cup of coffee all by oneself. At that moment, I knew that my mom would buy the house.

"Holly? Holly?" Mom called.

I emerged from the kitchen.

"It's perfect! Most of it is on the first floor, and there's a bedroom suite with a private sitting room that would be perfect for your grandparents." Her face fell. "But Delia and Carter are in the hospital. I don't even know the price."

"We have to return the key. Maybe someone at the office can help you."

Mom took another look around the house while I phoned Dave. "Carter is on his way. Any word on Delia?"

"Resting comfortably. I hate it when they tell me that. I guess it's good news, it's just not very informative."

"I know you're swamped, but Carter told us a pretty convincing story about what happened the last time he saw Boomer. The first thing he said was that Boomer must have poisoned the cookies."

Dave was silent for a moment. "Did he say he'd seen Boomer recently?"

"No." Still, I couldn't help thinking something strange was going on. "I suppose you don't think it's a coincidence that Carter's golf cart went rogue?"

"I'm keeping that in the back of my mind. But the repair guys tell me it's something that can happen without anyone tampering with the golf cart."

"Well, all I can say is someone went to the trouble of putting poison in those cookies and the chocolates, and they already managed to kill one person."

Trixie's Guide to Murder

One of the things to keep in mind is that we have a different view of the world than peoples because they walk on their hind legs. Plus, they're prone to dropping stuff. Who among you hasn't done a good-dog sit and waited for a piece of pizza or half a sandwich to land on the floor? (I won't mention taking food from babies. You know that's wrong. Right?) Murderers are likely to drop things or knock them over because they're usually pretty nervous. Not only can our noses lead us to things that peoples dropped or that rolled out of place, but we're lower to the ground and might see things that peoples don't notice.

Remember the bone you buried outside so no one else would take it? Sometimes peoples bury things that are important to them. How does that help solve a murder? You never know what your mom or dad will find useful. Not to mention that when they have enough time, murderers like to bury their victims. Peoples will walk right by places where somebody is buried, but we know somebody's there.

And while you're sniffing around, walk under tables and desks. You might be surprised by what you find.

Twenty-Seven

When Mom had thoroughly checked out the house, we walked over to Riddle Realty. The sidewalks were so congested that I picked up Trixie and carried her again.

Mom hurried inside, but I lingered at the doorstep, looking out at the people milling about. One of them had tried to kill Delia; her son, Carter; and me. I didn't see how it would benefit Boomer to murder Delia or me. But as I watched people shopping around the Christkindlmarket stalls, I couldn't help thinking that it would be very easy for Boomer to blend in. No one would be the wiser.

I finally entered the office and set Trixie down. She shook once as though I had ruffled her fur.

Mom whispered to me, "The house is in my price range. I'm trying to put down a deposit on it to hold it until Delia or Carter returns and can write up the contract."

The assistant was muttering to herself when she returned. "What a mess. You can go ahead and fill out some forms for me." She went to a filing cabinet and seemed perplexed about which forms she needed.

"I texted pictures of the house to your grandparents. They love it. Honey, it looks like I might be a while," said Mom. "Why don't you go on? I'll see you back at the inn."

I didn't relish the thought of sitting around while the two of them shuffled paperwork back and forth, so Trixie and I made our exit.

The sun shone in a gorgeous blue sky, and a slight nip was in the air. Perfect weather for holiday shopping, roasted chestnuts, which I smelled as I walked along, and happy holiday spirit. I marveled that very few of the people passing me had any idea what had transpired here earlier. Trixie darted into her favorite store, not because of their merchandise but because she knew she would receive a treat.

It worked out great, though. The owner nabbed me. "Holmes has been coming in here and eyeing that jacket. It looks like him, doesn't it?"

It did. The deep green color would look terrific on him, and it would be useful outdoors. "I'll take it."

"I'm going to wrap it here, so he won't accidentally see it," she said.

I paid for it, glad to know it was something he would like.

While Trixie collected her treat, I found a few more gifts and went back to the register.

At our next stop, Tall Tails Bookstore, I picked out some mysteries for Oma. As I was leaving, I ran into Holmes.

"I've been looking all over for you!" He beamed at me. "How about a bratwurst?"

Oof! They smelled so good. Did I dare try one? Maybe not quite yet. "I'll pass, but I'd be happy to sit with you."

I found a little table and sat down, glad to take a break.

Holmes returned with hot apple cider for both of us, bratwurst with mustard for himself, and a little sausage made just for dogs for Trixie.

"I heard what happened to Delia and Carter! What was that about?" asked Holmes.

"I wish I knew." I told him about the box of poisoned cookies with Mom's name on them as though they were a gift from her. "They came in a Pawsome Cookies box, but Bonnie says she hasn't used those boxes in months."

Holmes stopped eating and studied me. "Carter ate the cookies. Carter had a golf cart run amok. And Carter was scheduled to be at the Alcorn house when I was hit over the head."

"I'd forgotten about that."

"Thank you for erasing my concussion from your mind," he teased.

I made a face at him. "Dave says the golf cart incident could have occurred without being rigged. But if we add in the possibility that the blow to your head might have been meant for Carter, then it means that Carter is at the heart of this mess."

"But why? What did Carter do?"

I filled in Holmes on what I knew. "I thought the man in the tree must be either Penn, Boomer, or Jay Alcorn. But now I have met Penn and know he's alive. That leaves Boomer and Jay. Carter thinks Boomer is the one behind the poisoning. If that's the case, then Jay Alcorn may very likely be the man in the tree."

"We don't really have any clues about the person who attacked me," said Holmes. "And nothing on the golf cart. So let's focus on the cookies. Everyone in town knows about Pawsome Cookies and could have had an empty box."

"Agreed. But it had to be someone who bakes and knew how to get the poison into the cookies and the chocolates," I pointed out.

"And someone who knew where Delia lives."

"Good point. That probably narrows it down to local people."

"And Boomer, if he's alive," said Holmes.

"I was so sure it was Boomer in the tree. So many people had it in for him. Or had reason to be angry with him, at any rate."

"So what's next?" Holmes asked.

"I thought I might take a little trip to Snowball. Did you know Althea Alcorn's husband?"

He grinned. "I'll drive." He tossed our garbage in the trash and was ready to go.

But I led him to the Pawsome Cookies stall, which had virtually no business. "I'd like one of the Winter Wonderland packages of gingersnaps, please." While I paid for it, I asked, "What's going on? There's always a big line outside the main store."

The young man sighed. "There's a stupid rumor floating around that our cookies are making people sick. It's not true, of course. But how can you fight a rumor?"

"I'm really sorry about that. Maybe the visitors won't get wind of it."

The three of us walked to Holmes's car at the edge of town.

"This is turning into a nightmare for Wagtail. What do you want to bet I get a phone call from Oma very soon, telling me we have to stop this before it gets worse."

"Four people poisoned, one of them dead. It's hard to imagine anything worse," said Holmes.

An hour later, I scooped Trixie into my arms, and we walked up to the main building of the Snowball Retirement Center.

"Hi!" I said cheerfully. "We're here to see Mr. Alcorn."

The receptionist nodded pleasantly. "He will be delighted to have company. Go back the way you came in. Turn right and take the first right after that. He's in number 2004."

We thanked her, piled back into the car, and followed her directions.

"Interesting cluster houses!" said Holmes. "That's kind of cool."

"Four in a group?" I asked.

"Looks like it. They're joined in the back corners like a shamrock."

"I think we may have the wrong Mr. Alcorn. Supposedly he has Alzheimer's. I'm not sure he could live on his own. Although Carter said that Mr. Alcorn seemed fine to him."

"There's 2004. We're about to find out." Holmes pulled over and parked the car.

We walked about ten feet to the house. A mailbox mounted next to the door bore the name Tony Alcorn. Holmes knocked on the door.

A withered old man bent at the waist opened the door. "Hi, Joe."

Joe? My hopes sank. He was clearly confused.

"Mr. Alcorn, I'm Holmes Richardson. Do you remember me?"

The old man said nothing, just stared at Holmes. His face suddenly brightened with recognition. "Come on in, young man!"

We entered a tidy living room with a very large TV. A complex puzzle took up the better part of his coffee table. Somewhat small, the room was neat and tidy. As far as I could tell, it didn't appear a caretaker was there.

When I turned around, he had moseyed out the door and was peering up and down the street as though he was looking for something.

He finally joined us inside and closed the door. "Did you bring Althea?"

"No." Holmes shot me a confused look.

Tony Alcorn stood up straight. A broad smile lit his face. He shook Holmes's hand and hugged him, patting him on the back. "You grew up to be a fine-looking man. Is this your wife, Holmes?"

"Not yet," Holmes said. "This is Holly Miller, Liesel's granddaughter. She's co-owner of the inn now. And the little girl who wants your attention is Trixie."

He shook my hand and patted Trixie. "I'm pleased to meet you. I think the world of Liesel. How is she doing?"

"Very well, thank you. We brought along some gingersnap cookies for you." I held the package out to him.

"Pawsome Cookies. They're always delicious. Thank you!" He placed the cookies on the coffee table. "Please sit."

Trixie amused all of us by promptly sitting.

"To what do I owe this lovely visit? I'm sure you didn't drive over here just to see an old fellow like me."

"Actually, we did," I said. "I imagine you have heard about the man in the tree."

"Who hasn't? It's all anyone is talking about," he said. "That Orly, he was as ornery as Althea. Pity they didn't marry and destroy each other."

I looked at Holmes, thinking maybe the questions would be better received from him.

"Someone tried to poison Holly as well as Delia Riddle and her son, Carter. One woman has died."

Tony's eyes widened. This man didn't have Alzheimer's. He understood everything we were saying.

Holmes continued, "We think the poisoning is related to the man in the tree. It was brought to our attention that your son Jay disappeared."

Tony looked from Holmes to me. "He didn't disappear.

He ran away! There's a difference, you know. For that matter, I ran away, too."

"Ran away from what?" I asked.

"From Althea. The wicked witch of Wagtail." He cracked a smile and cackled at the title. "Kent is the only one who can stand her, and that's only because he wants to inherit her money."

"Are you saying Jay is alive?" Holmes asked.

"I assume so. I am, aren't I?"

"Do you know where Jay is?" I asked.

Tony inhaled deeply. "Althea was hard on that boy. He was smart." Tony pointed at Holmes. "Like you. Smart enough to stand up for himself."

"Were you there the night he left?" I asked.

"I was. Such nonsense about a girl. So what if she *was* Orly's daughter? Althea had a heart of stone. Thought she was better than anyone else. And she could not stand losing." He sat back. "You know what was so sad? She lost her son, and to her, that was a win. After she told him to get out, Jay came back. He said he wasn't seeing Orly's girl anymore. But Althea told him to get out. She said words to him that I never thought a mother would ever say to a son: 'You're dead to me.' That night was the last straw for me. I packed up my bags and never went back. Moved to Oklahoma and had a grand time. But when I got older and retired, I missed the mountains and came back here."

Oklahoma! That could be a lead to Jay.

"You divorced Althea?" asked Holmes.

"Nah. Never bothered. As long as she doesn't come around here, I'm okay."

"You're not sick, are you?" I asked. He seemed to be clear about everything except his son Jay. I was willing to bet he knew exactly where Jay was. What kind of parent would he be if he hadn't heard from his son for years and years and simply assumed he was all right?

"Alzheimer's? Is that what you heard? Now don't you go telling anyone that I'm clear as a bell. Believing I've lost my marbles is the only thing that keeps Althea from pestering me."

Holmes laughed at his comment. "We won't give away your secret."

"May I use your powder room?" I asked.

Trixie followed me as I passed the half bath and ventured into the master bedroom. I could hear Holmes talking about the interesting architectural design of the houses and asking questions about noise and neighbors.

An open rolltop desk drew my attention. I didn't dare peer in any drawers for fear they might squeak, but I nosed around the top.

I heard a scraping sound and wondered if Tony had a cat. It came from under the desk. I bent over, and to my complete horror, Trixie was sitting on her haunches, scratching at the underside of the desk. "Stop that!" I hissed. "You'll damage the furniture."

She pulled her ears back at the scolding and then she started right up again. That little rascal!

I dropped to my knees, hoping Tony wouldn't take that exact moment to look for me. I reached out to grab her, and something caught my hair. "Eww, eww, eww." A spider? A cobweb? I swiped the top of my head repeatedly.

Twenty-Eight

Contorting to see what it was, I spied an address taped to the underside of the desk. Trixie had knocked part of it loose, so it hung in the air. I angled my head to read it.

4702 Black Dog Lane
Austin, Texas 78753

I took a quick picture of the address, mashed the tape back into place, and hurried back to the living room with Trixie at my heels. "This is a really nice place," I said.

"It's not much, but it's the right size for me. Smaller means less cleaning."

"It must have been hard to leave your home in Wagtail. I saw it the other day and it's very impressive," I said.

"It belonged to Althea's parents. I don't have any claim on it. It's hers by right. I'd like to say I have fond memories of living there, but Althea made life miserable for all of us. I hope the family that buys it will bring joy back to that place."

"I have one last question, if you don't mind." I smiled at him.

"Yes, ma'am?"

"Is there anyone else who might have had a beef with Jay?" I asked.

"With Jay? Naw. Everybody loved Jay. Didn't they, Holmes? The ones who hated each other were Orly and Althea. But he's dead and she's still living, so I guess she won after all."

Holmes and I thanked him for his time and helpful information. We hopped back into the car.

"We're close to the hospital," Holmes pointed out.

"Delia and Carter! Oh, but I didn't bring them anything."

"They were just poisoned, I don't think they're hoping for boxes of cookies."

"Maybe we should pass. I doubt they'll allow Trixie inside the hospital, and they say never to leave a dog alone in a car."

"It's cool enough. Why not?" He eyed Trixie briefly. "Well, she might figure out how to drive off."

I giggled at the thought. "Apparently, people smash the windows to steal dogs."

"That's just sick!" he said. "I can wait in the car with Trixie while you run up to check on Delia and Carter. How's that? They won't want company anyway."

"I'd like that. Thanks for coming with me, Holmes. I think it helped a lot that you were there. Mr. Alcorn likes you."

"I like him, too. It's a shame he married Althea. He deserved better," said Holmes. "I'm sorry that he didn't have any helpful information, though."

"Oh, but he did. Trixie found an address in Austin, Texas."

"For Jay?"

"I'm not sure. It was taped under his desk, which leads me to think it could be his son's address."

Holmes glanced at me. "I hope so, but it could be his honey's address, too."

"Now that would be funny! But not terribly surprising. He seems like a nice man."

Holmes pulled the car up at the entrance to the hospital. I jumped out and dashed to the reception desk, where I was directed to the second floor. Delia and Carter were in adjoining intensive care rooms. I was shocked to see both of them on ventilators.

They appeared to be sleeping. I didn't want to wake them, but I stopped a nurse. "What are the ventilators for?"

"The biggest risk from gelsemium poison is that it depresses respiration. The ventilator will help them get through that. Shall I tell them they had a visitor?"

"That would be great, thanks. Holly Miller." I wondered if they had been sedated or if that was caused by the poison. And in the back of my mind I kept thinking, *That could have been me.*

I returned to the car quite somber, but Trixie's excitement at my return brightened my mood immediately.

"She was worried about you the whole time," said Holmes. "I promised that you would come back, but I don't think she believed me."

As we left Snowball, we admired the holiday lights that shone in the night.

Suddenly, Holmes said, "You must be starving."

"I am a little hungry."

"We could get takeout. Unless the poisoner works in that particular restaurant, you should be okay."

My phone buzzed. I checked my messages. "Must be the dinner hour. Oma says Cook left me sealed dishes to warm up."

"Sealed? How would you do that?" asked Holmes.

"I guess we're about to find out."

Mom, Oma, and Gingersnap met us at the registration lobby. More precisely, they were waiting for us there. They greeted us with the same enthusiasm as Trixie had.

"Uh, guys," I said. "What's going on here?"

"We were worried about you. Holmes, come with me to my kitchen. Cook stored safe food for Holly there. You can carry it to the private kitchen."

"This is ridiculous," I said.

Mom wrapped her arm around my shoulders for a little sideways hug. "We just have to figure out who has it in for you."

In the family kitchen, Mom rinsed the teakettle four times.

"I think that's enough."

"Maybe you're right. How do you suppose Jean got hold of those chocolates?" asked Mom.

"Someone must have dropped them off at the inn. Maybe she saw them and helped herself. The packaging is very cute and enticing."

"A lot of the shops in town are carrying things like that. They make such good stocking stuffers. I was thinking about buying some for our stockings. But not now!" She shuddered.

The door banged open, and Holmes rolled in a cart, with Oma right behind him.

"Dinner is served!" he joked.

"We'll have to warm up some of these things, I'm sure," said Mom.

I started taking lids off of them. "Not this beautiful

salad." Dark greens formed a base for cooked cranberries, orange slices, pecans, and rings of raw shallots.

Oma shook a glass cruet to blend the dressing.

"Oh my gosh," I said. "There's enough chicken and dumplings to feed us all and have plenty of leftovers."

Holmes lifted another lid. Apple halves lay on a pie-sized pastry. Glossy caramel shimmered on it.

"Ahhh," said Oma. "Apple tarte Tatin with whipped cream."

"And last but not least"—Holmes lifted lids on three smaller dishes—"looks like chicken dinners for Trixie, Gingersnap, and Twinkletoes."

We hurriedly set the table and sat down to eat the salad. But forks in hand, we all paused and gazed at the colorful salad. The room was silent, and our eyes met.

"Oh, for heaven's sake." Oma speared lettuce and ate it. "It's very good."

"Trixie and Twinkletoes aren't as silly as we are," noted Mom. "They're eating with gusto."

I went ahead and ate. Oma was right. Cook had prepared a delicious salad.

In short order, Mom brought the chicken and dumplings to the table. This time no one paused before digging in.

We were eating the tarte Tatin when Oma asked if we had any leads on the person who had poisoned Jean, Delia, Carter, and the WAG woman.

"I've been giving that some thought," said Mom. "I think it has to be someone who knows how to bake. I saw the last couple of cookies. They weren't an amateurish mess. I was thinking it might be someone who entered the gingerbread house contest, like maybe the winner, Kathleen Connor."

"Kathleen?" I asked in surprise.

"She's clearly very talented. She's in a rental house,

where she can cook and bake without the knowledge of anyone except her family. Think about it. How upset would you be if you found out the night before the wedding that your fiancé was also seeing someone else?"

"This is true," said Oma. "It could be enough to push a person over the edge."

"But why would they come back?" asked Holmes. "If I murdered someone and got away with it, then I would never go back to that place. Ever."

"How would she have gotten the box from Pawsome Cookies?" I asked. "And what about Orly? How did she get him to hide the body?"

"Orly could have been paid," suggested Oma.

"But doesn't that suggest a planned murder?" asked Holmes. "Not that I have ever murdered anyone, but isn't disposal of the body usually a big problem? For strangers to get Orly involved, or anyone really, wouldn't they have had to plan to murder? It's not as though you can murder someone and then take a few days to figure out how to get rid of the body. And for someone from out of town, they can't exactly ask around to find out who might bury a body for money."

Holmes made a very good point.

Trixie pawed my thigh.

"Did you like your dinner? You wish you had more?" I scratched behind her ears and thought how lucky I was to be home with my loved ones. It could so easily have been me in the morgue or the hospital. "Pepper!" I shouted, jumping to my feet.

Oma, Mom, and Holmes looked at me like I had lost my mind.

"Delia's dog, Pepper! Has anyone fed her? She can't be out by herself all night in this cold!"

"The three of you go get her," said Oma. "I'll clean up here."

I kissed Oma and thanked her. Mom, Holmes, Trixie, and I bundled up and dashed out to the golf carts armed with flashlights. Minutes later, we pulled up at Delia's house.

When Holmes turned off the engine, everything was dark. Only the light of the moon revealed the outlines of the house and the trees.

I couldn't help thinking of Carter's story about running through the woods with only the moon lighting the world. I was spooked by it now. It must have been terribly frightening for a little boy. I stepped out of the golf cart thinking that Boomer's motorcycle must have been parked just about where I stood.

Trixie ran around sniffing the ground, then vaulted up the stairs and pawed at the front door. Where was Pepper? If she'd been left outside, she would have greeted us by now.

Trixie whimpered by the door when we walked up the steps. I tried the door. It was locked. I thought I heard two tentative barks from inside the house.

"Poor baby!" said Mom. "She's been locked up in there all day. She must be about to burst."

Holmes ran his fingers across the trim over the door. "Nope. Nothing there."

"Carter would have a key, but he's in the hospital, too," I groaned.

"Maybe Delia's sister, Mira, has a key," suggested Mom.

We had turned to leave when Holmes said, "Hang on."

He studied the house number mounted on the wall next to the door. Four slate rectangles contained digits. Strips of wood across the top and the bottom held them in place. He pressed lightly against the final digit. It slid out, revealing a house key.

"I had no idea," I said. "I've never seen anything like that."

Holmes inserted the key and opened the door.

But there was no sign of Pepper.

Trixie sniffed the floor and led us to a closed door. When Holmes opened it, Pepper bolted out and made a mad run to the front door. I followed her and flung it open. She dashed out of the house and rushed to the grass. She ran around with Trixie for a few minutes, sniffing the driveway before they came back inside.

Meanwhile, Holmes had switched on outdoor spotlights and a light in the living room. "That was odd. Do you think Delia shuts Pepper in the bathroom every day?"

"That doesn't sound like the Delia I knew," said Mom. "But then nothing sounds like the old Delia anymore."

"Do we leave her here or take her home?" asked Holmes.

"We have to take her," I said. "She'll need to go out in the morning. It's okay. She can stay with Trixie and me."

"I guess we should see what she eats," said Mom. "We don't want to upset her stomach."

I followed Mom into Delia's kitchen, where she opened cabinets and closed them. "Hmm, where does she keep dog food?"

"Maybe she home cooks for Pepper."

Mom opened the trash can. "I don't think so."

Trixie's Guide to Murder

Training peoples takes a lot of patience. It's really the hardest part. We doggums can find the murder victims, but if your mom or dad doesn't understand what you're telling them, it can be very frustrating.

I recommend running toward the victim. If you yelp a few times, your peoples will probably follow you. Hard as it might be, you will have to ignore their pleas for you to return. They will be angry with you and may even use the dreaded "bad dog" phrase. This is where you must be persistent. When you reach the victim, sprint around the body in circles. I find a melancholy howl works well to explain to my mom that a murder has occurred. Sing the song of your doggum ancestors! Keep at it until your mom or dad can see the person. You may have to dig furiously to reveal the victim. Don't stop until the peoples understand.

However, it may take several murders before your peoples make the connection between your song and murder. When they figure it out, be sure to reward them with wags and kisses. It's the only way to teach them.

Twenty-Nine

"Did you find an empty can?" I asked.

"And more," said Mom.

I peered into the trash can. An empty container of dog food lay beside broken cookies that looked exactly like the poisonous ones that Delia and Carter had eaten. And farther down, round chocolates in perfect condition had caught on the trash.

Trixie sniffed around the trash can. "No, Trixie!" I shooed her away.

Mom placed her hands over her eyes for a moment. "I can't believe this. Not Delia!"

"Hey, Holly," called Holmes. "Looks like Trixie is on the trail of something."

"Okay," I yelled. "Don't let her eat anything. Pepper, either!" I stared at the contents of the trash can and closed the lid. "What are you saying, Mom? So some of the cookies broke and she threw them away."

Mom had grabbed two paper towels and used them to

open the refrigerator. She closed it and moved on, opening and closing cabinets again.

"I don't get it, what are you looking for?"

"A chocolate mold. And there it is," she pointed.

It didn't look like much. I wouldn't have even noticed it. A piece of plastic with a dozen round indentations lay on its edge, as though it had been filed.

"So?" I asked.

"Don't you see, Holly? Delia baked the cookies and made the chocolates."

A shout from Holmes got our attention. We shot down the hallway to a bedroom. Trixie stood on her hind legs with her paws on the edge of the bed and her tail wagging. On top of the bed, someone had left half a dozen colorful boxes of chocolates, exactly like the one that had contained the poisoned chocolates that killed Jean.

"But this doesn't make any sense," I said weakly. "Why would Delia poison herself and Carter?"

"She wouldn't," said Mom, sounding a little snarky.

"You think she baked two batches and ate the wrong one?" asked Holmes.

"I don't understand this. It's not like my Delia at all." Mom winced.

I was already pressing Officer Dave's phone number. When he answered, I said, "I think we may have found something at Delia's house."

In spite of the frigid temperature, the three of us decided it was best to leave the house until Dave arrived. We had already contaminated it with our fingerprints.

We stepped out onto the porch and Mom said, "I will never be able to come here again without imagining poor little Carter snatching his camera from that awful man, Boomer, and running for his life."

"Where did he run to?" asked Holmes.

"The bluff." I pulled my scarf tighter against the chill.

Holmes pointed. "It would be over that way."

"Carter told us he was screaming, and that Boomer shot at him. Wouldn't you think Delia would have heard a commotion like that?" I asked.

"The bluff is pretty far into the woods," said Holmes. "But you'd sure hear a gunshot."

"Any point in walking over there?" asked Mom.

"I don't think there's a trail. It would be easier in daylight. What I don't understand is why Carter never said anything. He followed Barry and me around. You'd think he would have told us about his mom and Boomer."

"Children hold in a lot of things, especially painful memories," said Mom. "If we believe Carter's story, then why would Delia be baking poisoned cookies? And why would she try to poison Holly?" Mom wrapped her arm around me.

I watched Pepper romp with Trixie. Pepper had been very well behaved. Why would Delia shut her in the bathroom? I couldn't imagine doing that unless a dog was out of control and in the way. She hadn't displayed that kind of behavior when we ate dinner at Delia's house. "Maybe she didn't."

Holmes and Mom gave me questioning looks.

"Don't you see? It's too obvious. We were meant to find all those things. She's been framed."

"That's why Pepper was in the bathroom." Holmes snapped his fingers. "Either she was being a pest because someone else was in the house, or that person didn't want Pepper to eat any of the poison."

"A dog-loving killer!" Mom blurted.

We were thrilled to see the headlights of Dave's golf cart. We explained the situation to him, glad to be inside, out of the cold again.

Dave stared at the contents of the trash can. "Nice of her to use a liner. It will be a lot easier to collect."

He checked the fridge. "And voilà, there's our poison."

The three of us peered around him.

"No touching," said Dave.

"I saw that earlier, but it looks so much like the dressing we had on our salad that I assumed it was salad dressing," said Mom.

Dave closed the refrigerator door and eyed us. "Is anyone dizzy? Having trouble breathing?"

"Our dinner was prepared for us by the inn cook," I clarified. "I'm sure it was fine."

We showed him the bedroom full of candy boxes. Dave was unimpressed. "A lot of guest rooms probably look like this right now. It's not uncommon for people to lay out gifts on a bed."

"Do you see any other gifts?" I asked. "This isn't Delia's Christmas wrapping room. This is a setup."

Mom seemed more hopeful. "Yeah! Seriously, would you dump perfectly good chocolates in the trash to empty the boxes? No! You would save the good ones to eat yourself or serve to your family."

Dave took a deep breath. "I wish Pepper could tell me what happened. You three head home. I'll collect what I can and take it over to Snowball for testing. And I'll get a guard to hang out here overnight."

We had to do some coaxing to convince Pepper it was okay to come with us. Eventually, she hopped onto the front seat with her buddy Trixie.

Back at the inn, we found Oma in the family kitchen with her feet up by a warm fire. Twinkletoes was curled up on her lap, and Gingersnap lounged beside her.

Twinkletoes watched Pepper curiously but didn't seem particularly distressed about her presence. We fed Pepper and filled in Oma about the cookies, chocolates, and poison at Delia's house.

Trixie and Gingersnap got a little bite of a second dinner. I didn't want them to be jealous of Pepper.

And then, feeling that Delia had been vindicated, we celebrated by making hot chocolate with a brand-new, never-before-opened bottle of Bailey's Irish Cream, topped it with whipped cream, and demolished the remainder of the tarte Tatin. Not to be left out, the dogs had a late dessert of Hamburger Kisses, little mounds of hamburger that ever so slightly resembled their chocolate cousins.

I woke early the next morning. My first thoughts were of poison, but work soon overpowered those notions. A lot of people would be checking out of the inn and driving home today. After a shower, I dressed in gray pants and a burgundy sweater. I knew from experience that the sliding doors to the registration lobby would be open a lot, allowing the chilly air in. I added a long necklace of freshwater pearls spaced apart on a strand of silver. Pearl earrings looked professional, but sneakers were an absolute necessity because I would be standing or on the run all day.

Trixie, Twinkletoes, and Pepper nosed around my walk-in closet. Pepper's festive plaid collar reminded me that Trixie and Twinkletoes weren't dressed for the holidays. The man in the tree, Kitty's disappearance, and the poisonings had completely distracted me. I readily found Twinkletoes's red velvet collar and put it on her. I swapped Trixie's collar for a red one that said *Santa's Little Helper.*

Mom's door was open. I stuck my head in to say good morning, but her bed was made and there was no sign of her.

Trixie, Twinkletoes, and Pepper scampered down the

grand staircase ahead of me. When I opened the front door, Trixie and Pepper dashed outside. Twinkletoes sniffed the air but turned and ambled toward the dining area, which undoubtedly smelled more enticing.

Shivering without a coat, I accompanied Trixie and Pepper outside. They romped joyfully in the cold air, completely oblivious to the chill.

But I was freezing. Feeling like a Scrooge, I cut their fun short and called them in for breakfast. Trixie led the way for her guest. By the time I caught up to them, they were getting pets and kisses from Mom, Oma, Mr. Huckle, and Officer Dave. A fire already crackled in the big fireplace.

"Everyone is up early this morning," I said.

Mom groaned. "Who could sleep? I tossed all night thinking about Delia and Carter." She shook her head. "There she is in the hospital suffering from poisoning, and meanwhile someone is trying to make her look like the poisoner!"

"No mother would allow her child to eat anything poisonous," said Oma. "I'm certain Delia did not do this."

Mr. Huckle drew up a chair for me.

"Thank you, Mr. Huckle."

"I apologize for not delivering tea to you this morning. Cook would not permit it. He said *from his hands to your mouth*, and booted me out of the kitchen!"

"He has been so kind to me."

Shelley arrived with a mug of steaming tea for me. She must have overheard Mr. Huckle because she whispered, "Don't tell him I brought you tea! I see we have a guest this morning. Is that Delia's dog?"

I nodded. "Pepper is staying with us while Delia's hospitalized."

"What can I bring you for breakfast?"

"Anything warm," I said. "Oatmeal?"

"No problem. Oatmeal for the pups, too? It's not sweet, of course. It comes with a chicken sauce and diced chicken breast with eggs. Salmon for Twinkletoes?"

"Yes, please. I think they would love that."

Dave's phone buzzed. He excused himself to take the call, but we watched his expression and waited for his return.

"There has been a development," said Oma. "I feel it."

Mom closed her eyes. "I hope Delia and Carter are all right."

Dave returned to the table.

"Well?" asked Oma.

Dave drained his coffee, and Shelley smiled at him when she refilled it.

"Thanks, Shelley. While we were sleeping, the people from the police lab were analyzing the items I brought to them from Delia's house. The mixture that was in the refrigerator is mashed gelsemium roots steeping in vodka."

"Vodka?" Shelley wrinkled her nose.

"Very clever," said Oma. "It would taint the liquid, which would make it easier to use in foods."

Dave continued, "The cookies in the trash contained poison. The chocolates in the garbage were fine, not poisonous at all."

"I knew it," said Mom. "That proves it wasn't Delia. She would have eaten the good chocolates."

"I don't know about that," said Dave. "Some people throw away perfectly good chocolates, but I think you're right about Delia being framed."

We stared at him in silence until Trixie yipped at Shelley.

"Don't say anything," said Shelley. "Not a word. Let me get their breakfasts."

She hurried off and returned in short order with a tray.

She set the bowls for the dogs and Twinkletoes on the floor, and then placed oatmeal in front of me along with a cruet of maple syrup, butter, and fresh raspberries in a raspberry sauce. "Okay, now you can continue."

I added syrup and raspberries to my bowl of oatmeal and ate while I listened.

"I struggled with the idea that Delia could be a killer. I've known her my whole life. Just like you, Nell, I knew she would protect Carter from anything. She loves her son! I couldn't imagine her harming him in any way. We were right to be doubtful. It turns out that there are no fingerprints on the bottle of poison or the boxes."

Oma squinted at him. "How is that possible?"

"Someone wiped everything down and wore gloves," Dave explained.

"Why couldn't Delia have done that?" asked Mr. Huckle.

Dave nodded. "She could have. But if she knew she was going to eat some, and that it was possible the police would search her house for the poison she ingested, wouldn't she have gotten rid of it? Thrown out the boxes of chocolates? Hidden the jar of poison? Why would she leave everything out in plain sight but go to the trouble of wiping off her fingerprints?"

Thirty

"So the real killer, the person who poisoned Jean, Delia, Carter, and the WAG woman, broke into Delia's house, shut Pepper in the bathroom, and planted all that stuff to throw suspicion on Delia," I said.

"Right. We're dealing with someone who is thinking this through very carefully." Dave's words hung in the air, ominous and horrifying.

"They are desperate," said Oma.

"But no one broke into the house," I pointed out.

"Anyone could have gotten in with the spare key, just like we did," said Mom. "I feel terrible for suspecting Delia for even an instant!" she exclaimed. "But why poison them?"

"Because they were there that night," I said. "They know what happened. They know who the man in the tree is and what happened to him."

Mom shot me a quizzical look. "We've heard Carter's version. He revealed an ugly side of Boomer, but he didn't mention anyone else. And Boomer rode off on his motorcycle. If it's Boomer in the tree, then whatever happened to him must have happened after he rode away."

"Unless," said Dave, "someone stole the motorcycle."

The sound of voices in the stairwell meant guests were up and about.

In a hushed voice, Dave said, "Here's what we're going to do. We're the only ones who know about this. We don't want any more poisonings. So we're going to pretend that we still believe Delia is the one who poisoned Jean. Got it?"

"How wickedly clever!" exclaimed Mr. Huckle. "The true culprit will relax and may slip up!"

"That's the idea," said Dave.

Oma bustled off to the office. I finished my oatmeal in a hurry and dashed upstairs to brush my teeth. The dogs and Twinkletoes followed me.

Mom found me in the apartment. "I'm coming down to help. Okay?"

"That would be great," I mumbled with toothpaste in my mouth.

We hurried down to the registration lobby. Thankfully no one waited in line yet. Twinkletoes leaped up on the registration desk and cleaned her whiskers as though she hadn't a care in the world. Trixie and Pepper sniffed every corner of the room.

"What do you think?" asked Mom.

"Someone else must have been there that night twenty years ago. Maybe Delia would tell *you* the truth."

"You think she lied to us? Her story fits with Carter's."

"Except for one thing," I pointed out. "He did not take off on his motorcycle until hours later."

Mom seemed disturbed. "Maybe she just didn't look out that way. She did dishes, probably gave her daughter a bath and put her to bed. She didn't notice."

"Maybe . . ."

Mom sighed. "I'll try to get it out of her." She grabbed a sheet of paper and wrote as she spoke. "The Connors, Penn and Kathleen. Stu Williams."

"Penny and Tommy Terrell. Bonnie Greene. Josie Biffle," I added.

"That's a lot of people. Can't we eliminate some of them?"

"Maybe Stu. I haven't heard anything that would have been a motive for him. He admits that he helped Orly with the concrete, though."

Mom struck through Stu's name. "If Bonnie was in love with Boomer, wouldn't she have killed Delia?"

"Maybe. Or she might have turned on him out of anger. But she probably wouldn't have brought him to my attention if she killed him. Not unless she thought Delia would bring him up and Bonnie wanted to beat her to it."

I pulled out my phone. "Yesterday, Holmes and I visited Mr. Alcorn, who is well. Trixie found this taped to the underside of a desk." I showed Mom and Googled the address.

Mom looked over my shoulder. It came up in a neighborhood site. I scrolled through the list of homeowners.

"There it is!" Mom said. "Regan Robertson," she read. "So much for that."

"Not so fast." I Googled Regan Robertson. "I think this could be her. An English professor at the university. Hah! This looks like a phone number."

Mom checked her watch. "It's a little early to call on a Sunday morning. Plus, it's an hour earlier there."

I jotted down the number as a gentleman walked in with Mr. Huckle, who carried his luggage.

Three hours sped by as guests checked out. Most were driving, but several were on their way to the closest airport.

During a lull, I phoned Regan Robertson.

Mom stood beside me with her head tilted to hear what Regan said.

A woman's voice spoke. "Hello?"

"Hi. This is Holly Miller calling. May I speak with Jay Alcorn?"

We could hear a sharp intake of breath. "You have the wrong number." She hung up.

"There was a pause!" Mom said gleefully. "Did you notice that? She gasped and paused!"

I had noticed it. "We have nothing. No confirmation. Nothing!"

"Call her back."

"Mom!" I whined. "She'll just hang up again."

"Tell her you're looking for Jay. Tell Regan about the man in the tree."

I called the number again.

"Hello?"

I could hear irritation in Regan's tone. "Hi. I'm terribly sorry to bother you. Is this Regan Robertson?"

I heard shuffling and she hissed to someone, "She knows *my* name!"

I didn't wait for her response. "I'm looking for Jay Alcorn."

This time there was a long pause. "How did you get this number?"

I couldn't exactly say that my dog found her address. "We have—" I skipped over the part about the tree. Who would believe that? "—found an unidentified body. It has been suggested that it could be Jay Alcorn. We're trying to find out if he's dead or alive."

She gasped again. I could hear her whispering. "They want to know if you're dead!"

A man came to the phone. "Who is calling, please?"

"Holly Miller. I'm calling because—" The line went dead. "So much for that," I grumbled.

"I hang up on a lot of people," said Mom. "It's those pesky robocalls. They're so annoying."

The inn phone rang. I picked it up and tried to sweeten my voice to hide my irritation. "Sugar Maple Inn. Holly speaking. How may I help you?"

I recognized the male voice immediately. "Sorry about that. Is Liesel Miller still alive?"

"Very much so. She's the mayor of Wagtail now. I'm her granddaughter. Sam's daughter?"

Mom took the phone out of my hand. "Hi, Jay! This is Nell. Holly is my little girl."

I leaned over to listen in.

"Nell DuPuy? I feel like I've stepped back in time! How are you?"

"Great, actually. Oh, Jay, you should see Wagtail now. It's a different place."

"Have you seen my dad?"

"No, but Holly visited him yesterday. She says he's doing well. Jay, they discovered a body inside an old tree on Orly Biffle's land. There's a rumor that you were dating Josie Biffle years ago and it made Orly so mad that he killed you."

"Did you say *in a tree*?"

"Can you believe it?"

"As you can tell, I'm alive and well. I don't know who they found, but it wasn't me." He snickered. "I didn't think anyone except my family knew about me dating Josie. We knew how much Orly and my mom would hate that. To tell the truth, we broke up right away. I think she had her eyes on someone else. About all we had in common were meddlesome parents. Dad tells me Mom is still alive and up to her fiendish ways."

"She's selling the house, Jay. I think she's slowing down. She can't manage it anymore."

"I hope the next family fills it with love and laughter instead of hatred and vitriol."

He really was his father's son. Hadn't Tony said almost the same thing?

Mom chatted a little longer while I helped the next guest depart.

When Mom hung up, she said, "We can cross Jay off the list. I guess that leaves Boomer or some unknown person."

Mom stared at me. "Holly, Jay asked me not to mention our conversation. I explained that we would have to tell Officer Dave, but he doesn't want his mom to know anything about him. Especially not where he lives."

"That's so sad. For both of them."

Mom shook her head. "Althea must regret what she did every single day."

Marie Johnson walked up to the registration desk carrying shopping bags. Kitty and Stuey followed her. And right behind them were Barry and his parents, Sue and Stu.

"I wanted to thank you for everything you have done for me, for us. You have been so kind to let us stay here. I'll be forever grateful," said Marie.

"I don't want to go," cried Kitty. "Poppy is going to have puppies and I want to see them."

"Honey, we'll be back next Friday. Maybe Poppy can wait a few days."

Barry grinned at Kitty and shrugged. "Maybe the puppies will be here when you come back!"

"And Santa will be here next weekend. I have to see him to tell him where we are," Kitty said earnestly.

"Should I reserve a room for you?" I asked, worried that we were probably already booked.

Marie seemed a little bit flustered. "Thank you, but

Sue and Stu have a rental unit where they're letting us stay temporarily."

Stu grinned at the kids. "We wouldn't let you miss Santa. Hey, Stu Too, want a piggyback ride?"

Stuey climbed on his back. "Let's go, Big Stu!"

They left, with Sue shaking her head.

Oma emerged from the office. "Ach, Marie! I am glad I caught you."

Thirty-One

Oma handed Marie an envelope. "It is the prize that Kitty won in the gingerbread house contest."

Marie tore open the envelope. "This is a lot of money."

"One thousand dollars."

Marie looked at her daughter. "This is a big surprise. They told me she won, but I thought she would get a trophy or a plaque."

Kitty crossed her fingers. "Is it enough to buy one of Poppy's puppies?"

Barry laughed. "I think Poppy will want you to have one of them for free."

Marie sucked in air. "Maybe this will go toward your college fund." She waved at us as she walked toward the door.

"Maybe half of it could go to the college fund?" asked Kitty.

The door whooshed closed, and all we could hear was the vacuum running upstairs.

"I hope things work out for them." Oma looked at her watch. "There should be a lull for about two hours before people will be checking in. I will watch the desk while you two grab lunch."

I figured the dogs needed to go out, so I slung on my vest. As we walked out of the lobby, I collected three clumps of Pepper's fur from the floor. No wonder Delia worried about fur in her house.

Mom joined us outside. The savory aromas of hot dogs and bratwurst floated to us.

Mom shook her head as though she was reading my thoughts. "Tempting but too risky, Holly."

"Cook probably made something equally delicious."

"Why does everyone call him Cook?" asked Mom. "It sounds so cold. I'm sure he has a name."

I laughed aloud. "I guess it does sound awful. He has a name. It's John Cook. He goes by Cook."

"Let's see what's cooking, then."

I groaned at her feeble humor.

Her phone rang as we returned to the inn. "Ugh. It's your stepfather. This is the first time he has called me since I left California. She pressed her finger to her phone. "Hello."

We kept walking toward the kitchen, but then Mom stopped dead in the main lobby. She motioned to me to go ahead.

When I entered the commercial kitchen, Cook dried his hands and hurried over. "We loaded up a cart for you. Oma needs to eat, too. Chicken hearts and ground turkey with pasta for all three dogs, and chicken pâté for Twinkletoes. You can tell which is which by the size of the bowls. Three butternut squash and apple soups with an assortment of sandwiches. And baked apples for dessert."

I thanked him and rolled the cart out of the kitchen

and into the lobby. Mom was pale, but her cheeks were flushed. I stopped and whispered, "Is everything okay?"

She nodded. Into the phone she said, "Let me work out the logistics and I'll call you back." She ended the call. "The California house sold."

"That's great news!"

"But they want possession by the first of the year! I never anticipated that. There's so much to do."

"First have lunch. I'll handle the registration desk this afternoon. You can start arranging for movers and see when you can close on the Wagtail house."

While we walked back to the office, Mom called her parents. I could hear my grandfather saying, "No problem. I'm ready to go!"

After lunch, Mom headed off to Delia's office to arrange the house purchase on this end.

And then Penn and Kathleen Connor stopped by. Kathleen introduced herself. "We're celebrating my father's seventy-fifth birthday next summer with a huge family gathering. Penn wanted me to see the inn. It's every bit as charming as he said."

Oma invited them into the office to see photos of other similar celebrations. Meanwhile, I dashed up two flights of stairs, with three dogs and one cat leaping along ahead of me. I was breathless by the time I reached the third floor. I carried the box of Penn's belongings out to the elevator. Trixie, who was afraid of confined spaces, refused to ride on the elevator, but I knew she would meet the rest of us downstairs. I suspected it might be Pepper's first experience in an elevator, but in true border collie fashion, she took it in stride.

Penn peered into the box, telling Oma, "Running off that day was the best and the worst thing we ever did."

"It was terrible of us," said Kathleen. "I should have

confronted Boomer and broken off the engagement. But there was almost a sense of adventure about it. Like when you go on a road trip with no itinerary and just see where life takes you."

Penn handed her the copy of Harry Potter. "It's been quite a trip, Kathleen." To Oma he said, "I never expected that anyone would keep these things. Thank you for doing that. It's sort of like a time capsule. It takes me back to that day when my life changed forever."

I watched him. If he meant the day he murdered his rival for Kathleen's affections, could he be so calm and confident?

Oma promised to send them information on the inn's parties, and I had to scurry off to check in a new guest.

By midafternoon we had a full house again and I turned to my next task, which was helping Mr. Huckle prepare the Dogwood Room for the town council's holiday party at seven o'clock.

Mr. Huckle and I brought up stanchions from the basement and hung red velvet ropes between them with a sign that said *Private Party.*

I placed poinsettias on the corners of the cloakroom counter, and we were set. Cook had prepared hors d'oeuvres and a delicious eggnog with cream from a local farmer. As six thirty approached, I helped Mr. Huckle set up the buffet in the Dogwood Room. We brought in bourbon for the eggnog, white wine, rum, brandy, and a blackberry liqueur made in Wagtail.

I took a quick look around the Dogwood Room. The lights on the tree and the mantel were really all the décor needed. A fire blazed in the fireplace, which added a cozy touch.

I dashed upstairs and swapped my sweater and pants for a dark green velvet dress. My pearls went with it perfectly, but the sneakers wouldn't do. It seemed like I rarely wore heels anymore, but they were right for tonight.

Mom was on my computer trying to find out just how fast she could have her furniture moved and promised to come down to Oma's party as soon as she figured a few things out.

Since I wasn't part of the town council, I settled at the front desk of the main lobby to answer questions and give our new guests directions around town so Oma could focus on her guests. Mr. Huckle stood by to take coats from guests as they arrived. Christmas music played softly in the background.

I hummed along to "Rockin' around the Christmas Tree," contemplating what we knew about the tree and the poisons. Or what I thought we knew. The man in the tree was most likely Boomer. Orly had hidden his body. I pulled out a sheet of paper and made a note. *Why would Orly hide the body? So he wouldn't go to prison for murdering Boomer. Or to protect someone else who killed Boomer. Or because he was paid to hide Boomer's body?*

The only reason I could think of that Orly would have killed Boomer was jealousy. Yet not a single person had mentioned anything of the sort. Only speculative rumors. So that seemed unlikely.

But he might have hidden Boomer in the tree to protect Delia. And she had reason to be very angry with Boomer. As did Kathleen, Bonnie, and Tommy, whose wife had been flirting with Boomer.

Dave thought Delia was not the poisoner. His reasoning was sound. Why would she wipe her fingerprints off the poison in her own home?

I gazed down at Pepper, who lay at my feet with Trixie. And who would lock Pepper in the bathroom?

I suspected Holmes was correct about Kathleen. She didn't have enough time to hire Orly to hide Boomer's body. And surely, she and Penn would never have returned to Wagtail even after all these years. Of course, a sane person wouldn't have returned, but a sane person wouldn't have killed Boomer in the first place.

Maybe Penn murdered Boomer, and Kathleen knew nothing about it. But I still had the problem about hiring Orly to get rid of the body. I decided I could strike them from my list of suspects.

That left Bonnie and Tommy. Bonnie claimed to have been at home cooking dinner and waiting for Boomer to come back after breaking off his engagement to Delia. But there wasn't any proof of that. She could easily have spied on him at Delia's house. Chill bumps prickled my arms as I imagined Bonnie hiding in the woods while Boomer enjoyed dinner at Delia's. If Delia's story was to be believed, they kissed as he left. That clearly would not have happened had he broken off the engagement. Had it triggered something in Bonnie?

But what about Carter's story? If Carter seized his camera from Boomer and ran through the woods, then wouldn't Bonnie have seen that if she was there? Had she caught up to Boomer and confronted him after Carter fled for home?

Now that was a possibility. I reviewed the scenario. Bonnie waited outside while Boomer ate dinner. He was supposed to break off the engagement and come to Bonnie's house for dinner. If she was outside Delia's house watching, then her anger would have reached a boiling point right about the time Delia and Boomer kissed outside.

But when Delia went inside the house, Carter swiped his camera from Boomer, who allegedly chased him for it. What had Bonnie done? Was she running through the woods intent on having it out with Boomer? Had she caught up to him and killed him? Had she pushed him over the bluff? But what happened to his motorcycle?

Either Bonnie or Tommy could have gone to Orly's house and asked for his help after killing Boomer. I didn't know if he was close enough to either of them to have hidden the body for them, but it was a possibility.

"Earth to Holly." A hand waved in front of me, jarring me out of my thoughts.

"Dave! Sorry." I lowered my voice to a whisper. "I was thinking about Boomer and who might have killed him."

Dave and I nodded at some guests as they entered.

He came around the desk and said in a low voice, "I collected Carter's camera this afternoon."

"And?" I asked hopefully.

"He has hundreds of memory disks. Someone really ought to put them together for a retrospective of Wagtail. He took pictures of everything. It's going to take days to go through them."

"Maybe we can get some people together, like Mom, Oma, Holmes, and Shelley, and work on it together."

"Let me see what I can set up. I'd better get over to the party."

I nodded and watched Bonnie walk in. Mr. Huckle took her black coat to hang it up. She smiled at me, and my breath caught as I gazed at her. She was one of my prime suspects.

"I see you caught desk duty tonight," she said.

"I might sneak over for some eggnog later."

She leaned toward me. "I hear it was Delia who has been poisoning everyone. She must have killed Boomer when he broke off their engagement, and Orly helped her hide his body."

I nodded at her. Either she was a very cool customer, or she wasn't the killer after all.

"Oh, look who's here! Pepper and Trixie!" She patted the dogs, who no doubt thought of her as the cookie lady and swished their tails happily.

Where had Twinkletoes wandered off to? I knew Gingersnap was in the Dogwood Room with Oma, enjoying the attention, but where was my sweet cat?

And then I heard Mr. Huckle ask, "How are your aunt and cousin?"

I looked up to see him taking Josie's coat.

She winced. "Our whole family is in shock over what happened to them. They're not well at all. We're hoping they'll pull through."

And as he took her bright red coat, I spied a clump of black fur on it. Fur that I had come to know over the past day because I had been collecting it as Pepper shed. I reminded myself that there were hundreds of dogs in Wagtail.

But then I heard soft growling at my feet. I looked down. Pepper was fixated on Josie. The growling persisted.

Josie looked at Pepper and Trixie with cold, calculating eyes. In her hurry to get to the party, she didn't bother to say anything to me. Not that she had to, but I wondered if she was worried about Pepper.

The more time I spent with dogs, the more I understood how smart they were. And one thing I had learned was that they had unbelievably good memories. Something had happened between Josie and Pepper.

I rose from my spot and found Josie's coat in the cloakroom. Only a scientist could confirm that the clump of fur on the back of Josie's coat came from Pepper. But it sure looked like Pepper's fur to me. And Pepper's attitude toward Josie meant something.

I had struck Josie as a potential suspect because Jay was alive. His words came back to me. Something about

Josie having her eye on someone else. Could Josie have dated Jay to make Boomer jealous? She must have known he was engaged to her aunt. Had she been the one waiting in the woods and watching for him to leave Delia's house all those years ago?

Even worse, had Josie been in Delia's house to plant the poison? Things began to click in place in my head. Delia hadn't left Pepper in the bathroom. It was Josie who had shut her in there. She had poisoned her own aunt and cousin!

I had to stop people from eating and drinking. She could be sprinkling poison on people's food or drinks at this very minute!

I stepped out of the cloakroom. The dogs were gone.

Thirty-Two

No! Oh no! Holiday music still tinkled softly. But the murmur of voices had stopped. I hurried over to the Dogwood Room only to find that Pepper had herded everyone into a group. Everyone, except Josie!

She had culled Josie from the group. Josie stood with her back to the Christmas tree, saying, "Shoo. Shoo. Get away from me!"

Trixie focused on Josie, too.

I had eliminated Josie Biffle from the list of possible suspects, but now one thing seemed very obvious. Her father certainly would have hidden the body for her.

"Really, can someone get these dogs away from me, please?" Josie reached into her pocket and threw something to the floor.

"No! I screamed. "They're poisonous. Don't let the dogs eat them."

I literally lunged for them. Lying on the floor, I picked

up the treats just in time. Trixie was already sniffing one. I looked up at Josie, furious.

And that was when an ornament bonked Josie on the head and Twinkletoes leaped from the tree onto Josie. And all I could think was that Shadow had done a great job of tying the tree to the wall so it wouldn't fall.

Josie screamed. Twinkletoes hissed. Pepper barked. And "Jingle Bell Rock" played in the background.

Thirty-Three

"It was you!" I cried. "You poisoned your own aunt and cousin!"

Officer Dave led Josie to a chair. I overheard him on his phone calling for transportation of a suspect to Snowball.

Bonnie offered me a hand and helped me up.

Mr. Huckle magically appeared with a first-aid kit.

And Pepper sat just out of reach of Josie, growling.

"Well now, this is the most exciting party I've been to in years," someone said.

Mom came flying into the Dogwood Room along with several guests of the inn.

"I thought I heard screaming," said Mom. "Oh my, Josie, honey, what happened to your face?"

Mr. Huckle was busy cleaning up the cat scratches that Josie had suffered.

"Did she poison the food?" someone asked.

Thankfully everyone pitched in loading food and beverages on trays. Mr. Huckle, Mom, and I carried them to the commercial kitchen. We washed our hands thoroughly and went in search of replacement dishes to serve.

"I believe there are additional hors d'oeuvres trays," said Mr. Huckle. "Oh yes! I have them."

I hit Oma's liquor stash. The guests would certainly want some stiff drinks after this. In no time at all, we had replenished the food and beverages.

"Do you want to tell us what happened?" Mom asked Josie.

"I'm not saying anything until my lawyer is present."

Dave nodded. "Okay. That's your right."

But Josie glared at Bonnie.

In a quiet, sensible voice, Bonnie said, "I realize now that Boomer was only stringing me along." She took a deep breath. "Delia had received all that money from her husband's insurance and was starting a business. I was starting my own cookie business. Kathleen came from a well-off family, and you, Josie, stood to inherit your dad's grocery business. None of us looked alike. We were tall and short, blond and brunette, different in every way except one. Boomer wanted money, and he would have done anything to get it."

"That's not true!" Josie shouted. "He really loved me."

Going out on a limb, I asked, "Then why did you try to make him jealous by dating Jay Alcorn?"

I heard my mother gasp. "That was a scam?"

"I didn't care about Jay," said Josie. "But it threw everyone off track. Delia was running around showing off her engagement ring. I had to see Boomer secretly! I mean, what would people have thought if I was going out with my aunt's fiancé?"

"Really?" I snorted. "That's what you were worried about? What were you going to do if he really married her?"

She stared at me with cold dark eyes, her face bitter.

"Oh my gosh!" cried Mom. "You were going to knock her off! Your own aunt!"

"But you killed Boomer instead," said Bonnie, again a voice of calm in the room.

"You were outside watching that night, weren't you?" I asked. "Delia probably mentioned that Boomer was coming over for dinner."

Josie's nostrils flared. "I loved him. And he loved me."

"Then why were you spying on him? And why did you bring a gun?" I asked.

"He was spending too much time with her. I was afraid he would dump me, and I couldn't stand that. And then I saw them kiss." Her tone grew hard. "And I knew. He wasn't going along with our plans. You don't kiss somebody that way unless you care about them. A lot."

She fell silent. I waited a moment before saying, "And then Carter showed up."

Her eyes met mine. "Boomer was carrying a camera and Carter ran out of the house, grabbed it from Boomer, and ran like crazy. Boomer called him ugly names and chased after him. Carter was just a little kid!"

"That's when you fired the gun?" asked Dave.

"I wanted to stop Boomer. He sounded like a crazed man, crashing through the woods and uttering ugly threats. I thought firing into the air might get his attention. Boomer would think Orly was up there and would run from him. But he didn't. I caught up to them at the bluff. Carter had gone over the edge and was holding on to tree roots, and Boomer showed a side of himself I had never seen. He had turned into a cruel and horrible man. He was kicking at Carter and trying to make him fall. I pushed him."

"Carter?" asked Oma.

"No. I pushed Boomer. It was the only way to save

Carter. Boomer crashed to the bottom. Carter pulled himself up and over the edge. I ran through the woods in hysterics. He never saw me. I walked down to where Boomer lay next to the edge of the lake, and I could tell he was dead. His leg was at this weird angle, and his eyes were open. Not blinking. Not seeing."

"Then you went to get Orly?" I asked.

"I told Dad what had happened. By that time, I'd lost it. I sobbed. About everything. About how stupid I had been to be sucked in by Boomer. About poor little Carter."

"Wait a minute," I said. "You tampered with Carter's golf cart."

Josie held up her forefinger. "I did not. That really was a weird malfunction. I had nothing to do with it."

"You poisoned Carter!" said Mom.

"That was an accident. How was I supposed to know Aunt Delia would give him some of her cookies?"

"Let's go back a minute, please," said Dave. "What did Orly do?"

"Dad told me to go to bed. When daylight broke, I went back to the bluff. Boomer was gone. So was his motorcycle. I saw Dad and Stu filling the tree with concrete, so I had a hunch where Boomer was. I asked Dad once about the motorcycle. He said it was a fish habitat. I guess it's in the lake."

"Who hit Holmes over the head?" asked Dave.

"I thought he was Kent Alcorn. I hoped you might think it was Jay in the tree and you wouldn't find out it was Boomer."

"Why did you poison Jean and Delia?" asked Dave.

"Delia was there that night. I was certain she knew what happened. And Jean stole the chocolates meant for Holly. I didn't want to be here, where I am now, handcuffed. Holly was getting too close to the truth. I left the chocolates at her door on Thanksgiving. I guess Jean found them and stole them." She shrugged.

Minutes later, uniformed Snowball police officers escorted Josie out of the inn in handcuffs. People mingled and talked about the saga of Boomer and what Josie had done for the next hour.

It was too bad she'd turned to poisoning people, because a number of them believed that she had done the right thing by saving Carter.

Thirty-Four

Monday morning, I woke feeling positively buoyant.

I showered and dressed in the brightest, reddest sweater I owned. I pulled on black tights and a pleated black wool skirt to go with it.

Trixie, Pepper, and Twinkletoes raced down the stairs. I opened the front door for them. Twinkletoes sat on the railing of the porch while I accompanied the dogs to the doggy restroom.

On our return, I picked up Twinkletoes and said something I never thought I would. "Thank you for climbing the Christmas tree and attacking Josie!"

She took it like a cat and scampered into the inn for breakfast. I followed her.

The odd thing about that day, I realized, was that while everyone was talking about Josie and Boomer, life had picked up as though everything was quite normal and nothing untoward had happened.

After a hearty breakfast of pumpkin pancakes, I walked the halls of the inn, noting the mundane. In the afternoon, Trixie, Pepper, Twinkletoes, and I stopped by Barry Williams's office to pick up heartworm preventative.

He saw me in the lobby and motioned to me to come to the back. Without a word, he opened a door revealing brand-new mama Poppy and her six puppies. They were tiny and black and wriggly. I petted Poppy and told her what beautiful babies she had.

"Holmes has already claimed this one." Barry sat on the floor beside me and picked one up. It had the beginnings of light brown eyebrows and the cutest tiny tail.

"Don't forget to save one for Kitty. She would be crushed if she didn't get to keep one."

Barry inhaled deeply. "Do you believe in kismet?"

"You mean like some things are out of our control and will happen anyway?"

"Exactly. I dated Kitty's mother when I was in vet school. She had to move out of state to take care of her grandmother, and we lost touch. I had looked for her on social media, and well, there are a lot of Johnsons. I had no luck at all finding her, but I never forgot about her. And then, suddenly, she showed up here. I can't help thinking that we were meant to be. Like some powerful force sent her this way."

I smiled at him. "I hope it works out between the two of you."

"Me, too."

Later that day, Officer Dave called to say that Delia and Carter were ready to come home. Mom and I picked them up at the hospital and drove them home. At

Delia's house, Dave met us with Trixie and Pepper, who acted like she hadn't seen them in years.

We told them how Pepper knew who had poisoned them and what a hero she was.

Delia just smiled. "I always knew she was a special baby."

We didn't talk much about Josie or Boomer. I assumed that would come later, when they felt better and had time to digest the situation.

Mom left for California on Tuesday. This time there were no sobs or regrets because she would soon be driving herself cross-country along with my grandparents. The housing situation was still somewhat wacky, but Mom had arranged to rent the new house in Wagtail until the closings could take place. Whether they would have furniture in the house on arrival back in Wagtail remained to be seen.

It promised to be a crazy Christmas and New Year.

Thirty-Five

After the mayhem, I was glad to have some time to Christmas shop. Before leaving Wagtail, Mom had been back to the house she bought several times, telling me all about how she planned to decorate it. That made holiday shopping all the easier.

I was in Purrfect Presents, which offered a nice selection of personalized items. I was waiting at the counter when I spied a stack of T-shirts. The one on top said *Big Stu*. It wasn't any of my business, but I didn't think there was any harm in peeking at the others. Maybe I would get some clever ideas.

The second T-shirt was clearly child size and said *Stu Too*. I knew who they were for. How many Stu Toos could there be?

The rest were more standard. *World's Best Grandma*, *World's Best Grandpa*, *World's Best Dad*, *Spoiled Granddaughter*. I smiled at them and returned my focus to the options displayed on the wall.

"Holly!"

I turned to find Marie Johnson. "Hi! It's nice to see you back in Wagtail." I gazed around for the children but didn't see them.

"Thanks. It looks like Kitty, Stuey, and I will be Wagtailites. We're moving here." She took a deep breath. "I'm really nervous about it, but there's nothing keeping us in Charlotte anymore."

I didn't mean to be nosy, but the words just came out of my mouth. "You've made a lot of friends in Wagtail. Especially the Williamses."

Marie's eyes widened. "That's what scares me. They took to all of us so fast. I never imagined that would happen."

"But you knew Barry already. Right?"

"Ten years ago! He was in vet school then. It's amazing how quickly we picked up where we left off." She gazed around the store. "Can I confide in you?"

"Sure." I hoped she wouldn't confess to murder.

"Barry is Kitty's father."

I stared at her in surprise. "What? Does he know?"

"I think he might suspect. He's smart, and he can certainly do the math. I'm going to tell them at Christmas. Sue and Stu already treat us like family, so I'm hoping it will come as happy news."

"What about Kitty?" I couldn't imagine how she would feel.

"Are you kidding? I can't get her out of Barry's vet clinic. She cannot get enough of Poppy's puppies. She's like Barry's little shadow already."

A couple of hours later I stood on the front porch of the inn with Mr. Huckles and Trixie, awaiting the arrival of Santa to his special chair, which I happened to know had been designed and built by Holmes, Carter, and Barry.

The town had commissioned a mock Santa sleigh.

Built on the frame of a golf cart, it certainly looked like the real thing. Children waiting on the plaza below us started to get excited as it came into view.

Santa aka Stu Williams wore his traditional red suit. Next to him sat Mrs. Claus, aka Oma. With her granny glasses and hat, I could barely recognize her. Her most trusted elf, Gingersnap, sat next to her wearing a green elf hat that had a bell on the end of it.

And on the front of the sleigh sat a certain calico kitty, in a little box made just for her. I was shocked to see that Twinkletoes's hat was still on her head, but I suspected that wouldn't be the case for long.

Best of all to me were the dogs, cats, and children of Wagtail, who followed the sleigh collecting the toys and treats that walking elves distributed, including one very tall elf who looked suspiciously like Holmes.

Trixie shot out to join them.

I thought of Josie, who sat in a cold jail cell. And Orly, who had made a desperate decision to save his only daughter. Boomer had caused chaos in a lot of families.

Snowflakes danced in the air as a few people began to make their way up the stairs and into the inn for afternoon tea. Mr. Huckle excused himself and hurried to receive them.

For a few minutes, I stood alone and watched an elderly woman walk slowly up the stairs in the company of two men, a woman, and a teenaged boy. I recognized one of the men as Kent Alcorn and realized with a start that the old woman was grouchy old Mrs. Alcorn.

The second man and the boy bore a startling resemblance to Kent. Jay! They had to be Jay Alcorn and Regan Robinson, and perhaps their son.

Christmas was truly the season of miracles.

Trixie's Guide to Murder

I know some cats are loners and not particularly friendly to us, but don't be afraid to work with them. They have excellent sniffers and are able to jump and climb much higher than most doggums, which can come in handy. And they are great at providing distractions for peoples. How many times have you been comfortably lounging when a cat appeared magically before you? You probably smelled the cat before you saw or heard it. They can sneak around without any peoples noticing their presence!

Here's a tip: Cats don't wag their tails like we do. When they flick their tails around, stand back, because they're upset. Sure they're small, but they spend a lot of time each day sharpening their claws. When they rub against us, that's a cat hug! They can be great allies. Don't underestimate them.

So that's it, fellow puppers. It's all about using your sniffers and training your mom and dad. Once the murderer has been taken away, it's time to enjoy well-earned cookies and snuggle up with your mom and dad, knowing they are safe and the world is right again.

Wishing you lots of cookies and tummy rubs,
Trixie

Recipes

❀ ❀ ❀ ❀ ❀

One of my dogs suffered from severe food allergies that did not allow him to eat commercial dog food. Consequently, I learned to cook for my dogs and have done so for many years. Consult your veterinarian if you want to switch your dog to home-cooked food. It's not as difficult as one might think. Keep in mind that, like children, dogs need a balanced diet, not just a hamburger. Any changes to your dog's diet should be made gradually, so your dog's stomach can adjust.

Chocolate, alcohol, caffeine, fatty foods, grapes, raisins, macadamia nuts, onions and garlic, xylitol (also known as birch sugar), and unbaked dough can be toxic (and even deadly) to dogs. For more information about foods your dog can and cannot eat, consult the American Kennel Club website at https://www.akc.org/expert-advice/nutrition/human-foods-dogs-can-and-cant-eat/.

If you have any reason to suspect your pet has ingested something toxic, please contact your veterinarian or the

Animal Poison Control Center's twenty-four-hour hotline at (888) 426-4435.

Maple Latte (cinnamon on top)

For people. NOT for dogs.

1 cup 2 percent milk
½ cup hot coffee
3 tablespoons maple syrup
Sweetened Whipped Cream (optional; see recipe below)
Cinnamon

Heat the milk gently. Pour the coffee into a mug, add the maple syrup, and stir. Whisk the milk vigorously to create foam. Gently pour the milk into the coffee. Top with the sweetened whipped cream (if using) and sprinkle with cinnamon.

Sweetened Whipped Cream

1 cup heavy whipping cream
⅓ cup powdered sugar
1 teaspoon vanilla

In an electric mixer or with an immersion blender, beat the cream. When it begins to take shape, add the powdered sugar and the vanilla. Whip until it holds a peak.

Pumpkin French Toast

For people, but dogs can have a bite.
Please note that nutmeg and cloves have been omitted from this recipe because dogs should not eat them. Do NOT substitute pumpkin pie spice, as it contains nutmeg and cloves.

4 large eggs
½ cup canned pumpkin purée (not pumpkin pie filling!)
½ cup 2 percent milk
2 tablespoons dark brown sugar
2 teaspoons vanilla
½ teaspoon cinnamon
8 ½-inch-thick slices challah
Canola oil
Maple syrup (for serving)

Combine the eggs, pumpkin purée, milk, sugar, vanilla, and cinnamon in a large bowl and whisk together until smooth.

Lay the bread slices in a large rimmed baking pan and pour the pumpkin mixture over them. Flip the bread to cover on both sides. Heat a skillet over medium to medium-high heat and add roughly ½ teaspoon canola oil. Place a couple of bread slices in the skillet with space between them and cook until lightly browned on both sides. Repeat with the remaining slices, adding oil and lowering the temperature as needed.

Serve with maple syrup.

Carrot-Pumpkin Soup

For people. NOT for dogs.

2 tablespoons butter
2 medium onions
¾ teaspoon rubbed sage
Pinch of thyme
2 celery ribs
5 large carrots
1 pear
4 cups chicken broth (vegetable broth would work fine)
Salt (to taste)
1 cup pumpkin purée
1 cup half-and-half
Toast or croutons

Melt the butter in a large soup pot over medium-low to medium heat. Dice the onions and add them to the pot. Give them an occasional stir while they cook. Add the sage and thyme. Slice the celery and add it to the pot.

Peel and slice the carrots while the onions cook to the point where they just begin to tinge a little bit brown. Add the carrots to the pot. Peel and core the pear and add it to the pot.

Add the broth and place a lid on the pot. Bring to a boil, then reduce the heat and simmer for about 45 minutes. The carrots should be soft. Use an immersion hand blender to purée the soup in the pot. It's up to you to decide how smooth you want the soup to be. Add salt to taste.

Add the pumpkin purée and half-and-half. Mix well and bring back to a boil briefly before serving.

Garnish with toast or croutons or serve with rustic bread and butter or cheese.

Apple Cider Cocktail

Makes 4 drinks. NOT for dogs.

2 teaspoons sugar
1 teaspoon cinnamon
2 cups apple cider
¼ cup dark rum
½ bottle (2 cups) sparkling wine

Mix the sugar and cinnamon in a shallow dish. Dip the rims of 4 tall champagne glasses in the apple cider and then in the sugar mixture.

In a pitcher, combine the apple cider, rum, and sparkling wine. Pour into each glass.

Gingerbread Cookies

For people.

These are soft gingerbread cookies, not thin crunchy ones. The amount of ginger seems like it is on the heavy side, but my tasters loved it. If you aren't a fan of ginger, you might want to reduce the amount to 1 or 2 tablespoons.

Makes 3–4 dozen, depending on size of cookies.

3 cups flour, plus more for dusting
1 teaspoon baking soda
½ teaspoon salt
3 tablespoons powdered ginger
1 tablespoon cinnamon
½ teaspoon allspice
10 tablespoons butter, softened
¾ cup dark brown sugar
1 large egg, room temperature
½ cup molasses
1 teaspoon vanilla
Icing (see recipe below)

In a large bowl combine the flour, baking soda, salt, ginger, cinnamon, and allspice. Set aside. Cream the butter with the sugar. Beat in the egg and then the molasses and vanilla. Gradually mix in the flour mixture.

Preheat oven to 350°F and prepare two baking sheets (to speed things up) with parchment paper.

Very lightly dust the area where you will roll out the dough. If it is too sticky to handle, refrigerate briefly. Divide the dough in fourths and roll out one fourth at a time to about ¼ inch thick. Cut out the dough with cookie cutters, place the cookies on one of the prepared baking sheets, and bake for 8 minutes. Meanwhile, roll out more dough and place the cookies on the second baking sheet.

Remove the baked cookies from the oven and place on baking racks to cool before icing.

When the icing has dried, store in an airtight container, separating layers with wax paper or parchment paper.

Icing

There are a lot of ways to decorate the gingerbread cookies. Use your imagination and have fun. I find that three buttons and two eyes (use a very small, round icing tip) are usually sufficient on gingerbread people.

2 cups confectioners' sugar
½ teaspoon vanilla
Pinch of salt
2 teaspoons light corn syrup (optional)
3–5 tablespoons water

Mix together the confectioners' sugar, vanilla, and salt. Gradually add the corn syrup (if using) and water until you reach a firm icing consistency. If it's too soft, add a little confectioners' sugar. If it's too stiff, add a little water.

Hamburger Kisses

For dogs.
People can eat these, but since they are not seasoned, dogs find them tastier than we do. These make good "special" training rewards. But make sure they're small! They also make great treats for dog birthday parties. They are not meant to be a meal, just a treat. Don't feed them too many. Please use **very lean** meat. Too much fat can cause upset dog tummies.

1 pound (more or less) 93% lean ground beef

Preheat oven to 375°F. Line a rimmed baking sheet with parchment paper. Place the entire pound of ground beef on the baking sheet and gently mold into a rectangle about ¾ inch thick. Slice lengthwise 6 times. Then slice in the other direction, cutting ½-inch squares (or smaller, depending on the size of your dog).

If the end pieces are too small, gently mold them together. Place the bits in rows across the baking sheet and bake for 8 minutes. Allow to cool slightly before serving to your dog.

Store in refrigerator in an airtight container.

Kitty Kisses

Dogs can eat these too. (Don't tell the cats!) Makes about 4 dozen.

Please be sure to use sardines **packed in water, with no other ingredients and no salt added**. These are meant to be an occasional treat, not a meal.

1 medium egg
1 teaspoon water from the sardine can
2 sardines packed in water, no salt added

Preheat oven to 350°F. Line a small baking sheet with parchment paper.

In a small bowl, whisk the egg until foamy. Add the water from the sardine can. Mix, then add the sardines and mash them. Using a ⅛-teaspoon measuring spoon, place about 1/16 teaspoon of the sardine mash on the parchment paper. Repeat with the remaining sardine mash and bake for 15 minutes. Allow to cool before serving. They will be a little bit moist.

Store the kisses by rolling them up in the parchment paper. Slide the paper into a freezer bag and place it in the freezer. To serve, remove one or two kisses at a time and let them come to room temperature.

Acknowledgments

Huge thanks go to Dave Barry for allowing me to use his quote. I first read it years ago and have never forgotten it. Every time I walk my dogs, I think about them reading the dog newspaper and wonder exactly what intrigues them enough to pause and take the time to check out a particular scent. We're so inferior! We don't see or smell anything at those spots!

Cats and dogs are at the heart of this particular mystery series. It might seem silly to some, but I have to thank my own cats and dogs for teaching me. They have been a big part of my life, and I have learned so much from each one of them. Who would have thought all those rascally and sweet and sometimes trying moments would be helpful in writing a book?

Many thanks go to my editor, Michelle Vega, who helped make this a better book. I'm so appreciative of her input. And thanks to my agent, Jessica Faust, who is always a step ahead of me and is a terrific dog mom.